River of Hidden Dreams

ALSO BY CONNIE MAY FOWLER

Sugar Cage

River of Hidden Dreams

Connie May Fowler

G. P. PUTNAM'S SONS · NEW YORK

This is a work of fiction. The events described are imaginary, and the characters are fictitious and not intended to represent specific living persons.

Published by G. P. Putnam's Sons
200 Madison Avenue
New York, NY 10016
Published simultaneously in Canada

Library of Congress Cataloging-in-Publication Data
Fowler, Connie May.
River of hidden dreams / Connie May Fowler.
p. cm.
ISBN 0-399-13912-5
1. Women—Florida—Fiction. I. Title.
PS3556.O8265R58 1993 93-34783 CIP
813'.54—dc20

The text of this book is set in Perpetua.
Book design by Chris Welch

Printed in the United States of America
1 2 3 4 5 6 7 8 9 10

This book is printed on acid-free, recycled paper.

ACKNOWLEDGMENTS

My thanks to Diana and Bob Smith for sharing their love of boats, Annie Ferran for her wings, Patrick Hamilton and Jean Dowdy for a dinner with "old salts," Karen Harvey for loaned reference works, Captain Brian Kelley for his able and perceptive tours of the Ten Thousand Islands, Jimmy Wheeler for sharing and treasuring the Everglades, the staff of the St. Augustine Historical Society for their generous guidance, the Florida Department of Cultural Affairs for its support, and Faith Sale and Joy Harris for their unwavering vigilance and care.

I also wish to acknowledge the works of Zora Neale Hurston and Marjory Stoneman Douglas, two writers whose love of Florida's natural and human treasures informs the spirit of this book.

C.M.F.

For my grandmother,
Oneida Hunter May,
and for Mika,
bearer of my dreams,
my wholeness

Those do not die who connect their endings
to their beginnings. Therefore, wander.

—Eric J. Leed, *The Mind of the Traveler*

River of Hidden Dreams

My mother and grandmother died while they were dancing. With each other. In a saloon in Chokoloskee. We'd been making our rounds through the Ten Thousand Islands, a world of water and mosquitoes and mangrove—a world that if you enter it, do so carefully, with wide eyes and a steady heart. Otherwise the dense swamps, the gators, the endless strings of rivers leading to dead-end bays might grab hold of your soul and tear it out.

There was never much surprising in the way visitors viewed the islands. Once they got over the shock of yellow flies and no-see-ums, they were awestruck by the area's beauty or saddened beyond belief by its enduring loneliness.

As for my mother and grandmother, they ignored

the pests, shunned the solitude, and celebrated the beauty. They were in love with the sky of the Ten Thousand Islands, for it is like no other. At the edge of the mangrove, looking out toward the Gulf of Mexico, there is no horizon. Water and sky become one vast stroke of blue, arching into a dome where clouds rest lazily, on and on—white and pure—eventually disappearing into the unseeable depths of heaven.

Those two women took it all in—the majesty and the harshness—and they knew they belonged there. To make a living they operated a floating general store, selling supplies like cigarettes and booze out of their boat to the backcountry crackers, people who had trouble with civilization and the law so they settled down in a place that had neither.

Whenever I think of my grandmother the first thing that comes to mind is her amazing face. Like wind-sculpted dunes, her features had been molded by time to the point that you could never have counted all her wrinkles. Not ever. Not even if your life depended on it.

But that didn't stop me.

When I was nothing but a two-pint runt I'd crawl onto her lap and trace those lines deepened by sun and sand and I'd try like the devil to add them up. She smelled like tobacco and flowers because she smoked cigars and always carried a vial of jasmine oil that she righteously dotted behind her ears and down her neck as though without that scent she might disappear. As far as I could tell, the jasmine oil was her only nod at vanity.

So there I'd sit, kicking my skinny suntanned legs against her skirt, thinking hard on coming up with the largest number I could imagine, and then I'd say something like "Mima"—that's what I called her—"you have eight hundred million zillion wrinkles."

She'd throw back her head in a motion that reminded me of a horse rearing and she'd laugh as if I was the most precious child on earth. Her laughter was full, without recrimination, formed by thick lips and tobacco-stained teeth. I remember running along the sandy shore of Pavilion Key, chasing shells tossed up by the surf, running in cadence with that laughter carried from gut to sky with wings brittle but sure.

As for my mother, she was a firecracker with waist-long salt-and-pepper hair and green eyes. She didn't share in Mima's passion for cigars or jasmine oil, but she loved to drink. She kept a flask of rum tucked in that canvas bag she called a purse. And even though my mother's hands resembled a man's because she wasn't ever scared of hard labor, she sipped from her flask like a lady. I don't think I ever saw her drunk, except during bad weather—at least not rip-roaring. She always approached me slowly, and when she held me it was with careful loving fingers, as though she'd given birth to a child with bird bones, easily snapped. And I can say this: I loved her good.

I remember my mother telling me about my father, although he is a man I never personally met. He floated in and out of her life like a mercurial breeze, showing up when she didn't want him and leaving when she did. But she said she never regretted sleeping with him despite the fact that he was a "no-good son of a bitch," because he was the only man who ever gave her children. By the time I was born, Mama had raised two boys—fully grown, fully on their own, fully and forever strangers to me. But Mama seemed content with all of it. She would tweak my nose and say, "I have never regretted a single one of you, not ever."

Then, of course, there is my grandpapa. Mama and Mima said he would have loved me best, above anyone else, even them, if he'd been around after I was born. You see, he is a ghost, but that doesn't mean he is lost to me. He is part of my blood-born memory, nourished by Mama's and Mima's stories. I would sit for hours listening to their tales about him and shutting my eyes so tight my lids ached, while I imagined him completely, even down to his bony knuckles and the scar along the crescent of his thumb put there by a fishhook.

Because most of our time was spent meandering through the islands, I wasn't around other children very often and I didn't realize Mama was old. It didn't seem odd to me that I had two grown brothers I'd never met. And never heard from. It didn't seem crazy to me that Mama and Mima were more like sisters than like mother and daughter, or that they shared equally in my raising, or that my grandpapa was the most important man in their lives and mine even though he was long dead. It's just how it was.

Here's another thing I remember: that saloon in Chokoloskee. It was a big cypress-shake building, all screened in to try to keep the mosquitoes and raccoons out. We'd been through three steady days of rain and wind and battling choppy waters, so finally we took shelter at the Crocodile Saloon.

It was owned by a man named Chester Tiger. He claimed to be a Seminole and dressed like so. Rumor was he didn't have an ounce of Indian blood in him, but just dreamed it. Folks whispered that he was black Irish and that his name was Mike O'Toole, but we only whispered it when he was out back scavenging through his storeroom.

Chester maintained a good supply of liquor and always on the bar there sat a stuffed 'dillo next to a plate of boiled eggs. The poor 'dillo, he had glassy eyes and when you looked into them all you could see was yourself, looking back out at you, reflecting off his dead irises.

I loved boiled eggs. And I was fascinated with the way Chester could take off their shells. He'd bend down to my eye level and hide the egg in his giant callused hand. I'd hear the shell crack, but when he opened his palm there was nothing but clean egg, no shell at all. When I was young I thought it was magic.

You could eat good at Chester's if you had to.

Gator tail and grilled fish and spicy rattlesnake stew. He wasn't married and I had a notion that maybe he and Mama might make a go of it. In fact, I'm sure something went on between them. But Mama and Mima, they had some kind of bond. I don't know what it was, and I heard them tell people that there was a time when they didn't even speak. They spun stories over it, laughing at their sad past like it was nothing but folly. The days when I knew them, though, were different. Wasn't nobody in all the world who could split them up. Nobody. I guess Chester Tiger wasn't prepared to marry the both of them.

So, I remember the rain and the howling wind. To this day I can close my eyes and hear the shutters banging like death rattles against the cypress. I can hear the roof and the walls groan as the wind begins to take its toll. I swear to Jesus, the walls moved. In and out. In and out. Like lungs.

But we didn't worry. We just did as always when there was a storm. We partied.

There was Mama, Mima, and me. Chester Tiger. The Emmett twins, Red and Shorty, who played mean fiddles. There were some trappers whose names I have long forgotten. There was a Seminole there who called himself Squirrel Joe, and his wife, Sue. And there were others, mostly men. Some I never saw again and others became friends of a sort. I would know their sons and daughters. I would come to know birthdays and I went to a few weddings. I've even slept with a few sons of men who were in the saloon that stormy evening. And Whitey Smith was there, an old fisherman, claimed to have been born in a chickee.

His mother, a fair blue-eyed blond woman, was brought down here when she was just fourteen by her husband, who, it was rumored, killed a man in cold blood up north in Alachua County, in a village named Micanopy.

As Whitey told it, his parents were out someplace in the scrub when his mama went into childbirth. The couple headed on horseback to the closest help they could find, a Seminole village on the western edge of the cypress swamp. The Indians made Whitey's daddy stay far away from his woman while the baby was birthing. And they made her drink snake venom, so she could hallucinate her pain away.

See, Whitey was full of such stories, and he liked me special. Even before it happened, he'd given me precious things—three gator teeth and one of those fish skeletons that look like Jesus on the cross. In perfect condition.

But the storm, it was getting nastier and the walls started breathing and Whitey leaned over and said, "Darling, don't you be frightened. It's just 'bout blown over."

Mama and Mima were deep into the rum by now and they asked the Emmett twins to "strike up the band!" That's what my mother yelled. She was gay and pretty, and despite living on a boat, she kept herself together in a womanly way.

Red and Shorty took up their fiddles and started picking. Shorty had a good voice. He was singing a song about being lonesome for the Tennessee mountains. It was a fast tune and we all began clapping. The men stomped to the music, and the flames from the hurricane lanterns cast wild, prancing shadows all across us.

Mama and Mima kicked off their shoes and took to their feet and began dancing like two little girls, in circles with each other. Their giant shadows kept time on the wall behind them. Mima couldn't exactly keep up—seemed to me she was a hundred years old—but she danced anyway. They were both laughing and cheering as if they were having the best time of their lives.

Sometimes I wake up in the middle of the night hearing the crash all over again in my head. The roof gave with a massive groan, and we were suddenly awash in rain and wind and falling cypress timbers.

Whitey grabbed me off the stool and ducked me beneath the bar. He squeezed in with me, smelling of rum and tobacco and too many days without a bath. And that's where we stayed for nearly hours. I don't know how many. It seemed like forever, like time's steady lope had been halted under the weight of that formidable storm. The wind rose up all around us, howling, grinding against our skin, exposing our belly-white fear. I hid my face in Whitey's chest, and put up with his rank odor, because the rain fell so furiously it stung.

Nobody ever let me see them. A cypress beam

had been ripped out of the roof like it was a toothpick. People were sad, but they loved the story—the Hunter women died while they were dancing.

Red wrote a song about them, and he and his brother played it at the funeral. I can't remember how it goes. But I'll never forget that plaintive weeping fiddle as we buried them at sea. The men, trying to be gentle, slipped Mama and Mima, shrouded and cocoon-shaped, into the turquoise water. In an instant their dead, heavy bodies disappeared and two silver-scaled tarpon flashed by, muscular and mighty and so swift that anyone who blinked missed them.

Mama and Mima had turned into two beautiful fish. That's what I prayed.

Yes, I remember the shrouds and the fiddles and the tarpon and also two frigate birds flying overhead, their scissor tails cutting across a wall of infinite blue.

For the next seven years, until he too finally gave up the ghost, Whitey took care of me. By general consensus he got the honor. And the boat. Which I still call home. My very own thirty-foot homemade trawler with a shallow draft and narrow nose for sneaking into tight spots and staying there.

I was nine when they died. I was nine when I lost my childhood and my women, and I was nine when I disappeared into my imagination. I fell silent, and Whitey did not provoke me. He was gentle. Even kind. But because he couldn't stand watching me stare down into the sweet blue waters of the Gulf as

I searched day after day for those silver-scaled fish, he supplied me with books. No matter whom we ran across, whether friend or foe or stranger, Whitey asked if they had any books they might want to give in order to lighten their load.

They almost always gave.

As a result, my education was not what you'd call formal. Instead, I cut my teeth on everything from dime-store pulps to college texts. One day I was caught up in the intrigue of Philip Marlowe and the next day I was adrift in a sea of geopolitical babble. The words dulled the pain of loss but didn't prevent me from being ever vigilant of my peripheral vision. The words did not stop me from peeking at the world just beyond the printed page in the hope that the two fish would clear the water in a moment of flash and triumph. Just one more time.

I am a woman who has made her own way in this world. The Gulf is so overfished there isn't enough to take and make a living anymore, at least not without guilt. So I turned to being a tour guide. I left the Ten Thousand Islands the day Whitey died—no reason to hang out in a place where every mangrove island and every trip up Ferguson River or sojourn through Alligator Bay provokes a flood of memories kept bittersweet because they reflect times that I can never reclaim.

I left at the tender age of sixteen, never to be tender again, and headed south to Key West. That's where I've stayed. I've never once gone back to Chokoloskee or Everglades City or the Big Cypress

Swamp, but their labyrinthine spirit is always with me. At any moment I can close my eyes and see the green and gold hues of the swamp, or hear the incessant chatter of the mangrove rookery, or remember the hot honest stare of a boy I once loved in Everglades City.

Now I take folks out to a gentler edge of the earth—to waters called backcountry, yes, but Key West style. In fact, most of the boys I grew up with would scoff at what the keys offer as untouched fare. But I don't. The mangrove swamps this far south are not as dense and lonely as in the Ten Thousand Islands. They don't stretch on from here to eternity—civilization is a quick ride away. The water is clear, not tannic black. The beauty here is fragile and obvious. The beauty of the Ten Thousand Islands is also fragile, but to an outsider the seemingly impenetrable wilderness can look solid and unyielding. It's not.

As for my tour guide business, I try to keep my prices low. Because I'm in an out-of-the-way marina that's nowhere near the godforsaken tourist district, my rent is modest by Key West standards. Folks have to search me out. For anywhere from a hundred to three hundred dollars a trip—depending on what you want and how long we're out—I'll take your party up through some pretty backcountry keys. Perhaps up to Dreguez and Sugarloaf. Maybe even to the Spanish Banks and Content Keys. Bring your own booze and food, fish if you want, party if you want, if I like you I'll tell you stories. Some of them I make up. Others are true. My repertoire is based on the stories I heard as a child, stories Mama and Mima told on themselves, stories that connect me precariously, as with a single gossamer thread, to my past and theirs.

But still I carry secrets, for the tale of the dancing women I keep to myself. That is a memory I never share.

Tonight as I sit alone on my boat, I watch a storm build out over the islands. It is a magnificent storm, better than any Fourth of July fireworks, nature at her most impressive. The clouds tower like mountains into the indigo sky. Lightning sears through them over and over, and I think that must be what birth pangs feel like—hot and electric and horribly sudden. I look out into the flashing darkness. The animals, I know, are all hunkered down, waiting it out, me under the bar.

I still have a few things that were theirs. The boat, of course. A handkerchief that Mima treasured as if it was gold. She never let me play with it, even though I knew it would make for a great headband when I played pirate.

And then there's the quilt. I used to watch Mama work on it. Mima patched it together years ago, Mama told me as she snaked needle and thread in and out of the deep colors of silk. Her broad, hopeful face would pinch up in concentration as she mumbled something about embroidering a story on it, our story, so that we would always have it, silk encrusted with thread drawings.

It's very nice. A gator all in white. A scrawny chicken. Buffalo charging around the edges. Fish everywhere. Important dates, like birthdays and separations. And names. Many, many names, some family and some not.

Before I could read and write I would point at a word and ask what it spelled and Mama would put the quilt aside for a moment and pull me onto her lap and she'd say, "That spells 'Mr. Sammy,' " or "That says 'Alice Motherwell,' " and then she'd begin to tell me about these people and most often as not Mima would join in, elaborating or correcting, jabbing the air with her thick brown fingers to make a point, and I would close my eyes and listen. In my imagination the threads would unravel, spinning themselves into real, live, flesh-and-blood folks as Mama and Mima, word by word, detail by detail, breathed life into their creation, which was far more than a quilt. It was their legacy. And mine. Sewn diligently, with loving and sometimes frantic hands. They wanted the quilt to be timeless, to freeze our history and heritage, a lasting snapshot that would act as a pathway to our familial past and offer among its constellation of drawings clues to my future.

But maybe my problem is the same one all storytellers must face: When is the story more real than the people themselves? When does fact become myth? And does it matter?

You see, the more I tell the stories stitched in this old quilt, the less certain I am that any one of them is true. And as time goes by, I don't miss Mama and

Mima any less. I miss them more, and in my sorrowful longing for them a bitterness rises so pure that I can taste it. For I feel cheated that I didn't know Mama and Mima longer and that my grandmother, who was born a Plains Indian but then underwent a forced transformation, was unable to pass on that part of her heritage. I don't feel as if I have any Indian blood in me, and I know my mother felt that way too. I regret that my memories offer few faces—I don't know what my daddy looked like, for instance, and as for the people I never met, their voices are in my memory through transfusion, through listening for hours on end to Mama and Mima. But still, all I possess are stories. As I get older I can't shake the belief that maybe that is not enough.

So here I sit, a premenopausal woman (if what I've heard is true, my good sense could evaporate at any moment), staring out into a majestic if violent sky, and because I am chilled I've pulled out the quilt and thrown it across my lap. I am completely alone. I've gone through two husbands—short-lived mistakes that derailed my independence by only a few months each—and I have successfully managed to never commit myself to anything, including children. I sleep where, when, and with whom I want and I do so with protection, guarding my womb from bearing like a tigress shielding the entrance to a holy cave.

This does not make Carlos happy. He is the closest thing I've got to a commitment. But it's a commitment you can discern only through a telescope. He's Cuban and a come-what-may fisherman and musician. The blues by Robert Johnson is all he'll sing—in English, that is. When he first got to Key West he moved in with a family in Little Bahamia, and the teenage son, evidently to Carlos's delight, played Robert Johnson nonstop. And it's strange, but when Carlos sings, he's not Cuban anymore but a gravel-voiced black man making deals with the devil.

When he's not singing, though, he's back to being Spanish, and believe me, all you've ever heard about Cuban machismo is true. It's a hoot. When he's all puffed up and telling me what I can and can't do, I laugh at him. And then I go out and sleep with somebody else.

I've developed the habit of carrying a rubber in my pocket or tucked in the cardboard carrier of my accompanying six-pack. Rarely have I met a man in this day and age who believes in mortality. They all think only gay men and sick people get it. "Listen, honey," I tell them, "you're not going to get any unless you wrap it up."

Carlos knows I sleep with other men. I make sure he knows. Just to keep the cement cracking. He doesn't hit or scream or mope or even threaten to leave. He stares me down, hurt and disappointment barely visible in his dark eyes, and he says, "One day, Mamacita"—he calls me "Mamacita" because he insists I have a motherly soul but just won't let it out, ha!—"you will see how good you are." As if that has anything to do with my sleeping around.

The real reason I do my damnedest to remain untrue is every time I feel myself slipping into a relationship that's a bit too comfy—with Carlos or anybody else—I bolt. It's a complete panic attack. The moment I know I'm close to making ties that bind, my throat closes up on me and I can't even breathe.

Everybody on the island thinks I'm tough, independent, a woman you don't fuck with. The truth is I still feel like a goddamned orphan. I'm tired of being alone but too scared to stop it. I'm tired of living on this old boat with only a haunted quilt for company. I am still that little girl cowering under the bar.

And I want out. I've had enough. But I don't know what to do or how to do it.

Ten miles west the sky blossoms with light. I finish my beer. I search the stars, which lead into clouds and speckled darkness, wondering if I'll ever be able to peel away the stories, to poke and prod at the ancient flesh that created them. Even with all the family tales, there are still holes. Like whether my brothers are dead or alive. Have they grown senile, sitting out on some windy porch in St. Augustine, way up in northeast Florida—that's where my people come from, via Oklahoma and a few other places—passing gas and swapping stories that I'm not in?

I read in *Time* magazine about folks in the Tyrolean Alps finding a frozen man who lived 5,300 years ago. The ice had preserved him, and now they are discovering all sorts of things. Like what he ate, and how he dressed, and that he even had tattoos, and all those smart scientists are surprised because they thought people didn't tattoo themselves until 2,500 years later.

But that's not the point. The point is they can figure out what a man had for a midday snack 5,300 years ago—sloeberries—and I can't say with dead certainty whether or not the oral history Mama and Mima were so determined to jam down my throat has any basis in fact or not.

It doesn't seem right. How come women from around the world are writing to these scientists desiring to be impregnated with the Iceman's sperm—they don't realize his phallus is mysteriously missing—when I don't even know what city or state my dead or undead brothers live in?

And if I became a grave robber and tracked down family burial sites and unearthed their old wormy corpses, what would I learn? Probably not a damn thing. Corpses speak only to a chosen few.

I ought to just forget it. Live my life. Maybe settle down with my dear macho Carlos. I ought not to worry about whether the past they left me is made up of lies and half-lies or the godly, unsullied truth.

But you see, I can't.

Because I know when I go to sleep tonight, warmed by the soft mantle of the quilt, at first I'll hear the sea gulls crying, and the water gently lapping, and the riggings of the fancy sailboats will ring, ring, ring all night long because we've got a pretty good breeze working, and all those noises will collide with the cacophony of stomping. And two furious fiddles. And that will give way to the patter of bare feet.

And then I'll see them in my dreams: two old drunk women laughing and singing and dancing.

Always dancing.

I wake up not to the salty fresh smell of the sea but to Carlos's aftershave. Old Spice. He loves the stuff. Douses it on as if it's going to protect him from evil or something.

But what it really acts as is a fingerprint you can smell. I don't even have to leave my cabin to know he's come aboard and stood on the deck, snooping, light just beginning to crack the sky. And I know he has already snuck back to his apartment, happy with himself because I was sleeping alone, after all, and he thinks he has snooped undetected.

I have never told him his liberal use of Old Spice results in his leaving a trail. I don't want him to know. It means I maintain the upper hand.

Carlos came to America by mistake. It was during the crazy Carter years, when Fidel Castro decided to play an international joke: an infamous little something called the Mariel boatlift. Carlos says a second cousin, José Something-or-other, decided that coming to America would make all his problems, whatever they were, disappear. José dreamed of owning a big American car that wasn't two decades old and kept together only through the desperate ingenuity that a blowtorch and sacrificial auto parts can provide, so he decided to take his chances among the criminally insane and other misfits gleefully being loaded onto the boats.

But here was Carlos's mistake: He boarded a crowded vessel and found José and attempted to persuade him to disembark, to stay in Cuba and wait Castro out. For Carlos and his family the issue wasn't political, it was about keeping the family together. They would all go or none would. And since the former was impossible, Carlos had been sent as an emissary, whose instructions from his mother were clear: through means violent or peaceful, get his cousin off that boat.

And he tried. I really believe he did. As he sat with his cousin under the hot Cuban sun, and as the boat came close to sinking under the weight of fleeing humanity, Carlos spoke quietly but firmly about the importance of not leaving Cuban soil: "Stay," he said, "for the good of the women and children."

As he spoke his eyes probably glazed over with tears, because Carlos is a very passionate man; and because sometimes he focuses his attention too precisely, a laser beam unaware of his surroundings, he did not hear the motor start up. Plus, there was so much noise, people crying and cheering and sea gulls honking, that he was not aware that he had left his friends and family and the only world he had ever known, until the speedboat, whose mahogany nameplate identified it as the *Patriot* from Tampa, had drifted a few yards from the dock and then was pushed into overdrive by a captain who feared Fidel might experience a change of heart.

Carlos argued with the captain. Demanded he be returned. But of course, even if the captain had been of a mind to accommodate, none of the desperate men aboard would have allowed it.

And now he can't return home because no one would ever believe he'd gotten on that boat by mistake. They'd say he was a deserter, a traitor who'd changed his mind. He'd be tossed in prison and forgotten. Or shot and forgotten.

So Carlos lives in America now, a wild-hearted but loyal man who is haunted—whether he'll admit it or not—by the knowledge that his mama and papa and brothers and sisters and aunts and uncles think not only that he abandoned them but that he did so without courage, that he acted as a thief, promising to bring José home and instead stealing himself and his cousin away.

Even though he has lived over a decade of his life on American shores, he doesn't speak good English. Most people can't understand him. He is self-taught, his first lesson being aboard that Chris-Craft headed out of Cuba. Some well-meaning smart-ass, as they traversed the ninety miles to exile or freedom, depending on your point of view, taught Carlos several indispensable phrases. They included "Yes, sir," "Yes, ma'am," "Please, may I have a glass of water," "Political asylum," and "Fuck you"—all anyone needed to know in his circumstances.

Besides murdering up the English language, he has an accent so heavy I suspect even other Cubans can't understand him.

The worst thing about all this is that any communication problems that occur because of his language impairment he blames on me. He raises his palm heavenward as if he were the Pope and yells in that thick tongue of his that he can't understand me.

As if it's my fault.

I tell him, "Why don't you go take some lessons at night school and learn to speak right. It's not me with the tongue made of marbles."

In response he wraps his arms around me and scans my face as I watch his beautiful Latin eyes with those curly lashes I covet and he whispers in Spanish. I can't understand what he's saying, because, of course, that is not my language. I do make out the word *amor,* and I know what that means. He is speaking the language of love, and I have to admit it always does the trick. Then he sighs into my hair and says, "Our secret, Mamacita. Language no good. So we understand with our hearts."

You can see how difficult it is to completely shoo away a man like that.

But I do my best.

In fact, this morning I am angry. I don't like being snooped on. I don't like him feeling he has some right to me.

I throw back the quilt and pull on my robe. I need coffee. Bad. I've got a party of three coming over in an hour. Yuppies, no doubt, from Jersey. My fucking favorite. They left their names scrawled on the sign-up sheet I keep on a stand on the dock in front of my boat. Each one penned his name—Tom, Dick, and Harry, or something equally mayonnaise—and each even went to the trouble of adding "Hoboken, New Jersey."

Like I needed to know.

They're the kind who usually cluck that it's a shame we haven't developed all the islands down here. They think we marry our cousins, and say so to our faces. They mimic our accents and hint that we're dumb.

Whenever I get that type I'm patient, like an old gator stalking supper. I wait until we are far into the backcountry, where the wilderness is as lovely as it is frightening, and in the meantime I've planted tidbits, like how the area is teeming with man-eating crocs. And then at the next Southern-bashing thing they say, I mention my .38 and what a good marksman I am.

I say, "You ever hear what us stupid rednecks do to Yankees who come down here who are too full of themselves?"

I cut off the motor.

Life in the prehistoric mangrove rings.

I smile big.

The eyes start darting back and forth, snatching glances, each trying to get from the others whether this crazy cracker woman is serious or not. The Yankees sort of laugh, but the laughter is full of nerves jangling, and then they shut up with the kind of talk that so riled me in the first place.

As the coffee brews, I consider what stories I might spin today, and I decide that since I'm feeling so lonesome, and since something is building up in the back of my brain—like maybe I'll tell Carlos to kiss off for good and maybe I'll sell this old boat that Mama and Mima said is part of our heritage and take up bartending or something—I decide that maybe I should tell the beginning of the story. Just start at square one. For my own good. Whether they want to hear it or not.

See, people who charter trips with me don't know until after I've already begun that I might tell them tales. And most of them pipe down and listen because the stories are important. But sometimes they don't shut up. Sometimes they aren't aware at all of the beauty of the mangrove islands. Sometimes their mouths don't stop moving long enough to hear the heron cry.

When that happens I continue telling the story, but only to myself. In my head I spin the tale, and I am not a part of the people who won't be quiet and listen. I am someone they'll never know or appreciate.

And so is the land.

FIVE MINUTES EARLY they walked up to my boat and from the dock one of them called, ''Hello, hello! Anyone home?'' in that funny accent, and I didn't respond. I stayed below and did absolutely nothing, pretending I was deaf—just to knock them off kilter.

But in fact, they are pretty nice folks. For Yankees. Three college kids and still full of hope. Imagine that. Frayed cut-off jeans and faded T-shirts. Peach fuzz from not shaving this morning, and bright eyes.

I like the blond one best. He's got curly hair almost to his shoulders and wire-rimmed glasses and a band of rawhide around his wrist—don't you know he'd be fun to lay down with—like he's trying to preserve the sixties or something. Except his favorite word appears to be ''awesome.'' I don't believe any of us as we bumbled around in search of love, peace, and hope ever uttered that adjective.

It is a beautiful day. We've got a light breeze, which will take the sting out of the heat. I suspect we'll see yellowtail and dolphin, and maybe, when we get into the backcountry, barracuda and bonefish will show.

I never get tired of the scenery. The mangrove roots that curve into the water like natural harps and then form an impenetrable thicket unless you're a bird or a fish or some kind of larva—being out here among them always calms me. And so does the sight of the curlew or cormorant lit on the deep-green crown of the mangrove. This is the world ancient and wonderful, before destruction.

The boys are behaving. Each has a beer surgically attached to his right hand. Beer for breakfast. Their faces have the glow of youth, that gloss of getting away with something their parents would frown on, so I'm guessing that fermented hops is not their usual a.m. grain of choice. The faster I go, the louder my boat's old motor hums. The boys are quiet. Evidently they don't feel like shouting over the din. I push my face into the wind, happy to be leaving land behind.

As I begin to steer us through ribbonlike twists and turns, and as we get farther and farther from town, and as the world becomes a waterscape jeweled with islands, I hear her voice. Just a whisper at first amid the mist and secret hollows of the estuaries, rising from a depth I cannot measure or pinpoint.

Then, as always, her words gather strength from the water and sun and fossil-rich soil. I know it won't be long before a flurry of vowels and consonants rolls across my tongue, needling me to speak. But it will be Mima telling the stories, life as she remembered it, as she related it.

Sometimes I wonder if her memories and my mother's and my grandfather's don't actually stretch across the ages. Maybe it is their memories that live and I am the one who is not real. Maybe I'm just a chorus of voices housed within a casing of flesh.

A long hyphenated line of pelicans zooms overhead, and amid the Yankee boys' exclamations of "Awesome!" Mima begins to speak, telling her tale for anyone who'll listen:

THESE, SADIE, are the things I know, scraps of memory I've retrieved from my past, stumbled upon by accident but retold purposely, carefully, so that we never again forget.

According to the white man's calendar, the year was 1875. I was just a baby, a speck on that golden Oklahoma prairie, playing my favorite game. I threw myself down on the earth, spreading out my arms and legs as if they were wings, and I flew in place, staring at the immense hard sky, pretending I was a redtail hawk soaring on the shoulders of a brisk wind; then I hopped up and studied the smashed grass and I delighted in the image I'd made: an angel reedy and yellow, distinct enough to catch the eye of any bird of prey.

I have a memory of a time when I was even younger. I was running through a field after a cloud of pin-sized prairie-colored birds, and I was happy—I know that—and I heard my father say,

"There she goes again. Chasing birds. Our little sparrow hunter."

Thus my name, what my parents called me, always: Sparrow Hunter.

What they did not realize is that the birds who really fascinated me were the big ones, the hawks, the eagles, the owls, and, yes, even the vultures. Because they saw everything, knew everything, and they never let it bother them.

I was not supposed to be in the field that day, so far from camp. I was not supposed to be playing games or lifting my face to the cold breeze or opening my arms wide from my body, letting the chill cut through the animal skin I wore, causing me to shake, to harden like a block of ice.

What my mother wanted was for me to stay in camp by her side and pray over the fires that the women had burned day and night, ever since the soldiers rode in on their gorgeous horses, bearing rifles that through some act of sorcery never ran out of bullets.

For three days and nights the fires blazed, and in that time we had not seen my father or almost anyone else's father because the soldiers had forced them as if they were cattle to their encampment several miles west of ours. They took nearly all the men, young and old, sick and strong.

Some of the children cried and clung like helpless wild babies to their mothers' legs. Not me. I was a tough child. I think I understood, even back then, that crying would only push frayed nerves to snap more quickly, more harshly, that it would do nothing to bring back my father.

We had no clue to what the soldiers planned to do with our men. But I kept watch those three days, searching my mother's eyes for a sign. When they shone deeply, like the hopeful color of the spring blackberry, I knew she was imagining our men's return. She saw them walking back into camp, good men who'd survived their captivity, happy to be home, eating a good supper, and then lying down for a long-deserved sleep.

But sometimes I foresaw another future as I gazed at her. Without warning my mother's eyes would dull and a gray light would steal the vibrant color of spring and I would recognize the berry in winter right before it tumbles off the vine. Then I would demand to be held and I would push my face into hers, eyebrow to eyebrow, and I would share in her death thoughts.

Now, as an old woman trying to remember the morning the soldiers captured my father, I hold only these faint impulses, testing for accuracy, pushing for more: gray clouds dusting a pink horizon, gunfire and sulfur, white men shouting orders as if they owned us.

As these events occurred I soaked in every detail until I was overflowing with memories of destroyed villages, fields, animals, friends. But time and fate came along and steadily, slowly wrung out my past. Drop by drop, I began to forget. My memory became selective, only I had no power over the choices. So today, Sadie, while the actual arrest of my father is vague, the days that followed are clear. As if it all took place yesterday. I don't know why. But it's so.

The women unbraided their hair. The very old ones stayed in their tents and chanted, their voices rising and falling like the haunted breath of wolves. The younger ones, like my mother, offered dead things to the fires.

They began with small items that were sweet-smelling: bundles of grass, yellow and pink prairie flowers that hadn't yet succumbed to winter.

When that didn't work they tried larger offerings such as rabbit and fox.

Still the men didn't return, and someone suggested that what the fire spirits wanted were buffalo, which was impossible because there were hardly any buffalo left. They were gone, shot out, a relic.

The women knew this. But it was difficult for them to admit that without the buffalo our prayers were weak, traveling starbound on the fire's smoke but then falling back to the earth like wingless birds, unable to penetrate that omnipotent cold stare of the sky.

Child, listen to me, now. Everything about our religion belonged to another time, another sort of world, a world before the hunters and the soldiers aimed their endless bullets at the bent heads of the Great Animal, a world in which the spirits still listened. A world lost.

Before we understood how close our culture was

to being wiped out, how close we were to becoming nothing more than a collection of bones on display in a white man's museum, when we still thought we could hold on to the old earth, my mother would brag loud enough for everyone to hear that my father had what she called "the body of a moose and the soul of a dove."

"That's why your father is such a good buffalo hunter. He has the strength to hunt them and the heart to save them," she would boast in front of the other women as she pulled back my hair until it hurt, and then braided it with such speed and grace that I imagined her fingers were actually brown wings stirring the wind as they fluttered over my head.

But me, the little girl who stubbornly insisted on making grass angels for the hawks even after I'd been told not to leave camp, decided my father's dual nature was what caused the soldiers to ride in at dawn and capture him. He killed two white men—two criminals who had been slaughtering buffalo for months.

And my father wasn't alone. Almost everyone had come to the conclusion that the only way to stop the slaughter was to kill the killers.

Where was the morality in such a decision? It was there, lying hopelessly in a rubbled earth that would never again appear as if it were on fire, a glorious mirage created by thunderheads of dust kicked up by the pounding hooves of vast herds on the move.

This was where morality lay: on a prairie where as far as the eye could wander one saw dead buffalo heaped up like blisters beneath black clouds of vultures. Animals, carriers of our dreams, now skinned and rotting, offering the only thing left: a stench so putrid we had to cover our faces with whatever we could find, and stop breathing for as long as our bodies could take it.

During the time of the slaughters, it became a game among us kids to see who could hold her breath the longest. We called it the Dead Game. Of course, this enraged our parents. It was the buffalo, they lectured, that had given us clothing, food, shelter, a reason for praying. Any good fortune came our way because we sacrificed a calf in the sun dance. The bladder or eye or hoof of the buffalo enriched our prayers and helped ensure our success in love and marriage and hunting and medicine.

Our parents' eyes darkened as they spoke, and their gazes shifted from our faces to the marred horizon, and then they fell silent because they realized the unspeakable: We were losing everything.

Still, I was persuaded by their argument and I decided to believe wholeheartedly in this spiritual connection to the animal even if it was facing extinction. Most of us stopped playing the Dead Game, and the ones who continued made sure none of the adults knew it.

So our morality became this: The men who hunted down the buffalo-killers were heroes, defenders of our lands, and beliefs, and dreams.

As our world was turned upside down, our songs and stories changed too. Gone were the tales of spirits helping us hunt the Great Animal. We would huddle under a vast black sky and listen to night sounds: the distant howl of a coyote, the hollow cry of an owl, the rush and push of prairie grass beneath the weight of the evening wind. Then someone would begin to spin a story about the bravery of the Great Animal, but it would inevitably wither into a lamentation or a curse, a wish that the white man would die.

To come to terms with the bloodletting, we decided that the soldiers and the hunters they brought with them were less than human. One morning—it was in the spring and the wildflowers were scattering the prairie with color, so it was hard to imagine bad things happening—I asked my mother where were the children of these white men.

"Silly," she snapped, "monsters aren't capable of fathering babies."

We convinced ourselves that they were without human hearts, soulless, above having to answer to even their own people.

But still, as we struggled to maintain the old ways, to preserve the old earth, our imaginations never spun cruelly enough. No. Until it was too late none of us had an inkling as to what swift and efficient killers these people were.

I remember my mother one night by the fire, when our men were still with us, the flames softening her face—which had begun to hold and not release her sadness—murmuring into the smoke, "It happened so fast, this silencing of the Great Animal."

And it's true. One day we were talking about ways to stop the slaughter and the next day people were having visions of the last herd dissolving first into mist and then into pure spirit.

I had been a happy child before they took away my father. And I was a hopeful child the day my mother, through acts both impressive and pathetic, found a way for us to stay with him. But that is another story. What happened when they slaughtered our buffalo, and stole our land, and imprisoned our people, and raped our women, is the story of a world falling apart. It's a story about being cast into hell while you are still alive. It's a story about all faith and all things familiar being ripped expertly away. It's about losing the innocent spark of childhood.

And the soldiers enjoyed it. I saw them smile. I saw the mean-spirited light in their eyes. I saw how they never swerved from their course. I saw it and was afraid.

That is why, on a clear, cool November morning in 1875, before I had reached my sixth year, I stood on the heart of my grass angel and I spread my arms out wide and I threw my head back and searched the clear sky for a hawk. And when she came, circling high and majestically overhead, I prayed harder than I ever had that she would swoop down to the earth and take me by the shoulders in her iron talons and that we would fly far, far away. Away from the absence of buffalo. Away from shackled fathers. Away from women whose eyes reflected only the fever of worry. Away from the fires whose smoke curled furiously into a now godless sky.

As the hawk descended I tried to remain still and calm. I wanted to see the spirit in her yellow eyes when she snatched me.

Telling Mima's story to my captive trio, I watch them grow uncomfortable. They dare not look at one another. Rather, they stare into the rippling water. And fidget.

Sometimes rawboned truth, especially when it's truth coming from a woman, rankles a man like sandpaper up his craw.

I don't hold this against the boys. If I was younger perhaps I'd be mad. But not now. As I've gotten older, things that once riled me only serve to amuse.

Yes, as Mima told it, they took her daddy and all the rest of the men. They weren't shot and tossed into a mass grave, as you might be thinking. That would have been too easy. Instead, an ambitious young captain in the United States Army came up with the brilliant idea of jailing his ragtag string of Indians and schooling them. That's right. He decided to teach the Indian blood right out of each and every one.

But before he could accomplish what he thought was his God-mandated duty, he had to deal with Mima's mother, an iron-spined woman who was determined that she and Mima would go with the men, no matter where it was or how awful.

Sometimes women have to fight with what they are born with: those primitive feminine stones at the base of our spines. My great-grandmama didn't have a weapon like a gun or a rifle, and one would have been useless anyway against all those upstanding soldiers of the U.S. Army. But she did have this: a sky-shattering scream and a stubborn temperament and a burning desire to see her family stay together.

She threw a fit the fury of which must have haunted those men until the day they died.

She did so twice.

The first time was in Oklahoma. This is what my grandmama told me. The prairie looked like glass because the night had brought with it a hard freeze and the morning sun was too weak to burn the ice away. The shackled men were being loaded onto wagons and the women were being told that they would not be allowed to accompany their husbands. My great-grandmama, evidently a believer in transcendent strength in moments of terror, fell to the cold earth, screaming and hollering as if her butt was on fire and grabbing hold of the shackles binding her husband's legs, desperately trying to snap the chain.

Of course she couldn't snap iron, but the soldiers couldn't pull her away either. As men do, there was a flurry of suggestions and disagreements and nothing got done. But finally one voice rose above the others to suggest, ''Here, throw this on her.''

They doused my great-grandmama with a bucket of water, and it certainly did prove to be a baptism of the flesh, because the water sealed her hands to the iron, and then a government man pried them loose, frozen finger by frozen finger, leaving behind strips of faintly bleeding skin between my great-granddaddy's legs.

Still her hollering and wailing did not stop, and the man in charge finally gave in, allowing this proud and stubborn woman and her little girl to go with them, but only as far as the next transfer. Where that was, though, only the white men knew.

I guess if something works for you once, you might as well try it again. And she did. At Fort Leavenworth, Kansas. Threw a fit right there in front of the waiting, steam-gasping train just as the soldiers were about to take her husband away once more.

The captain, hawk-nosed and self-important, somewhere underneath all his careful layers of uniform and underclothes and buttons and soft white flesh must have held on to a scrap or two of soul, because he looked at that wild, bellowing woman and looked at her scared little girl and then looked at the icy ground and said, ''Let them go with him. What harm can it do?''

Mima swore that as the train chugged eastward with its cargo of shackled, numbed people, away from all they had ever known, her old skin started slipping away. It took years before the skinning was complete, but she swore that's when it began.

And also she swore this: When they crossed the Mississippi she looked down into that muddy water and saw a shadow pass. She knew what it was. "Good-bye, spirit buffalo," she said.

And then she closed her eyes and dozed, but her sleep was filled with dreams of the spirit buffalo, flying underwater, animals with huge green eyes and gentle dispositions, flying her somewhere.

Somewhere.

I DOCK THE *SPARROW HUNTER* and see him. Carlos in his oversized blood-red Bermuda shorts, a white, crisply bleached T-shirt, clutching a bouquet of purple peonies. His gold Saint Christopher medal glints in the sun. He's all macho and delight in a freshly shaved package.

The sight of him stirs in me an irrational effect: I am twinly happy and peeved. Why does love affect me this way? Why does the sight of a man who adores me send me into a schizophrenic two-step?

I secure the boat and say good-bye to the boys. As they disembark, Carlos bows ceremoniously, a crazy grin and a shock of black hair. I know he's being a jerk, jealous that I spent the day with a trio of young men.

They think he's boisterously friendly.

"Mamacita! Sadie Baby!" he sings.

"Hey, there." I push my hair back off my face. "Who are the flowers for?"

Ignoring the ladder, he jumps aboard the *Sparrow*. I watch his arm muscles strain under the white cotton as he grips the railing and hefts himself through the air and back down. His movements are graceful but not sissified. They suggest a man comfortable in his own skin. Plus, Carlos has a good physique, which sure does help. Some women say it's the legs or the eyes that send them up. For me, it's those wide shoulders angling into a circlet of a waist. Bingo! I'm still a woman.

He holds out the peonies as if offering a pot of gold. He isn't smiling. In fact, he's as serious as daybreak, with dark eyes that smolder under heavy lids. It's his look of ardor, the one that says he wants to own me. The salt air struggles against the knock-you-down-dead scent of Old Spice. "For you, lady, they are my heart," he says.

"I hope they don't die soon, then," I joke, but he doesn't laugh.

Instead, he touches my cheek with two fingers that are brown and callused from handling nets and ropes. He murmurs, a near whisper, "You know the old saying, The secret for living is water."

"You're a regular walking, talking poem today, aren't you," I dryly offer, holding the peonies in one hand and poking him in the chest with the other. I move to take the flowers below, but before I can get away he has me in his arms and we're kissing. I start to give in, to really enjoy myself, and then I remember what I woke up to. The reason for the flowers becomes suddenly clear: to ward off my nailing him for being nosy. It won't work. I pull away. "Why were you snooping on me this morning?" I demand.

"Snooping?" His voice rises an octave and his eyes widen to enhance the appearance of incomprehension and shock. He shakes his head as if disappointed in me and then touches my hair. "Oh, baby, baby, baby. I no snoop on you. Never. It was the moon," he says, as if that is a rational explanation.

I can't help it. I'm taken by him for a moment: that long Roman nose and those fine, delicate bones, and lips that make me crazy. They are full lips, definitely lips—you know, the kind you can really, really kiss. Then my mind veers sharply. I decide his face reminds me of a tree in winter, a tree whose loss of leaves heightens its seasonal stark beauty. What in the hell am I thinking? His poetry is infectious, like VD. I sluff off my moment of temporary insanity, this tendency to be romantic.

I shake the flowers at him. "What does that mean exactly, Carlos, 'It was the moon'?"

He drapes his arm over my shoulder. "It makes people see"—and he points to his beautiful eyes—"things that can only be visioned at night, things not always real."

"Carlos, that is not an answer. That's evasion."

Why am I trying to talk to him sanely? He doesn't even know what "evasion" means. Nor does he care. He's bearing down on me with those eyes I can't shrink from. Their beauty and blatant desire swallow me up. But there is sorrow underneath all that sex appeal and sweetness. I think it's a sorrow peculiar to Latins, as if they view love and death as different sides of the same penny.

"*Sí,* Mamacita," he says simply, "the moon."

And then he begins to chatter, and he sounds utterly sincere but I don't have the slightest idea what he's saying because he's speaking in Cuban.

"Will you stop!" I snap, and turn away. If I could, I would kick myself in the butt. Here is a man full of life. Busting with passion. He's like the female part of me that's missing, that got left behind in the afterbirth. But when he's around, I harden. Inexplicably. Subzero on a tropical day. There's no winning. He's never going to admit he snoops. I'm never going to be some romantic piece of fluff. And he's always going to spout off in that foreign language of his each and every time I've got him cornered.

So I give up. For now. Because if I push, the fact that I've lost this round will become more obvious to him. And he doesn't need any help noticing that. I brush past him and go below, where I put the peonies in a water glass and get us a couple of beers. I return to the deck and sit with him, the two of us in plastic armchairs facing the orange-and-blue sunset.

Before long it will explode into red and purple. I let him hold my hand.

He says, "You are a wild girl, Sadie. And mean."

"Yep. You're right about that." I toss back my head—it's a motion that's effective only if you have long hair, a female's nonviolent equivalent of a slap in the face. I don't have long hair. In fact, I keep mine, which is black with a few strands of gray, chopped off at the chin. I cut it myself, just like my grandmother. It looks like hell, but it's functional. And like a dog who chases his tail even if he's been born without, I feel in my subconscious the tresses I don't have slap against my back.

Someone belonging to the sailboat the next slip over trundles down the dock, his arms full of groceries. "Hey," I yell, "what's for supper?"

He is dressed in white tennis shorts and a baseball cap. He smiles stupidly and shouts something, but the wind whips his words into the ether.

Carlos stands up and fiddles with the tape player I keep by the helm. He's punching all the buttons as if there's some secret code or magical sequence to make it play.

"It's on the fritz," I say.

He looks over his shoulder at me. "Really?"

"Really."

He stares back at it like he can't believe it's broken. "We'll get you one new," he says, and he slumps back down beside me. He takes my hand in his again. And we're silent.

I watch cormorants far in the distance, darts against the kaleidoscope-colored sky, aiming for the heart of the sun. Poor, foolish Carlos, I think, always insistently hunting for my heart beneath the patch of brambles and thorns I use to protect it. What keeps him going, searching? How does he even know if I have a heart to share?

He hums softly. The dying light softens his sharp features. He follows the lines in my palm, concentrating on them like a fortune-teller seeking money or truth. The sun blossoms into a poppy-red orb, partially descending behind a bank of purple-and-gold clouds. I wonder what he dreams about. I almost ask him, and then decide he'd laugh at me.

He looks up from my hand. "That's good," he says.

"What's good?" I stare at my palm, but its squiggled lines mean nothing. I don't believe in signs or palm reading or tea leaf reading or anything else outside my control.

"Woman, you are going to live the long life," he says matter-of-factly, as if revealing grass is green.

"Yeah? I think I've already done that." I tuck my hands under my legs. I want him to quit staring at me. I look up at the sky and pretend I'm fascinated by it.

He leans into me—I'm getting angry—and whispers, "It will be a life full of sex."

With a set jaw I say, "I think you've got our palms confused. Let's see." I take his thick, scarred hand in mine. "Yep, yep, looks like you'll spend your days fucking like a rabbit, making little grand-babies your mother won't ever see.''

God damn it. I did it again. Sadie Hunter, master of hitting below the belt. I wish I could stuff the words back into my mouth, but of course, it's way too late.

He takes a huge swallow of beer and then sets the can on the rail carefully, as if it's a glass vase, as if he's slowing down, weighing the wickedness of his response. He turns to me and his eyes are shining and his lips are curved up in something close to a grin and his head is tilted back so he's looking down at me, but I can't tell whether the eyes and lips and tilt of the head add up to a challenge or just one giant smirk. ''Stand up!'' he says.

''What?''

''Stand up! Don't you understand English, Miss America?'' He's on his feet and offering me his hand. A mess of black hair has fallen in his eyes and now not a stitch of a smile. The air is hot and close. The breeze, for the moment, has died. There's no room for bargaining.

I take his hand and allow myself to be pulled out of my chair only because I'm guilty over shooting off my mouth.

He jerks me toward him and says, ''Let's dance.'' But he's not suggesting. He's insisting.

''You're crazy. There's no music.'' His arms are strong. I think that if I were a shot bird falling end over end through the sky, he would catch me.

He tries to sway or spin, but I'm not budging.

"We make our own music," and he starts singing—he does have a good voice—but I don't understand the foreign words. I won't give him one turn, not one rhythmic step. And even though it feels wonderful to be held by him, I will never admit it.

He stops singing and pulls away, taking me by the shoulders. "Who gives you this idea? That I want to go back to Cuba? Me, Carlos Octavio Perez. Have it made in this country."

I can't help myself. I start laughing. He sounds like an investment banker with two houses and a stable of race cars instead of a fisherman who makes enough to pay his rent but not enough to buy that Harley he's so wet-mouthed over.

I look into his tanned, boyish face—both honesty and blue-blooded cockiness reside there—pondering my response. I could tell him I recognize the homesick pall in his eyes as he stares into the horizon toward his homeland and softly hums a Cuban folk song. I could tell him he looks close to tears when he talks about his kid sister's slight overbite and her beautiful guitar playing or his mother's love of good tobacco and her luscious coconut cake. I could tell him I've caught him daydreaming and I'd bet my boat that his dreams were of home and of his village and of the colors of the Cuban mountains rising placidly into a storm of tropical sunlight.

I could tell him all of this. And I'd be right. But I don't feel like striking another blow at his heart right now, I'm just not able, so I gaze into that face that could make me tremble if I were a sweeter woman, and say, "How about a Popsicle?"

"No dance?"

"Nuh-uh," and I turn on my heel and head below.

"So, your work today. How did it go? Those boys pay you?" he asks as he follows me, evidently content not to press on with a discussion that could easily have mushroomed into an argument.

I peer into my runt refrigerator and at its inch-high freezer. I start to ask, "What boys?" and then I remember the trio from Jersey. "Of course they paid me. It's what I do for a living." I hand him the orange one and keep the lime for myself. Popsicles and beer—a Key West tradition.

We stretch out on my bunk. It's hot and the air is thick, close to being visible. Carlos hands me his Popsicle and takes off his shirt. He makes a pronouncement in Cuban. I think it has to do with how hot it is. The only sound I make out as a distinct word is *muy*. I hand him back his Popsicle. There's something about the way he smells when he sweats. It's a guy thing and it makes me feel vulnerable. I hate it.

"Mmmm. Good stuff," he says as he takes a bite out of his orange sugar-on-a-stick.

"Yep. It'll make you fat and rot out your teeth."

"You tell them stories?" He looks as if he's got cheap neon-orange lipstick smeared on, and I start to make fun of him and then realize my lips are probably green. I wipe my mouth off with the back of my hand, hoping I'm wrong.

"What else am I going to do out there but tell stories? I'm certainly not going to try to make small talk."

He nods, takes another bite, and with his mouth full says, "True. You're no good at that."

To prove him wrong I say, "Your day? How was it? Catch anything?" I keep my voice light, interested.

Life as a commercial fisherman isn't so grand. Especially if you don't own the boat. He tells me he had a good haul, though, mainly yellowtail and dolphin and skate. Lots of skate, which they pound out with round things that resemble cookie cutters, and the restaurants serve them up as scallops. But he didn't get the price he wanted. "Everybody poor-mouthing," he says.

He finishes off his Popsicle and takes my half-eaten one and sets it in my clamshell ashtray. He leans back, resting his head on one hand, fiddling with my blouse with the other. He kisses me, and a scent of citrus mixes with Old Spice. I know his tongue is stained neon orange and he's probably transferring the toxic dyes they put in this stuff straight down my throat. So now I have a double dose of toxins. I know I am not thinking in particularly romantic terms, but perhaps that's a gift you're born with, or maybe it's an acquired talent, like drinking single-malt Scotch without making a face.

"Sadie Baby," he says.

"What, Carlos?"

I'm listening but I'm also planning, like maybe I'll take the boat out again. Not far, just a few miles, and watch the end of the sunset.

"I have this question."

"Shoot." I see myself puttering off into the light.

"Sadie"—he slips a finger inside my blouse—"I been thinking. You live on this old boat all day, all night. No flowers to make grow. No yard to tend or water. No, how you say, solid ground. Nothing to take care of."

"I don't want to hear this, Carlos," I snap. He slips his finger behind my bra cup. He's fishing, all right.

"No, no, no! It's a good boat. Yes. Old and good. Like you," he teases, and I slap his hand away. He smiles, flashing those perfect white teeth. He is cute, I'll give him that. "Woman," he says, each syllable falling from his lips in a puff of Popsicle-sweetened breath, "just think of this for me. No deciding now. Just think. You can move into my place and we see how it goes. We can make love 'round the clock. See if we can stand it. Maybe you'll plant a garden. And I'll help you. Cucumbers. Onions. Even tomatoes. On the patio. Keep the old boat and this—this business enterprise. But Sadie Baby, it might not be bad. You might like it. Everything calms down when you grow a garden. Plus, rent free. If you want."

He's looking at me so earnestly, scanning my face as if I'm of value, that my throat closes up. Anger flies all over me. I can't even find humor in this new insistence that I become Farmer Jane. All I know is that suddenly, and again, I am a drowning woman. Why can't he just leave me alone? Why can't he leave me to fuck up my life any way I see fit?

I try to stare him down but can't. His eyes are too deep. And his heart is bigger than I thought that first day I met him, two years ago, under the banyan, when I ran smack into him because I wasn't watching where I was going but taunting some redneck with a beer belly for brains who'd yelled at me in a passing truck. Why doesn't he understand that I can't let him inside my skin? He thinks my hard shell protects a soft heart, the heart of a *mamacita*. He's wrong. Mine is a heart of shattered glass. My tough shell simply keeps the shards inside, so not too many people get cut.

I sit up and I bury my face in my hands. I'm suffocating. I don't know what to do. I need space. I feel like beating on him, making him go back into the shadows he came from.

But instead I say, "Go home, Carlos. I don't want to talk to you right now."

And this is what a kind man he is. He does not argue or pitch any hint of a fit. He sits up and kisses my forehead. Sweetly.

"*Sí,* Sadie Baby," he says, and I catch no hint of judgment nor a play at pity. There is only a sincere and patient sadness. He starts to lean over and kiss me again, but I shoot him a warning look. The one that means, Don't even try it.

So he turns around and walks out of my cabin and off my boat and down the dock, and then I am alone.

But he has left his T-shirt behind. Its cologne-heavy scent rises like smoke into the sweltering air.

I'M OUT FARTHER than I intended. Gas isn't cheap, and here I am, motoring to get away from a man who loves me, to watch a sunset that's almost over and that I could have seen as well from land. Plus, I have to avoid the party barges—the cats and dining boats that take Yankee lovebirds out for champagne sunset "cruises."

Anchored farther west than the party barges go, I'm pretty much by myself. There are a few sailboats scattered about, but they are beyond shouting distance.

As the sun sinks lower and lower, as it becomes more a suggestive glow than a fiery stone, my discontent with Carlos and with my behavior grows. Even though in my rational brain I know he did nothing, said nothing, intended nothing, to harm me, my irrational brain is still furious. I can't shake it. Maybe it's some sort of inherited dysfunction on my part.

I'm hot from my long day and I know if Carlos were with me now, kissing my naked skin, he would taste salt. And he would be joyous about it, ingesting my sweat as if it were truly part of me and not just exhaust. Guilt springs eternal as I remember his stubborn but hurt expression when he left the boat. If I'm not careful, I'm going to lose him. I know that. And then I will have accomplished what I seem bent on even though it's what I fear most: I'll be alone in the world. Again.

I look toward the eastern horizon and see that the moon is already dawning, a three-quarter white disk amid the still blue but darkening sky. Sometimes I believe my body and psyche really are invisibly tied to that bright light traveling up there among the stars, its path, always so predictable, mapped out by skinny scientists in close rooms who chart its movement like shamans scrawling in the sand. Except that the shamans were looking for larger truths, willing to believe that the moon's soft white light not only shone down from the heavens but penetrated our skin to take a good long look at our souls.

The water is so inviting. It begins to shimmer as the moon rises higher. A few stars sprinkle the sky. A memory flashes. Mama in Chester Tiger's kitchen tossing sugar across star-shaped pieces of dough.

I take off my clothes. I don't care if anybody sees me. I've always been amazed at the ability of a naked body to send grown people into spasms of stupidity.

I dive overboard, and as the warm water envelops me, calms me, I consider Carlos and the troubled love I stingily offer. I dive deeper into the salty darkness and try to imagine his face that I so appreciate. But instead I see Mr. Sammy—that's what Mama and Mima called my granddaddy. In the deepest part of my heart I think I mix up Carlos and Mr. Sammy fairly often. For example, sometimes when I'm dreaming, they switch places. I might be dreaming of swimming with Carlos, and the next thing I know we've turned into silver-skinned fish and are cutting through the water. Brilliantly. Except the fish I'm with is no longer Carlos. It's Mr. Sammy. And right now, even though I'm awake and really swimming down, down, down, I try to think of Carlos, but it is Mr. Sammy I see. I mean, the way I've decided he looks. The way I pretend he was: slight of build, cinnamon-colored, and eyes so sweet, so patient—like Carlos's—that I long for them.

I reverse course, spinning like a child in the womb, aiming toward the moonlight, and I surface. The air is cold against my face. It's a clear evening. The constellations are defined and sharp, but my astronomy is no good. I can't tell the Big Dipper from my big toe. I rise out of the water a little so that I can float on my back and watch the sky.

Suspended in water and space, meandering among the constellations, I swim toward a day and time before I was born.

You may think I'm off my rocker, but right there in the southern sky, with a zigzag of stars on his shoulder and the moon rising at his feet, I see my Mr. Sammy. And I listen:

FIRST TIME I laid eyes on her I weren't but five years old, and she the same. I was a little mulatto boy who'd seen the hidden heart of seeds and stones and birds. She was a pint-sized Injun girl who, I would come to realize, had seen magic animals racing that huge sky and endless prairie she come from.

What our eyes had witnessed when we were still too young to have figured out ways to filter out the pain was what made us different, is what above all else turned us, even as little children, into outsiders.

Wouldn't you think such eye-to-eye backgrounds would make for an unbreakable bond?

It did, 'cept she was so hardheaded she kept trying to break it. Kept trying to say that our love didn't exist despite us both smelling it. Every time we saw each other the air grew thick like it weren't air at all but jasmine honey.

I admit, on the surface our attitudes and circumstances seemed as different as corn bread to French bread. But really, we was dough cast from the same hand. She just had a dickens of a time ever confessing to it.

I was with my parents that warm dark night, fishing off the new San Sebastian bridge. The city had finally gone ahead and spent the coin to build it. The old bridge had been tore up during the Civil War.

Nobody ever explained to me how it got tore up, since there weren't never any battles in St. Augustine. All that folks said was, "Yeah. The old bridge got tore up during the war. Replaced it with this ferry." The ferry was a memory too, and now we had a good fishing bridge, and it was pretty easy once more to get from east town to west town.

So me and Mama and Papa were leaning 'gainst the rail, our long cane poles dangling out over the black water, expecting the most excitement we might have that night would be catching a fish big enough that we didn't have to toss it back in and wait for it to grow up.

There wasn't no moon in the sky, so I weren't even sure why we was out. The brighter the moon, the better your chances not to go home empty-handed, 'cause the fish get attracted to all the pretty light floating on the surface. I guess Papa just had his heart set on throwing out a line. That's all.

So there we was, defying nature, fishing without so much as a hint of the moon in that inky sky. Mama's head was wrapped in a yellow feed-sack kerchief with tiny white flowers. Papa wore a brown sliver-brimmed hat tilted way back. They was both the color of chocolate milk cut by half with sweet cream. Mama's eyes were big and brown but Papa's was green, like mine. A spooky eat-your-vegetables green.

This here is what they told me, about how we had such a confused bloodline topped off with high-toned skin. Both my grandmamas had been forced to do duty to their masters, pardon me, and the result was two little mulatto babies. Grandma Jones gave birth to Papa, and Grandma Wilson gave birth to Mama. Even though the babies was half white, their slave-owning grandpapas wouldn't have nothing to do with them 'cept enslave them. Mama's papa couldn't even look at her. He sold her and her mama to the owner of an indigo plantation north of town. The owner just happened to be my papa's granddaddy, but never mind that, 'cause like I said, he still put him in chains. That's how Mama and Papa met. They grew up together, owned by the same man, till they became freedmen at the beginning of the year in 1863.

'Cept it took a while for word to filter down this far 'bout any freedom, and it took even longer for anybody to pay attention to it. Plus, the war battled on for another two years. No matter that St. Augustine was held by the North almost the entire time, 'cause nobody put much pressure on the slave owners to do what they was supposed to do under the law. There just wasn't any will to challenge them. Northern heads could turn as easy as Southern ones. That's why it wasn't till sometime in 1865 did anybody tell Mama and Papa they was free.

But once told, on the very day they opened the plantation's iron gates and set their feet into the world as freedmen, they took their wedding vows. Said them to each other under a live oak with two chickens and a skeptical lost cow as witnesses.

And they never looked over their shoulders at that

plantation, which wasn't much of a plantation any-more, seeing's how both the war and the weather had taken their toll. All the fields had gone to seed and everybody said Ol' Massa done lost his mind, 'cause one night during the hottest part of summer—during the time that your clothes stick to your skin like wet bandages—he set fire to the whole damn plantation and almost even burned his own house down 'cept a rainstorm blew in and put out the fire.

So anyways, Mama and Papa, free as two ex-slaves can ever be, became squatters along the San Sebastian River with a slew of other freedmen. 'Cause nobody in town would sell food or clothes or anything else to the freedmen, slowly they started their own places of commerce and somebody got the bright idea of calling it Lincolnville. And that name stuck.

And because of my light skin and white man's eyes, lots of colored folks make fun of me and lots of whites let me in the stores. I'm lighter than even some of the Minorcans in town.

But the trouble, then and now, is that moods change with the breeze. One day a mulatto boy is considered at least decent enough to allow inside the store and sell penny candy to, and the next day he might be run out and called a nigger.

In a town like St. Augustine the breeze never blows the same way twice.

But that night, with our poles hanging lazily over the railing, it seemed as if the only thing the wind was full of was the salty scent of oyster beds and the ocean roaring just beyond the safety of the harbor. Everything was calm, 'cept I was growing fidgety. I wasn't yet a patient fisherman, desiring as I was for my line to be struck the second it drifted underwater. Back then, too, I prayed a lot when I fished. But I'd grow bored with the praying, so I'd huff, loud and long, and Papa, he'd grin at me like I was a knee-high joke.

And then he'd start telling me stories. That was the only thing I didn't grow bored with, his stories.

Mama had just said, "I think a crab got my bait." She pulled her line in, and sure enough, even without a moon we could tell the wiggler was gone.

I found this a good time to show off my impatience, so I huffed.

Mama just set to rebaiting her hook, the worm winding like a snake 'round her finger.

That's when Papa says, "Sammy, I ever tell you 'bout your uncle turning hisself into a gator? How his soft skin could turn dry and hard and grow big old gator scales? How he could slither off into Mad Man's Swamp and wait like a bumpy log, just his snout and beady eyes above the water, for that master of his to canoe down those black waters, your uncle waiting to gobble that man up?"

I said, "No, sir, you ain't never told me that story." Which wasn't true and he knew it, but it was such a good tale that I could never get enough of it.

I slapped a skeeter off my face and Mama grinned

out at the water and Papa said, "Son, you and me come from a long line of gator men."

Then the wind gusted, but instead of the expected salt smell rolling over us, the scent of jasmine flowered all 'round. It was enough to make Papa shut his mouth, 'cause we'd had a late freeze and the common set-to all over town was that the freeze burned back the jasmine and everything else so we weren't in for a very sweet-smelling spring. But there it was, a scent so full of pollen it could make a nun drunk.

And then as we were still stunned by the sudden jasmine, we heard horses, lots of them, to the west. Moonless nights don't do anything to ease a nervous soul, and I looked to Papa, who was a man who saw ghosts easily, sometimes even in daylight, and I knew he was afeared. 'Cause the smile he had on his face when he fixed to tell me the gator man story collapsed into a thin line and his eyes darted fast to the west.

"Papa, what do you think is going on?" Mama whispered, but the whispering wasn't solely 'cause she was afeared. It was 'cause her and Papa almost always whispered to each other. A habit left over from slave days, when if they got caught talking together it might mean the whip.

Papa whispered back, "Mama, I think I see a light out there." Then they look at each other as though they've got it figured out, but they don't say anything 'cause they don't want to scare me.

But I already am afeared, because I might have

only been five but I knew what they was thinking 'cause I'd heard the rumors the grownups shared with one another. Out there, in the darkness, with their flames burning brighter and brighter as they rode closer and closer, was what we feared most in them days: a lynching party full of dead men. Folks said that the ghosts of Confederate soldiers haunted these parts, gaining revenge by lynching good honest people.

As much as I didn't want to be lynched, I didn't want to see no ghost, rebel or not. I started to cry.

Mama set her pole down and pulled me into her arms. "Don't worry, baby, we're all right," she whispered. And instead of smelling of cinnamon—Mama liked to dab it behind her ears when she could get it—the jasmine smell grew so strong that my tongue turned bitter.

Papa said, "If we run, they'll catch us for sure. We're just gonna have to stand on this bridge, as still as we possibly can, and we're gonna become real dark. You hear me? So dark they ain't gonna be able to see us in all this night."

We snapped our lines out the water and set the poles on the ground. Mama put her arm 'round me to steady me, which is a good thing, 'cause I was so afeared I thought I might wet myself.

With her help I stood on that new wooden bridge still as the dead ought to be, and even when a skeeter landed on my arm and bit me I did not swat him off. I was trying to think of nothing 'cept blending into the night, but I could not block the sound out of my ears: horses and ghosts and chains.

Barely breathing but eyes wide, we watched them approach, their torches casting flame-light over their faces, and each of us—Papa, Mama, and me—had to hold in a gasp of pure surprise when we realized what we was seeing.

They was soldiers, all right, but they weren't ghost rebels. No, sir. They was government men with fat, long rifles, and they was herding over the bridge and into town not cattle but a long line of chained human souls. Human souls like we'd never seen before, 'cause they was Injuns, with long black hair and eyes that snapped in the torchlit night.

Many of 'em wore beads 'round their necks, and as if to defy the night's heat, wild-patterned blankets draped over their shoulders like armor.

No one spoke, not the ghost soldiers or the ghost Injuns, but hovering above the sound of the horse hooves 'gainst the wooden bridge planks was the sound of iron chains, like tambourines shattering the night.

Despite my fear, I took full notice that among all those grown-up and chained Injun men walked one spectral girl, holding her mama's hand and clutching a pretty, pretty black-haired doll that looked just like her.

I know of this resemblance 'cause she passed within inches of me. I saw her dirty hands gripping that look-alike doll and I saw her stubborn face that even at that young age was firmly beautiful. I saw how dark and perfect her wide eyes was.

And this is the truth: She passed by so slowly I was wounded. Yes, sir, I knew we had not succeeded in becoming invisible because she stared straight at me and I at her and all the shadows fell away. The wind gusted, fat with jasmine, and my mouth turned sour, as if it was chock-full of petals. The flames bent wildly but survived. Our eyes locked, and in that pure moment, without anything—man or law or god or shadow—blocking our view, I perceived that she was looking at me with an overflowing bowl of hate.

As the last ghost crossed the bridge, the wooden planks creaked and the smell wafted off into the night. But the taste lingered.

My papa whispered, "Those was the strangest ghosts I ever did see. They was in chains, Mama." His voice was thick with sadness, weighed down with memory and fear.

"Let's get on home," Mama said. "We done enough fishing for tonight."

They was both so shook, the sight of ghosts in chains being something too awful to think about. With our poles over our shoulders and the worm bucket in Papa's hand, we shuffled off into the darkness and none of us said nothing, not a word, till we got home.

Once there, Mama and Papa, without even lighting the lantern, sat down at our old pine table and started whispering to each other, fumbling with a single rosary, sharing in some sort of catechism.

I went on back outside and pumped water and tried to wash the bitter jasmine out of my mouth, but it wouldn't be cleansed.

That night I slept as if I was in a fever, tossing and tumbling through pictures of that Injun girl glowering at me with nothing but hate. I must have cried out, 'cause Mama woke me up and wiped tears off my face. She held me 'gainst her breast and said, "Hush, sweet baby," but I wouldn't be stilled.

I just kept babbling on 'bout what my dream had told me, trying to convince her that those chained-up souls weren't ghosts at all but living, breathing savages done forced at gunpoint into our town.

I weren't never peaceful again. That is, not until the Christmas of 1885. 'Cause without warning that girl's face would gather in my mind and I didn't know whether to cry or go find her. But like I'm saying, that was before Christmas and Miss Raison and Saint John the Conqueror. This here is what I mean:

Lots of white people just 'bout bought the stores out come Christmas, but not us. Being poor to the point gifts were out of the question, my mama and papa and I gave each other stories. Mama would fix wild boar or turkey, whatever Papa had gone out and shot. Plus, if our garden had cooperated, which often it did not, we'd have pole beans or cabbage. Sometimes, if we could get together enough coin for the grain man, there was a big skillet of sweet corn bread. If it was a fortunate year, a jug of liquor appeared on the table, which I got a sip of, and which Mama and Papa enjoyed a glass or two of. We were and still are moderate folks.

After Christmas supper we'd have our story time. They weren't new stories necessarily, but honed. As if we'd spent the past twelve months putting the tales to the fire, burning away the excess, so that when we finally sat down at our table to celebrate the birth of Jesus the words that did come out of our mouths were pure. Mama would start out, then me, then Papa, 'cause his stories was always best. And they was true, even the one about our people being able to turn into reptiles, and the one about there being a white gator somewhere in the Florida swamp capable of great good, a gator who had made hisself known through dreams to the menfolk in my family. As for me, I hadn't yet caught any whiff or sign of him. I was confident once I became a man, though, that I too would be blessed with a white gator vision.

But see here, on the particular Christmas morning I'm speaking of, I'd gone outside to pass the time till supper was ready. I was tossing stones at some tins I'd set up on a stump, when I looked down at the dirt in disgust for having missed a shot and saw the destruction one of our chickens had wrought. I said, "Oh, Miss Raison, Mama's gonna have your scrawny butt for Christmas supper."

Miss Raison, being a chicken of little substance, in all likelihood never would have ended up on the chopping block, but I sure thought Mama might kill her anyways 'cause there she was pecking away and ingesting the entire Saint John the Conqueror garden Mama had done planted last spring.

Mama placed a lot of stock in that garden 'cause Saint John the Conqueror was as good as you could get as a saint. Some folks called him the Merrymaker, and back in slave days he wandered the countryside disguised as a poor raggedy-clothed beggar. But them slaves who could see the other world knew who they was looking at. And while their bodies was still enslaved, after a visit by the Merrymaker their spirits were free. At night their souls, made slippery with mutton grease blessed by Saint John, slid from their irons and floated out over still waters, where they was replenished.

Mama used the Saint John the Conqueror plant in teas to ease gout or asthma, to cure depression or a weak character. Folks came to her all hours of the day and night in need of the tea. So this garden, as you can well see, was mighty important to her. Yet when I ran inside and told her what Miss Raison had done, she set down her batter bowl and with her calico apron wiped sweat out her eyes. She clapped her hands together and said, "Praise the Lord!"

Then she hurried to the garden and saw for herself and she put her arms around me and said, "Son, we have got us a magic chicken."

Which pleased me but didn't knock me over. 'Cause as soon as Mama said, "Son, we have got us a magic chicken," I made a wish that a bucket full of gold would fall from the sky and land at my feet. It didn't happen. I would come to see that Miss Raison's magic was slow and steady. The very best kind. For instance, from that day forward nothing bad happened to Mama or Papa or me. Nothing world-changing took hold, like we didn't find no passel of money or get some mansion or anything like that. But mean folks left us alone. Papa bagged venison. I reeled in sea bass. Mama grew less scared of white people. Anybody who visited our shack by the river said something to the sort, "It sure is peaceful here." And everything we stuck in the ground grew. Beans and corn and potatoes and oranges, they grew so well that we was always able to share with our neighbors. And sometimes they didn't have a thing 'cept what we gave them.

Now, over the years I never forgot the Injun girl we saw that dark hot night when I was just an upstart. The memory of her beauty and hatred flitted like a firefly along my thoughts, here and there, and until the Christmas of 1885 I remained sorely confused. I couldn't figure out that combination of unprovoked hate and searing beauty. But once Miss Raison ate the Conqueror root, once me and my family began to believe nothing bad could befall us, then some nights as I drifted off to sleep I would remember her child's face and then try to conjure what she might look like as a young woman, and then I would whisper into my moss pillow, "Bring her on."

UNDER A STAR-PIERCED SKY I swim back to the boat and struggle aboard. Moonlight trips across my skin and I wonder if I'm any better for it. If I were in a phosphorescent lagoon, one of those rare places unsullied by human exhaust, my skin would appear diamond-studded. And in reality what it would be is a zillion infinitesimal luminescent critters who show themselves not for what they are but as points of light. Maybe that is their true selves—light dots—and maybe Mama and Mima were really fish all along, and Mr. Sammy was a gator, and I could just never see it.

I grab a towel that is draped over the beer cooler and dry off. Then I throw on a clean T-shirt and shorts, and feeling far less morose than when I came out here, I kick up the motor and head back to town. The moon has gotten smaller as it's risen higher. But it's much brighter. And intensely white.

Poor Mr. Sammy. That first night he laid eyes on Mima must have shaken him right down to his gizzard. But of course he was right. He wasn't seeing ghosts. They were alive, flesh-and-blood people, being herded into St. Augustine's massive old fort. And while he grew older, never letting go of his vision of that little girl—even aging her in his imagination—she was undergoing transformations that went well beyond the inevitable march from childhood to adolescence.

What occurred was the mutation of her spirit, and it began in the fort where Mima, her parents, and the rest of them stayed imprisoned while the captain, under the auspices of the U.S. Government, systematically and effectively brainwashed them, insisting day in and day out that they give up and accept the lie that everything about them was wrong.

This is what the soldiers did to my people, this is what I know—they cut their hair, they put the men in army uniforms and forced them to perform drills for hours on end, they didn't allow them to speak their native tongue and taught them English. If the Indians were caught speaking their own language, they were beaten.

They were told they were savages, damned in the eyes of the great white god. Christianity was the only true religion, they were told, and after several attempts at revolt and escape, they all buckled down. They settled into a routine of drills and classes and punishments, eventually muttering their amens and losing their souls.

The world is such a wily place. The human heart, especially a young one, can change allegiances as quickly as a swallow flying through a crystal sky can soar toward the sun and then plummet, without warning, toward earth, catching an insect on the wing. That's what happened to Mima. When they first locked her up in the fort, she possessed an Indian heart. But as the months turned into years, it got tangled in the brambles of religion and culture and change. She plummeted to the earth, all right, sizing up the insect first from afar and then internally as that poor bug beat its wings against the soft tissue of her mouth.

She told me that by the end of the incarceration she wanted one thing above all else: to be a little white girl. She said her parents had become strangers to her. And worse. She said she was embarrassed by them.

After three years of spiritual and cultural rape, the government decided to try out its experiment on a fresh group of Indians. The plan was to send Mima's people back west, where they were to act as missionaries for the white cause.

But one of the women from town who taught at the fort had taken a special interest in Mima. Alice Motherwell. It seems she couldn't bear the thought of this child, who'd been so successfully transformed, returning to life among "savages." Indeed, Mima's new heart conspired with Miss Motherwell's genteel Southern one made of steel. And the captain, believing Mima was his greatest success, was more than willing, along with Miss Motherwell, to try to persuade her parents to give her up, or at least to bring his weight to bear in telling them that they no longer had a daughter.

Even as an old woman, when Mima told this story she would cry cold hard tears.

The captain, in a voice that Mima likened to thunder, demanded she tell her parents what she—all on her own, he smugly lied—had come to realize. As she told them, she was careful to keep her eyes aimed at her new buff-white button-up boots that so wonderfully pinched her toes—a gift from Miss Motherwell. Her father insisted that he would never allow his daughter to be taken from him. "No! No! No!" Mima said he shouted.

But Mima's mother, the same woman who'd fought so hard on the prairie to keep their family together, the woman who at one time believed she could snap iron, must have truly lost herself in that fort. Somehow they got to her good. All the preaching about the false gods of the prairies, and their savage souls burning in hell, and being forced for three years to think and speak in the ways of another culture at the expense of her own must have indelibly cracked her, because she looked at her daughter dead-on and said, "No. She must stay. She isn't ours anymore."

I wonder if Mima swallowed it whole, or if it took her a while to get used to her new self, or if she spit out the wings.

Mima told me she didn't remember the little boy on the bridge the night she was herded into the fort. She didn't spend her nights re-creating his image in her mind and musing about the sound of his voice or the touch of his skin. He didn't enter her consciousness until years later, when, as love-starved teenagers, they crossed paths in a Catholic church. "I was seventeen," Mima would say, and she'd slit her eyes and gaze into the distance, as if it held her past, and then she'd say wistfully, "And he and I were beautiful."

I remember her sitting on the shore of some unnamed key, ignoring the yellow fly that had lit on her shoulder, her face softening with the glow of the past: *And he and I were beautiful*—suddenly I am adrift in that nagging issue of her reliability, because to believe her without question is like believing in religion. It's not about their beauty, it's about projection—maybe her memory lens was warped and scratched. Maybe Mama's and Mima's stories were never meant to project reality, but some sort of dream time, a state not unlike sleep, where death and laughter and the impossible intermingle freely. Did Mr. Sammy exist? Or did they create him out of longing for a man who was faithful and all-suffering and through-and-through good? And like Doubting Thomas, who asks, "How do I know?" I am befuddled by the perennial response: "Have faith."

As I approach the marina, I throw the *Sparrow* into idle. I hear the slap of a mullet jumping. I've got friends who swear mullet jump for fun. I think they do it because they're spooked, thinking any second Mr. Dolphin is going to make himself some supper.

As I aim the *Sparrow* toward the dock, I see Carlos. There's the bright fiery end of his cigarette—he smokes when he's nervous—and he's in shadow, just standing, waiting. I can't see clearly, but I know it's him. I know the slight hunch of his shoulders, the patient tilt of his head.

This is good, I decide. I can try to make some

amends. Try to make my apologies for being such a jackass earlier. I'll try to watch my nasty mouth. I'll try with all my heart and soul to be nice. I hope I don't look too bedraggled. He never seems to mind when I look like shit. Maybe there's something wrong with him.

I motor past a forty-foot yacht decked out in radar and a depth finder and all sorts of other unnecessary toys. In gold leaf and mariner blue, it proclaims itself to be *Babe's Boy* from Delaware. Rich folks on their way to the islands.

I clear *Babe* and make the turn straight for my slip. Maybe I'll ask Carlos to stay over. Maybe I'll offer to give him a massage and I'll break out the chips and beer and I'll kiss his face and we'll coo like love doves.

I look ashore and wave, but I'm saluting empty space. He's gone. Vanished. A phantom. A brief curl of smoke.

And then I have a most frightening thought. Maybe that shadowed figure wasn't Carlos at all. Maybe there wasn't anyone standing there, maybe it was a figure of purely hopeful invention. It can't be, I tell myself. Being uncertain as to whether I'm making up the past is one thing. But to have the same doubts about the present is too much.

Even for me.

I AM HAVING such a peaceful sleep. It is a slumber without nightmares or dreams. As I awaken, I know this. I feel satisfied up to my eyeballs that I didn't wake in the middle of the night, scared. I do that sometimes. For whatever reason. I don't have to be having a nightmare. Sometimes I just wake up, a sudden bright fear coursing through my veins as if the Sandman had visited me with a syringe full of ill wind.

As I become more aware of my new day, I realize not only that my sleep was untroubled but that I am not alone. Carlos has reappeared. The Phantom snuck in sometime during the night and is holding me close, sweetly. Much as I hate to admit it, it's nice waking up in your lover's arms. I was so sure that was Carlos standing like a sentinel on the dock, the stark lit end of his cigarette burning a hole in the night. How can he disappear and then reappear so quietly? The Cuban Ghost—that's a fitting handle. Carlos may be passionate, but he's also spooky. And I think he has a stubborn streak equal to mine. That's the only way he survives me.

I watch him sleep. My quilt is bunched around his ankles—all Mama's and Mima's hard work kicked to the foot of the bed. He's naked. I like it that he's not very hairy. His Saint Christopher medal lies shipwrecked amid what chest hairs he does have. I've told him Saint Christopher was defrocked, that he's not really a saint anymore. He refuses to believe it. He says Saint Christopher is who brought him safely to America, across ninety miles of choppy water, even if it was by mistake, and it is Saint Christopher, he swears, who will carry him home.

He also swears that as a boy back in Cuba he had visions of Saint Christopher. Only he doesn't believe they were visions. Visions suggest unreality. This was real, he insists. He says he was four or five and very sick. He tells me the name of his affliction but he says it in Cuban, so I haven't a clue as to what was wrong with him except that it sounds more like a tropical drink than a disease. But Carlos claims he was close to dying and that his mama and papa and aunts and uncles and cousins were all gathered around his bed, smudged with incense and ashes, crying, saying the rosary, looking up to heaven and doing whatever else folks do when they're holding a death vigil.

The room was dark, wisdom being that shadows soothed the ailing. But amid all that darkness was one blot of color put there by Carlos's pious aunt Viola: a vase of red hibiscus on the side table next to his deathbed, blood of a resurrected Christ.

Carlos opened his glazed eyes and scanned the anguished, mirthless faces clustered around like concerned birds jostling for space. He tried to raise his head from his pillow, an attempt to say good-bye. But then he paused and reconsidered. Perhaps it wasn't time to leave this earth, he thought, because right there, squeezed in between his sobbing mama and his even-more-beautiful-when-she's-sad cousin Margaria, stood Saint Christopher. In a brown dress, Carlos says.

I've told him to call it a tunic or robe or anything other than a dress. But he insists—no matter who he is telling the story to—that Saint Christopher was wearing a brown dress.

Anyway, the saint holds out his hand to sick Carlos, and damned if Carlos didn't take it and get right up from that deathbed and walk around that sunless room and then all around the house, which was lit up by a zillion holy candles. Carlos even ventured outside and peed, the band of deathwatchers following behind him as if he were the Pied Piper.

At first his mama pleaded with him to go back to bed. Carlos says she screamed, "He's *loco* from fever! *Loco* from fever!" and she beat her bosom until her husband held her hands still.

But then his aunt Viola, a woman who Carlos says was the best of Catholics—went to mass every morning when such things were still possible and was constantly reminding people to go to confession even after such a thing was no longer possible because the Church had been ordered out of the village—implored her relatives, "Can't you see? This is a miracle. The baby has been touched by God. We are having a miracle!"

Carlos says that his entire village for three days and nights held a fiesta. They ate yellow rice and chicken and drank homemade liquor and the children gorged on so many sugar-coated sweets that many of them threw up, and when the pious aunt asked him what had happened and he said Saint Christopher, suddenly every house in the village had to have a carved wooden figure of the holy saint protecting it.

Carlos's papa was good with his hands, and it was said that the most powerful statues came from the knife of the risen boy's papa. He charged just a few cents each, so despite the fact that these were poor villagers, he did manage to make some extra change.

Carlos remembers walking in the dandelion field beside his house, where his papa did the carving, amid dozens of ankle- and knee-high Saint Christophers, the actual one shadowing just behind.

Then came the revolution. Carlos isn't sure what happened to all the statues. He knows some were destroyed when the village was burned out by a band of guerrillas. He doesn't know which side the guerrillas were on. Carlos wasn't then nor is he now political. He's simply passionate, indiscriminately. But whatever side they were on, the guerrillas descended like a blanket of locusts and burned the village. Carlos insists some people buried their Saint Christophers. They tilled their destroyed fields and planted statues, giant seedpods that never bloomed. In fact, he swears that if he went there today and began digging, what he would find is an entire army of Saint Christophers buried beneath the rubble.

He claims that until he reached puberty Saint

Christopher visited him on occasion. There was no pattern to when he showed up and when he didn't. At least not one Carlos could discern. Carlos would be alone, except for animals. He might be standing in the shade of a guava tree with his dog, Pepe, or his pet goat, Carmen, and lo and behold, along would come Saint Christopher, his brown dress rustling in the fragrant Cuban breeze.

"What did he want?" I always ask when he gets to this part of his story.

"Oh"—Carlos looks over my head, his open face closes, there are secrets even Carlos holds dear—"just to talk."

And his story is over. I can't ever get any more out of him.

He looks so innocent as he sleeps; his youth still lightly veils his face. I can clearly imagine him as that barefoot boy, in ragged clothes, scattering the chickens as he walks, believing he is in the company of a saint.

I touch him softly. I feel not at all like stone but like a lover. Carlos moans, stirs, kisses me. His body, if not his mind, is fully awake.

And then, we begin.

It's a dance we do so well, so effortlessly, like two old herons remembering each other after a long, cold winter.

THAT MORNING everything is easy between us. I'm happy that he snuck aboard and slept with me. I've decided to let slide his request that I move in with him. I am at my best—capable of having a good time without worrying too much about traps or obligations. It's a rare mood.

He fixes us scrambled eggs Cuban style, with onions and green peppers and Tabasco. He's wearing nothing but a towel around his hips. He's shaking the skillet across the burner as if he's panning for gold.

I squeeze some orange juice. He is singing in Cuban.

"What's that song about?" I ask.

He sprinkles garlic powder on the fleshy yellow eggs. "You, Mamacita," he says, "and about a love so deep the man cannot sleep unless he is with her."

I can't help myself: I smile. And fiddle with my hair. And because I'm embarrassed I turn my back to him and gaze out the door. The day is gorgeously blue. And the air is wild with scents because it is spring. I love this season, a time when both well-tended yards and untouched nature are renewed as tender green shoots aim their buds toward the sun. I want to go out among it. I want to see the hatchlings in the mangrove. And the baby turtles sunning themselves on fallen timber. I want to hear the new life chirping so insistently that you know the mama birds must go slightly mad.

"Breakfast is served, Mamacita." Carlos interrupts my thoughts. I turn around. He's spreading newspaper on my mattress—our version of breakfast in bed. He sets the plates on the newspaper. In addition to the eggs, we're having fried potatoes and sliced mangoes. He's a much better cook than I am. I could live forever on TV dinners. Carlos holds up his glass of orange juice. "To you and your breasts, Mamacita," he says, and then downs it in one gulp.

"To my breasts," I agree.

As he sits on the bed his towel falls away. But he doesn't appear to notice. He could walk down Duval on a Saturday night completely naked and feel comfortable. In fact, he'd probably enjoy the stares.

He doesn't touch a bite until I do. He watches me as I try the spicy eggs. "Good, yes?" he asks hopefully.

"Delicious. You should open a restaurant."

He nods. "Maybe." He shovels in some eggs, and as he chews I reach over and wipe away a parsley flake stuck to his lip. He tries to kiss my hand, but I move away fast. "Now, Mamacita," he says, "what are your plans today?"

I stab a potato. "I don't know. Nobody has signed up for a tour. So maybe I'll just do some chores. Clean the deck or something."

He sets down his fork and runs his finger along my knuckles. I wish my hands were smooth and soft, like a mall hag's—you know, the kind of woman who spends so much time and money at the shopping plex that by the time she leaves the place she looks just like a mannequin. But my hands are tough and scarred, like Mama's and Mima's. "What about we don't work today?" he suggests. "We can take your *Sparrow* and wander around or fish or swim"—he pauses—"or make love," and he smiles at me innocently.

"We already did that." I smile back. Just as sweetly.

"We can again," and he's not smiling. He's doing his I-know-I-can-make-you-melt look.

"Okay, I vote for a picnic. Out in the backcountry," I say. I scoop up another forkful of eggs and, with my mouth full, mumble, "We should hurry, then. We've got to clean this mess up and get going. In case it rains later."

He leans over our plates and kisses me. Slowly. I mean, he really takes his time. Our breath is a bouquet of garlic and green onion. But it's okay because we're equally offensive.

"Mamacita," he whispers, "we're not going to rush anything today."

We're babes together, skinny-dipping in water that most people stay out of. They think they might get eaten by a water moccasin or a croc. I believe you can't let such threats stop you from having a good time.

Still, when Carlos, without my knowing, slips underwater and grabs my leg, I scream like a banshee and shoot straight up into the air. I fall into his arms, laughing, and as I look at his precise, lovely face, my heart soars. I know every dimple. Every early wrinkle. I know he's got a freckle the size of a well-sharpened pencil tip just to the left of his nose.

And I know that when he looks at this enduring primordial waterscape he takes it in aggressively. I've looked into the eyes of ospreys and hawks and seen the same aggression. It's a very male thing, I believe, to massively snatch details from the world and hold them in your heart until later. To not take them out and consider them gently until you're alone. Even my Carlos, who doesn't seem all that shy about crying in public, snatches his details, tucks them into his heart, and carries them home, where he savors them. Privately.

"Now listen," I tell him. "I'm going to try some synchronized swimming. So watch me." And he does, looking just as serious as one of those Olympic judges as I twirl around in the water like a ballerina on acid.

I'm having so much fun. As I spin about, images of spring tumble through my head. I have a few criteria for a good spring. There must be lots of color. Take William Street, for example. Mrs. Jefferson's gardenias must blossom next to Mrs. Reyes's fist-sized peach roses. I know her roses have a proper name—

the Damascus or something—but I don't know what it is. I just know they are fist-sized. And gorgeous. Especially next to Mrs. Jefferson's cream-colored gardenias. And around the corner from Hemingway's house is a yard full of well-tended bird-of-paradise, whose beak blossoms thrive beneath the purple canopy of a jacaranda. From balconies all over town bougainvilleas explode in cascading rivers of deep pink and violet and brilliant white.

And when I go into the backcountry this is what I long for: amid all that mangrove green I want to see splashes of white and roseate and teal—the colors of my birds.

I want to get drunk on it all, to let it overwhelm me and stir within me the unpredictable. That's the essence of spring—unpredictability. It's what makes spring the most beautiful and most violent of seasons. Yes, late summer holds the threat of big blows, but spring holds the promise of sudden rains so intense they blind you.

That's what happened to us.

Esther Williams—that's me—smiling as I cut through the water, toes pointed. Carlos is Tarzan, bellowing out a jungle call to show his approval. We are having so much fun that we don't notice the thunderhead until it is upon us. The bright shades of spring darken quickly and the wind rapidly picks up out of the north. The mangrove, which had been silent except for the occasional cackle of heron and egret at their nests, rings with disconcerting disjointed warning cries, an orchestra in panic as it tunes up. Shadows pass overhead: seabirds flying for cover.

"We'd better get out of here," I yell over the wind. Carlos nods in agreement, and we climb aboard the *Sparrow*. I'm considering whether I want to stay put and let it pass or whether we ought to race southward and try to make port before it's too late.

But the sky breaks open. First the thunder, as if the heavens are actually cracking, and then the awful stinging rain as the gray sky, which is all around us, pulses, the erratic heartbeat of lightning.

"Go below," Carlos shouts, and he tries to cradle me as we hurry into the cabin. The *Sparrow* is rocking violently, and I'm afraid of taking on water. I tell Carlos we ought to start the motor and try to race out of it, but he tells me no, it's too dangerous.

"Zero see," he says, meaning visibility, and I know he's right. No telling where we'd end up if we just took off. He pulls me into his arms and holds me tight. My mind wanders into my past. Whitey huddling with me under the bar, holding me against his stinky chest as the wind and rain howl. I can't help myself. I start to cry. I'm about a lifetime older, but the vulnerability of that time is unchanged.

As the *Sparrow* lurches in the angry tide, Carlos coos into my ear. "Mamacita, Mamacita," he murmurs, "everything is fine." He says the words over and over. The repetition is soothing.

And he is right. Before long, the rain and wind lessen and the thunder becomes less distinct, no longer able to hold its crisp edges.

"Thank God it's a fast mover," I say, and Carlos tries to wipe my tears. But I feel like an idiot for crying, so I pull away and head to the deck. It is still raining lightly.

The sun filters through the mist and the birds begin singing. People think I'm making it up, but I know birds celebrate when a storm has passed. They sing the prettiest songs then, just after a storm.

I check out the boat. Thanks to the short duration of the bad weather, we're in fine shape. I don't want to die at sea in the middle of violent skies. I know I can't choose my final poison, but death by drowning seems to me the worst. I look to the north and notice something floating in the water.

Carlos hands me a towel—we're still naked—and I say, "What do you think that is?"

He squints into the distance and then we both light up. We don't have to say what we're thinking. Maybe it's a marijuana bale—square grouper, as it's known around here. I have friends and acquaintances who regularly scout these waters in hopes of nailing just such a species.

Square grouper finds used to be more plentiful, but since Reagan's War on Drugs took aim at south Florida, smugglers started flying different routes. But still I hear the rumors. Every now and then some down-and-out fisherman will suddenly set up the entire bar with drinks, and locals wink at one another and pat the fisherman on the back and ask him if he kept any for himself. And the fisherman, with wide-eyed surprise, will ask, ''Kept what?'' And then he'll return the wink.

You never know, though. Square grouper stories are like fish stories. One bale becomes five, et cetera. However, exaggeration notwithstanding, if you're lucky enough to run into one and you can be discreet, it's like finding money. It's as though the smuggler had dropped hundred-dollar bills out of his plane.

Of course, there's always the possibility that it's not reefer but cocaine. I won't have anything to do with the white stuff. Morally, it's just too scary. If it's coke we'll let it float by. If it's reefer we'll take it straightaway to Bobby Joe Burke's. He'll know what to do with it. And he won't cheat us. Not too badly anyway.

The rain has stopped and Carlos has taken out the binoculars. ''Yeah, yeah, yeah,'' he says as he focuses on our prize. It's heading straight for us. Like a gift from God. Then he breathes heavily through his teeth, almost a hiss. I don't know what that means.

''What? What?'' I demand, and try to take the binoculars from him, but he's not letting go.

''Don't know,'' he says.

''Let me see.'' He hands me the glasses and walks over to the motor, keeping his sights on the bundle. I have a hard time focusing but finally do. He's right. It's not a bale. At least not one in the traditional fashion. I think it's nothing but a block of wood. Or maybe a wooden box. Yes, a box. My mind springs from dope to doubloons to jewels. Maybe the storm dislodged someone's ancient sea-wrecked treasure from the bottom.

Carlos doesn't wait to find out. He jumps overboard and swims toward it. "Be careful," I call to him, stupidly. What do I think is going to happen to him—a traffic accident?

He gets to the box and then holds it in the air to show he's in possession. "Yay!" I yell, and I wave at him. He starts to swim back to the boat. Dollar signs—big ones—are taking over my brain. I can fix up the *Sparrow,* quit the tour business, cruise the Caribbean for a year or two, and if it's really a lot of money I'll give some to charity, and I'll . . . My list-making is cut short because he's back at the *Sparrow* and lifting the box up to me.

"Here," he says, out of breath. "No heavy."

He's laboring to come aboard, but I ignore him. I'm fascinated with our new treasure. The box is solid wood, not veneer. It's mahogany, I believe. They used mahogany a lot more in the nineteenth century than they do today. If my memory serves me, most of the mahogany forests in Cuba and Haiti were pretty much clear-cut early in this century. So it's old, I decide. Perhaps the property of some long-dead, tragically lost-at-sea aristocratic grande dame. And it's full of rubies and gold. I just know it. The old iron lock is corroded shut. I hold the box to my ear and shake it, and decide that what I hear is the rustle of jewels.

Carlos grabs it from me. "No shaking," he says crossly.

"How are we going to get it open?"

"Toolbox," he says like a surgeon requesting a scalpel.

I search through my storage bin and retrieve my rusty tool catchall. Over the years, I've accumulated an excellent assortment of bits and ratchets and hammers and such. They keep this old boat sputtering.

Carlos, using a crowbar and hammer, tries to force the lock from the wood. It doesn't look good. He has managed to lodge the tongue of the bar between the wood and the mount, but he's having a difficult time pulling the lock completely away. His biceps are all blossomed out. His neck veins are blood-engorged. He's making a face like a power lifter, and when the metal finally pops from the wood he breathes out hard, as if he's been punched in the gut.

"Great!" I say. "Come on, luck. I'm betting on rubies."

We set the box on the bench between us. This is a momentous occasion. I can't believe our good fortune. Carlos looks me in the eye. "Ready?" he asks.

"Ready," I say.

He removes the lid and sets it aside. We are staring into layers of blood-red silk. Delicately and slowly, Carlos tries to move the cloth, but it crumbles into dust at his touch.

And then we see it, below the ashes of silk. I cry out and look away.

But not Carlos. He whispers, "Jesus, Mary, and Joseph!"

I turn back around, but the surprises are not over. Carlos is removing the dead child from the mahogany casket. It is mummified, so it resembles a little brown doll, like one of the carved Saint Christophers of Carlos's childhood.

I am saddened and thoroughly aghast. Because there is Carlos holding it up to the sun, marveling.

FIVE DAYS have passed since we found the baby, and still Carlos refuses to let me bury it. He is an obsessed man, both fascinated and repulsed. He thinks the child is here to reveal secrets, or cure us of something we don't even know is wrong. Saint Christopher, mummified, trying to speak, such are the thoughts floating through Carlos's mind. Why, I wonder, can't he accept the fact that not everything has a hidden meaning, or meaning at all, for that matter?

Upon finding the child and after clearing my head of its useless dollar signs, I told Carlos we had to take it to the sheriff. He'd know what to do. Not that I thought the baby was a crime victim or anything. I think it's an artifact. I think that the box had been buried in the muck of one of the islands and the muck protected it until the storm blew in and it was dislodged and swept away. That's all. No mystery.

But I don't want it around. It's too eerie.

Carlos, however, insisted we keep it. "Sheriff?" he said, eyes popping, as if I had started babbling in Russian for no particular reason.

"Yes, Carlos. We don't want it. What in the world would we do with it? Use it as a masthead? Come on."

"Fine, Mamacita," he said so calmly that anyone else might have actually thought he was sane. "The baby goes with me."

And it did. He took the dead child home.

And we've not gotten along since. This is far more than my being stubborn or afraid to let Carlos take seed inside my heart. Now our fights center around the important as well as the ridiculous. We fight about the baby and what to do with it. We fight about what to have for supper or what TV show to watch. We fight about what color to paint my toenails and whether some actor, whose name we don't even know, wears a rug or not. We just fight.

So. I go to Carlos's to try to smooth things out. That is my intention.

He lives in a rambling, magnolia-shaded turn-of-the-century clapboard house that has been divided into apartments. Across the street is the cemetery, which is lovely and not spooky at all, because the ornate tombs are aboveground and resemble ruins of an ancient city. It's a perfect resting place for the dead: placid and comforting. Often, nighttime finds us sitting on Carlos's fire escape watching the stars sparkle down on tombstones embedded with glass-domed photos of the departed, and we make up stories about, say, Luisa María Sánchez Smith, born in Cuba in 1870, who died the fifteen-year-old bride of a white man in Key West.

The house has thin Florida walls and not an ounce of insulation, so you hear everything: the gay couple upstairs making love, the construction worker next door whose body emits the most amazing sounds from no telling which orifice, the whiny four-year-old two doors down and her pleading mother, and Carlos and me either arguing or else having the best time you've ever eavesdropped on.

I don't knock or anything. His door is cracked open. He does that a lot. I tell him not to. I tell him that he doesn't necessarily know his neighbors as well as he thinks he does—even if he can hear their private mutterings—and why risk getting robbed?

He tells me I don't know how to trust.

So I open the door and go on in. A blanket is thrown across his couch, and his pillow hangs precariously off one end. A tennis shoe is by the door, its mate under the glass-and-wicker coffee table. A cereal bowl is on the table, its residue of Wheaties hardening like flakes of concrete. The kitchen is just off the living room and I see his shadow splashed like ink on the terra-cotta tile floor.

I walk in and he's just sitting there, balancing the dead thing on his lap, whispering gibberish to it. Some kind of Catholic hocus-pocus, no doubt.

"Carlos, what's wrong with you?" I demand, not a very gentle beginning, granted, but this is really getting out of hand.

"I no know, Mamacita," he says. "I no know. I just can't let go of him." Then he shoots me a look as if he's about to reveal wisdom of the greatest magnitude. "It is a he. I checked," he says.

I'm at my wits' end. I snap, "Don't call me Mamacita. Okay?" Sometimes the term is endearing, but not now. Not since he's gone off the deep end with this mummy. I look around the kitchen. There's a stack of dirty dishes in the sink—no time to clean his house, but he's bought a new plastic crucifix. It's nailed to the wall over his kitchen table. Plus, two religious candles, the kind they sell in the supermarket down here, with an image of the Holy Mother glued on, flicker and dance next to the mahogany casket.

I throw open his refrigerator. Maybe I can entice him back to his senses with food. But of course not. He hasn't got a damn thing to eat. Just a chewed-on deviled crab and a bottle of Yoo-Hoo. The hell with it. I'm thirsty. I pop open the Yoo-Hoo and take a slug. "Jesus!" I sputter. "How do you drink this stuff?" It tastes like chocolate milk of magnesia cut with sugar.

I lean against the fridge and eye my problem: Carlos, a grown man I know intimately, is losing his mind. It's a terrible sight, him cradling the dead thing as if it—excuse me: he—is a real baby.

But I know that the child is not real. I know that he's someone petrified. Someone inert. Someone who shouldn't concern us.

I pull out a chair and sit. "Carlos, this isn't good," I plead. "I want you back, the Carlos I know. Not this guy sitting around his dirty kitchen praying over an artifact. Please, let's just go rebury him and forget we ever found him."

He looks at me sharply, as though all the world's details that he so aggressively snatches have turned on me. He's got at least two days' worth of beard. "Where is your heart, Mamacita? And yes, what about your soul?"

I drink more of the Yoo-Hoo just because I'm irritated. I slam the bottle back down on the table more loudly than I mean to. Then I demand, "What do my heart and soul have to do with this, this, this thing that's more stone than baby?" I try to keep my tone calm, but even I can hear the high soprano edging in.

Carlos's thick lips curl into a mean smile. He holds up the baby and stares it in the face. The child looks tiny and vulnerable, but I know that's impossible. The dead are not vulnerable, I remind myself.

At some point, I guess when he died, he was wrapped in a sheath of muslin or some such fabric, but the cloth has decayed in places and the baby's stony skin peeks through. His eyes are shut. He's thoroughly embalmed. Whoever prepared the body knew what he was doing. Maybe the mummy ought to be in a museum. On display. He has what my mama always called a button nose, but then most babies do, and his lips are neither smiling nor grimacing. They are just there, mute and ungiving.

"Here," Carlos says, "if it's a stone only, then hold it. I dare you."

Damn him to hell. That's what I'm thinking.

"Scared." He tires to sum me up in one crappy word.

"You're an imbecile." But my insult doesn't penetrate. The smirk remains. And he's holding the baby out to me, like a gift.

He leaves me no choice, the bastard. But I stall for time anyway. "Carlos, this baby was pulled out of its grave by mistake. Now why don't we do the right thing and put it to rest again?"

He cradles the mummy in one arm. "This was no mistake. This baby sailed the sea straight to us. Open your eyes. See what's happening. He has come to tell us something. It's like . . ." But Carlos's voice trails off.

"It's like what?" I challenge. "You were going to say some bullshit about being visited by that fake saint of yours? Is that it?"

Carlos's sweet face is tinged in red. Those veins are bulging again. "You know nothing!" he yells. "You no know what the life is. You no know how to love!" And then he spurts out some more, but it's in Cuban so I can't understand him.

I don't think he has ever yelled at me before. But I

won't let myself be stunned by it. I yell back, with plenty of cussing, and then he cusses. I presume that's what he's doing.

"Speak English!" I finally shout.

And he says, "Then hold the baby."

"Fine, I don't have any problem holding this piece of nothing."

He holds the child aloft, an offering.

I move to take him. I'll hold him. So what? What could be so terribly special or important about holding this dead baby?

I take him into my arms. He is stiff, but warm from Carlos's touch. I start to hand him right back. But then I look down into that silent face—those pinched lips, the curved nose, cheeks like two small balloons, and a high proud forehead. He is brown and hard, yet despite that, something soft lingers just below the stony surface, like a flint strike struggling to take on life, struggling to hold on to one bright flash until it becomes a sure flame. If only I'd allow it, he could be more than an inanimate stone of the past. He could be something affecting my life. Now. Something just this side of real. If I allow it.

But I won't. The idea is too awful. I won't let my heart be moved. "Here," I say. "I held him. Satisfied?"

Carlos takes the baby and sets him gently back in the casket. "Your stubbornness, it cracked," he says as he touches the baby's face and then shuts the lid. "For one second."

Now I am really mad. I scoot back my chair,

scraping it loudly against his tile floor that needs a good mopping. "Fuck you, Carlos," I say. "Only a child or a crazy man would sit here playing with a mummy like it was a doll. When you grow up, come see me. But don't show up till you do."

He's not looking at me. He's gazing into dead space as if I'm not even here.

To try to get my point across, to try to make him understand how angry I am, I blow out both of his stupid holy candles. "I mean it, Carlos," I say.

But he has shut down, or at least shut me out. When he's really upset there's no cascade of Cuban words. There is only silence. Carlos and the dead baby and silence.

So I leave.

I HAVEN'T HEARD a word from Carlos in two days. Yet all around, spring bears its new life without any subtlety whatsoever.

The birds are noisy. They thrash through the dead twigs of winter, searching out the ones that are strong, sticks that have retained enough sap to avoid becoming brittle. Building nests, I've come to know, is an exact, painstaking process.

The birds that have already laid eggs chortle and squawk as they try to protect them from marauding coons. And I, as I make my way along the uneven sidewalks carpeted in fallen petals of purple and pink, white and blue, keep an eye skyward because in the spring marsh hawks and redtails swoop boldly into town in search of the newborn delicacies chirping in unprotected nests. If I see one stalking I make a commotion. People think they are passing a lunatic as I suddenly flail my arms and yell at the hawk. I simply want the baby birds to have a chance to fly at least once. That's why I do it.

I've spent my time of late just walking around. I removed my sign-up sheet. I can't stand the thought of carting a bunch of sunburned tourists to the backcountry. And for all my bitching about it, I'm disturbed that there has been no Carlos, flickering within the scent of his cologne, spying on me in the early morning or late at night. I wake up to the salty smell of the sea. That's all.

In town the bushes droop with the weight of brilliantly colored flowers, and bees buzz over the petals; and those flowers that are womb-shaped, like the hibiscus and the lily, offer to the insects a pollen-lined sanctuary that they enter for minutes on end and then withdraw from, gold-soaked and dizzy on the wing.

But still, given all this, I feel no rebirth. Spring is not cracking me. I feel not the hope that new life offers but the despair of being surrounded by death, as if that mummy we snatched from the storm-roiled waters has somehow tainted Carlos and me, making us unfit for the ritual dances of spring.

No. I don't feel the exhilaration this season should

inspire. Rather, I feel as if I've been sucked into Limbo. Mima always called it that, although Mama would correct her. "Purgatory," she'd mumble, as if she'd been there too. But really, I feel unable to move on, as though my actions are those of a mime and don't have any effect on the world, as if I could swipe my hand through the air without stirring the faintest wind. So, after forty-eight hours in Limbo, I awoke today with a hangover—a pitfall of drinking beer alone—and my thoughts centered on betrayal.

My walking hasn't purged these thoughts either. From the wharf to Fort Taylor to the lovely old conch houses around Southard, I play the same refrain: The only way to get my life back and to make Carlos snap out of his temporary insanity is for us to rid ourselves of the dead thing.

I decide to go to the sheriff all on my own. In fact, I fantasize about how to steal the mummy so I can deliver him to the authorities and be done with it. I will go to Carlos's apartment and pretend that the mummy's strange face, so dark and round it reminds me of a tobacco-stained moon, no longer bothers me, and when Carlos's guard is down I'll snatch the coffin off the kitchen table and flee into the street with it. I'll run down the petal-scattered sidewalk, enveloped in the freshness of this new season, holding the poor dead child in my arms, and I'll save us from him. Forget the sheriff. I'll simply toss the child away, and Carlos and I can go on with whatever it is we do.

We can continue to measure out our days with

uncertain hands, but we won't be staring death straight in the face. I can choose to shut down the past and refuse the future on my terms, without the added pressure of a brown, muslin-wrapped corpse mutely holding court, silently but effectively judging me. Yes, together or separately—it doesn't matter—Carlos and I will go on with our half-drunken stumble toward death, but we won't have to be overly conscious about it. Perhaps we won't even recognize it.

These are my thoughts, you see, as I wind my way through town and back to the *Sparrow.* I go into the cabin and start fixing myself a sandwich. I decide that when I'm done eating I'll march over to Carlos's apartment and simply take the mummy from him. I settle down with a bag of chips, and I'm actually sort of enjoying myself, because I know that the pall that has settled over Carlos and me will soon end. Once the mummy is gone, we can slip back into glorious ignorance. But my good mood never has the chance to become congratulatory, because that familiar stink rises up. Old Spice.

Carlos is at hand. And then I hear them, several people speaking gibberish all at once. I emerge from my cabin into a morning that's become violently bright, to find Carlos, the coffin under his arm, and a silver-haired, black-eyed, dark-skinned couple by his side. Beaming at me.

"Sadie Baby!" Carlos calls.

"What are you doing, Carlos?" I am not friendly.

The two people nod at me, still beaming, as if

they expected to be greeted by a nice person and reality hasn't caught up with them yet.

"Business for you. Please meet María and Pablo Vasquez. New friends from Cuba. Two months in America they've only been."

I halfheartedly wave—I don't have it in me to be completely rude—and they, in a language I can't fathom, begin jabbering at me. I look back at Carlos, who appears to be the most pleased person on the planet, and he explains, "They go on your boat. For a sail. I said to them, 'She's a most good storyteller.' They want to hear one. But they no speak English. So I translate."

"Are you out of your mind?" I ask. The sun is directly in my eyes, so I'm squinting, but I don't miss the pause that eclipses his face.

Carlos withdraws his shades from his T-shirt breast pocket and puts them on, hiding behind them, making sure neither fear nor mirth nor anger is allowed to jumble the space between us.

He says something to the couple, and I'm expecting to see a flash of disappointment and then polite smiles as they turn on their bunioned feet and go away, but instead they break into celebratory chatter and Carlos offers the aged Latin beauty his hand and helps her board. Then, gallantly, he offers Pablo his arm, which the old man manages to accept with dignity, as if age hasn't diminished his manliness but has simply added a dimension akin to royalty.

I brush away Carlos's two small acts of kindness and start cussing, a good long string, but he only smiles in response, a placid grin, unpeggable—is it triumph or arrogance?—because the intent is hidden by two black ovals that protect his eyes from the sun and my comprehension.

Once aboard, holding the coffin in front of him as though he's bearing a tray of crystal, he says, "I'll put him below. For safety." Then he whispers, "They came on a boat so small, like a toy. Coast Guard plucked them."

That's nice, I think. My tax dollars at work. "Do you take him with you everywhere you go?" I ask sarcastically, pointing at the dead thing. But Carlos ignores me and heads into the cabin with it.

So I say to María and Pablo, "You know you're in the company of a madman, don't you? What did he tell you, that the box contains his lunch? Listen, friends, that isn't a picnic basket. It's a coffin, and inside is not a bologna sandwich but a dead child, so you all ought to run while you can."

María looks up at Pablo, concern shading her penny-colored face. But Pablo says something gentle that sounds like a coo, and the concern vanishes, carried away by his words. They giggle conspiratorially and then nod at me, white grins breaking across their dark skin.

Jesus fucking Christ.

I'm a woman who knows when her options are all played out. As Carlos rejoins us, I walk over to the helm and give in. "Okay, buster, you win," I mutter. "But don't expect me to be entertaining."

I take them to a small island south of Content

Keys. Two dolphins shadowed us almost the entire trip, which excited my passengers no end. But now that I've cut the motor and set the anchor, they are looking at Carlos and me expectantly, two old schoolchildren who never managed to graduate. They are a most handsome couple, he in his guayabera, she in her flower-embroidered white cotton dress. Despite my not wanting them here and not being able to understand a single word they say, I feel an openness, a sweetness, that makes them quite likable.

I look to Carlos, who has spent his time on the outward bound gabbing at them. "Carlos, dear," I say, "how do you plan to do this? Your English isn't exactly flawless."

He takes off his shades and looks at me with that honest stare full of sex, and for a moment there is nothing in a box below reminding me that life sucks. I can't help it, I feel myself blush. The two old folks grin and shoot knowing glances, and Carlos says, perfectly, "Just tell your story. It will take care of itself."

"Fine," I say. "But try to keep up."

I look to María, to her beautiful, time-carved face. The sunlight reveals everything, allowing her to hide nothing. I gaze hungrily at her, conjuring images of Mima, as María shyly diverts her eyes to her sandal-clad feet. I know I'm being rude, blatantly staring, but it's my boat and my stories, so I'll do as I please. I try to imagine María young, and before long it works. I see Mima, a teenager in a small town, growing up in an era when girls were raised to be mothers, wives, and servants. I see her dressed in a long skirt and a high-necked blouse with a cameo at the neck. I see her during a time when she called herself Susannah.

So many changes, so many turnabouts, had taken place in Mima's life in the years following her incarceration in the fort. Above all, Alice Motherwell happened to her, a woman whose beauty and despair lingered not silently but like silver bells sewn into the folds of her skirts, ringing softly and unmistakably with each lovely step.

These are the sad facts Mima told me about the woman who raised her, facts gleaned from townspeople who claimed to know:

Alice Motherwell had a daughter, who was a decent and popular child, spoiled but nonetheless loving, with strawberry-blond hair and blue eyes like her mother's. Her husband had been a most eligible bachelor, not only coming from a well-respected and moneyed English family but also handsome to the degree that when parents suggested to their daughters that they get to know him, the girls did not turn their backs and roll their dewy eyes. No, they pursued him. With all the wiles they could muster. Alice Motherwell was no exception. And she won. So she thought.

After they married, he invested his inherited money in indigo and sugar, and although the War Between the States was hard on him, his plantation outside the city held its own because St. Augustine was Union-occupied and the Yankee garrison soldiers needed and wanted sugar as badly as anyone else.

After the war, however, was another matter. Reconstruction didn't do much to reconstruct anything except ill will, so her husband journeyed south, for he had heard that the land around the Okeechobee—the big lake that serves as the headwater for the 'Glades—was well suited for growing cane. His plan was to see for himself, and if he liked it he just might move his family to what then was considered the frontier.

So with provisions enough to last a month he headed downstate toward the great lake, a body of water so large that people who saw it for the first time often thought they had stumbled onto the ocean.

The Seminole Wars were still fresh in the minds of Floridians, most of whom thought they hadn't really ended. Rumors of skirmishes persisted even into the Civil War. The United States Government had been routinely capturing Seminoles and shipping them west to try to rid the state of them completely. Not only were they a pesky problem; many were black Seminoles, runaway slaves who'd sought freedom among the Indians. The government tried to eradicate the "savages" of both colors by means twofold: war-sanctioned murder, and exile to sparsely populated areas out west. I don't know how they kept it all straight, as busy as they were sending some tribes east and others west.

But they were certainly in over their heads when it came to the Seminoles. No one knows for sure how many Indians fled into the swamps and the 'Glades, but it was enough to keep them from extinction. The soldiers tried flushing them out and failed, as these boys from the cold north were no match for the swamp and the men and women who understood it.

Alice Motherwell's husband, for whatever good qualities he may have had, didn't understand the swamp or the Indians or that there are areas of nature that just need to be left alone. He wandered into that world of water and river grass and cypress and was never heard from again.

Perhaps he fell prey to a bear or a panther or his own ignorance. Maybe a gator got him or he succumbed to the madness incessant mosquitoes can inflict. Perhaps, for whatever reason, he decided to never return to his blue-eyed wife and his daughter, whose skin was so soft and properly pale it reminded him of gardenias.

No, abandonment was a possibility too vile, with too many unpleasant reverberations, to consider. Folks up in St. Augustine decided he'd been murdered by the Seminoles. They had no proof. They didn't need any. For they had their fear. And Alice Motherwell went along with every frightened rumor they uttered. Any newcomer who made an inquiry was told her husband had been murdered by Injuns. And because they said it, it became accepted as fact.

But Alice Motherwell's bad luck wasn't to run

out. Within a year of her husband's disappearance, her little girl was playing in the street one afternoon, chasing a ball she'd been given by a man in town who considered himself a possible suitor to her mother, when the milk-carriage horse, spooked by a rifle blast down at the docks—apparently shot off in glee over a particularly good haul—reared and landed on the child, who was of a singular mind just after that ball. She lasted the afternoon and then died, with Alice Motherwell looking on.

Mima told me town legend held that the woman entered her stately house overlooking the harbor and fort and didn't leave it for a solid year. The yard that had been the pride of St. Augustine, with its well-pruned white roses and its branching spikes of sea lavender, all of it went to seed. The neglected garden grew gray and gnarled, and even an occasional thunderstorm couldn't stop it from turning to dust.

But when the woman finally did open her shutters and let the light of day into the shadows of her house, and even as she ventured out among it all, the town's rumor mill went into action full tilt. The first to notice was the butcher, and then the clerk at the mercantile, and then Mrs. Masters from next door. And then the priest, having heard something was shockingly wrong with the young widow, took it upon himself to pay a special visit.

The lovely woman spoke calmly and softly and her gaze was direct, but the priest was not fooled into thinking the Widow Motherwell had spent the past twelve months immersed in careful mourning.

Because, as fantastic as it sounds, she was no longer blue-eyed.

Oh, the left eye was still blue, for sure. But her right eye had turned brown, like a blossom dying, like madness leaving its mark.

Some folks thought the eye had darkened slowly, taking the entire mourning period to change color. Others insisted it must have happened in one sparkling insane moment. A few souls who were more careful claimed the eye had always been brown. But these people were dismissed as nonbelievers and, therefore, not to be trusted.

Mima believed the legend, which she heard first from her classmates and then later from old women whom she'd occasionally speak to as they fed pigeons in the town plaza.

I don't know exactly what Mima thought of the woman who, for all intents and purposes, raised her. I think she loved her. And was a bit scared of her. Those eyes were mismatched, after all. But I'm not sure that Mima ever really considered why Alice Motherwell took her away from her parents in the first place.

I have my theories. I believe it was with a mixture of self-righteous charity and soul-spoiling revenge that Miss Motherwell took Mima into her home. As she tried to lighten my grandmama's hair with lemon juice and as she told her that for the rest of her days she would be known not by an Indian name but called Susannah and as she taught her Southern manners and dressed her in lovely clothes picked out of mail-order catalogues, she must have been giddy with all the bloodletting, just absolutely satiated by the belief that she was destroying the Indian part of my grandmama. But also she must have felt like God as she resurrected in Sparrow-now-Susannah the image of her dead daughter.

A heron glides past us, low and smooth, toward the islet on our leeward side. I size up this couple, this clearly happy couple, who in the waning years of their lives took the big ride, the big gamble, out of Cuba and to freedom. I wonder if they're finding it here. Is this place what they thought it would be, or are they experiencing moments when they curse themselves for leaving their home?

But I stop questioning, for the magnitude of their action begins to stun me. They are not here through a comedy of errors like Carlos. No. These are two old people willing to risk their lives and leave everything they have ever known for an idea.

I decide quickly and with utter certainty that they must love each other very much.

I think I actually smile at them.

Then I look to Carlos, who is forever patient and all-suffering, missing his family, whom he believes he has dishonored, and dealing with me. No wonder he sings the blues.

He shuts his eyes once, sweetly, as if to give me encouragement. Or strength.

''Okay,'' I whisper, letting the word hang in the

air between us. Even though it is a small sound, it is one full of possibility, as if by saying yes you are saying maybe to love, or at least the notion of love.

''Okay,'' he echoes, such a good translator.

''This,'' we begin, his voice flying just behind mine in a world of light and water, ''is a love story'':

Listen to me, Sadie, this is what I was like as a budding young woman: beautiful and obedient and wild. Sometimes I managed to be all three at once—an ability firmly rooted in youth.

I remember the day Miss Alice took me away from my captors and family and brought me to her house, which was just across the street from the fort and had a fragrant garden of white roses. The rose beds were thick and well kept and were edged in seashells. But I didn't know that yet. The only thing I knew about up to that day was the fort, its dankness, its stale smell of death.

The day of my departure, I was standing on the fort terreplein with my parents. My father was looking out to sea and my mother was fitfully stringing a necklace of shells, and I had my hand on her skirt but she wasn't looking at me. She hadn't looked at me in two days, not since it was decided I would not return west with them. I had become, you see, enraptured with the idea of living in the looming house that faced the bay, with its gingerbread scrollwork and its rooms filled with treasures and its owner, Miss Alice, who would care for and nurture me as if I was a worthy Christian child and had never been a "savage." I hated that term, and my new self held great disdain for anyone who was a "savage." I thought I could leave my mother and father because I wasn't like them anymore. But then, as the act of leaving became more than just a fanciful idea and progressed to the point that the matter had, as the captain announced, "been settled," my resolve weakened and I found myself wishing that my mother and father could move with me into that grand house. But it was too late. The die had been cast.

A slack-jawed soldier walked up the narrow steps and past a cannon and over to me and muttered, "Let's go." I didn't fully understand what was happening, I didn't recognize the finality of the unfolding events. I tried to put my arms around my mother's neck. She pulled away and said, "Go, now." And then she touched my hair, but her gaze never met mine. I looked to my father, who still had his back to me. He said something softly and in a language I no longer wanted to understand. I turned to the soldier to see if he'd heard that forbidden tongue. If he did he chose to ignore it, pushing me toward the stairs and warning, "Don't give me any trouble."

He held on to my arm as he led me to the captain's office. But the captain wasn't there. No one was. The soldier told me to wait inside and to not touch anything. I didn't. I tried to do what I was told. But I was alone and fearful: Maybe Miss Alice wasn't coming for me. Maybe they were going to send me to yet another strange and awful place. I had to bite back my tears. I listened to the captain's mantel clock tick tick tick tick. The sound echoed off the thick coquina walls like water dripping into an empty pail. I wanted to spin the big hand around to see if time would tick by faster. I may have even reached toward the clock. But then I heard the door open and I jumped back and Miss Alice was standing in the doorway, dressed in a proper charcoal skirt and bustle and white silk blouse. She said, ''Susannah, dear, I'm so glad to see you. I've come to take you home!''

She walked over to me and put her hands on my shoulders. She knelt down—her skirts rustling like crumpled paper—so that we were eye to eye. I knew that she was a powerful person, maybe even capable of sorcery, for surely anyone marked by God with eyes of brown and blue knew and saw things beyond this world.

''Susannah, child,'' she said, ''when you leave this fort you will begin a new life. The past for you doesn't exist. You are my child now. The savage in you is dead.'' She squeezed my fingers and prayerfully shut her eyes as she said, ''And a God-fearing white child is born.'' Then she looked at me intently, as if my answer mattered, and said, "Do you understand?"

I responded the way a good child should: "Yes, ma'am." Then, with one hand on my back, she guided me out of the captain's office and away from the ticking clock, past three soldiers, through the courtyard and out the massive door, over the moat, and we started down the fort's rolling green. But I thought I heard wailing. My mother wailing.

I looked over my shoulder, toward the sound. Suddenly I wanted to run back to my mother, crawl into her lap, and tell her everything was fine. I didn't want her to be sad.

But I couldn't stop. Miss Alice grabbed my arm and we walked swiftly. I couldn't keep up. Each time I stumbled she pulled me so that even though I wasn't exactly walking I was always headed in forward motion, propelled by her iron grip until we were across the street and standing among her roses.

It was strange to me then and is strange to me now, but as soon as Miss Alice opened her front door, the wailing stopped. I never heard it again. Except sometimes in the early morning, upon waking, I would look out my bedroom window with its view of the bay and the fort and I was almost positive that I'd listened to it all night long in my dreams. But I could never be sure.

That is how I left my past life and entered a world of godly piety and crystal. Miss Alice taught me with a missionary zeal, and before I knew it the years were spinning past and the only place I considered home was my elegant house with its white rose beds. She was my mother and I was her child, and my savage parents and the prairie were a faraway nightmare remembered only in the vagueness of twilight and dusk. My days were busy as Miss Alice taught me the manners and tricks girls needed to know: How to act shy and embarrassed even if you weren't. How to be polite and courteous even if someone was throwing sand in your face. How to talk softly yet make a big impression.

When I reached puberty her lessons and gentle advice had less to do with good manners than with how to gain the attention of boys. This necessarily involved beauty. And in my case, it meant the bleaching not only of my soul but of my skin. On my fifteenth birthday, she gave me a half-doll brush. The accompanying brochure explained that Emmaline, as she was referred to, was cast from fine Bavarian porcelain and hand-painted by master artists. With her cold blond hair and rosebud cheeks and light complexion, she was quite an image to live up to. But I gave it a good try as I used the soft-as-silk horsehair brush to sweep powder across my face, light powder meant to hide from the world one fact that could never be completely covered over: my skin that was not the color of pale wine but reflected the earth-toned shades of the prairie.

Miss Alice's husband had left her well-off, and she and I dressed as such. Each spring when the new mail-order catalogues arrived from the Northeast, we would sit in the parlor—she in the mahogany rocker with the petit-point cushion and I on the damask-covered couch that was about as comfortable as a church pew—and we would choose a handful of blouses and skirts and perhaps a brooch or two and always a hat, one for her and one for me.

Her mismatched eyes would scan the fresh, never-before-turned pages of the catalogue, up and down, back and forth. I would watch, fascinated, and I would breathe deeply, for Miss Alice smelled of roses and cold cream and sadness.

Sometimes as we sat together, perhaps doing white work—she taught me how to use a needle and thread handily—I would imagine her dreams for me. She wanted me to marry well, of course. Someone from a good family, educated, with a strong head for business. She wanted me to bear her grandchildren, and they would pop from my womb with only the slightest resistance, and they, boys and girls, would miraculously look like her.

We never spoke in such terms, but I read her actions and her mind and I'm sure it was so.

You can well understand, then, her discontent when the time came for me to attend my first cotillion and no one asked me to go. You see, the prevailing wisdom was that if you couldn't find a date for the Spring Cotillion, you certainly would never find a husband.

As the fresh spring days sped by without my procuring an invitation, she and I grew desperate, and in our desperation we became harsh with each other, silently placing the blame for our failure at feet not our own, unwilling to admit that the town would view me never as Alice Motherwell's daughter but always as that Injun girl she took in.

Each passing day her eyes grew stonier and her lips, usually curled in a pleasant, polite demi-smile, grew thinner and thinner until they all but disappeared. Her patience with me burned quick. Stitches in a coverlet that once would have been praised now became "sloppy" or "uneven" or "unacceptable."

As for me, I took her criticism in silent but holy stride. I decided—and I believe to this day I was right—that only an act of God would change the hearts and minds of the town's eligible young men and their parents. In my pursuit of divine intervention, I fasted and prayed and read the Scriptures, which was a major mistake because I got snagged on the Song of Solomon. I even memorized parts I found especially romantic: "How fair is thy love, my sister, my spouse! how much better is thy love than wine! and the smell of thine ointments than all spices!"

Me, a reformed "savage," asked God for a miracle. I was to discover that fasting can be quite a rigorous price to pay, but I was willing. Two days prior to the cotillion, after a day and a half of taking nothing but water, I wandered, hungry and weak, into the cathedral downtown to show Him how serious I was. I bargained. Please, God, if you'll only grant me my prayer and get me a date, I'll never cheat on a math exam again. I'll never tell off-color stories to the other girls or listen to theirs. I'll never wish bad things on Miss Alice. I'll never dream of my body being touched in an intimate manner by a boy. Ever. Ever.

The result was that I fainted, not from being overcome by spiritual ecstasy but from starvation.

And also this resulted: I was picked up and removed from the shadows of the cathedral's looming crucifix and revived with a tender hand and fed a snack of Holy Communion wine and hosts by a young man who was paid to sweep out the cathedral twice a week.

Those are the facts.

But here's my heart:

I don't remember fainting, but I remember opening my eyes and staring into the loveliest face I had ever seen. Eyes so green you could drown in them. And bones that were prominent yet amazingly frail, as if they were a jeweler's setting for those emerald eyes. His black hair fell in curls down his neck. His skin was lightly tanned and it held its color well.

He was leaning over me, watching me, patting my face with a checkered handkerchief, his handkerchief, and it smelled so sweet and slightly floral that I winced, so strong I thought was this scent of love.

"Miss, are you okay?" he asked.

It was too much: the lack of food, his handsome face, the smell of jasmine. I began to spin once more into unconsciousness and he said, "Oh no, Injun girl, don't you faint no more."

And he slapped my face.

I managed to say, "How dare you!"

He smiled, I thought radiantly. "That's right, you're coming along now. Let's try to get you sitting up."

I allowed him to help me from the floor and into the closest pew. Even though it was a fleeting touch, I was most impressed with what it felt like to have his arms around me. He said, "Don't go anywhere. I'll be right back."

I told myself to get out of that church then and there. This ill-spoken, beautiful boy certainly could not have been what God had in mind for me. But before I mustered enough strength to leave, he was back, with a tray full of hosts and a glass of Holy Communion wine.

"I'm sorry, Miss, but this is all I can find. I think you ought to eat it, though, 'cause you sure do look like you need nourishment."

I was elated that my welfare interested him. But all that good breeding Miss Alice had instilled showed itself. As I took a handful of hosts I said, "You called me Injun girl. I would like an apology." I started eating the hosts. I was ravenous.

He sat down beside me. I could feel his body's warmth as if it were an aura. I looked at him, waiting for an apology, and I swallowed the chalky disks. His face darkened with sadness as he said, "I am sorry, Miss, except I do know who you are. You are that Injun girl I first saw on a hot night years ago when the government men was taking you and the others into the fort. Don't think me forward, it's just I know because that little girl I saw was so beautiful—so beautiful that she frightened me. And so do you." Then he looked down at the church floor and said, "Besides, I wasn't being mean. I just don't know your name."

The hosts were filling my stomach, but this boy was filling my heart in that way only teenagers know. I whispered, "Susannah Motherwell. And yours?"

He handed me the glass of Communion wine. "Samuel Abraham Lincoln Jones. But my friends call me Mr. Sammy."

I took a sip of the bittersweet wine and I could feel myself stepping into another world, as if the door of Miss Alice's house was suddenly ripped off its hinges and I was running past the well-pruned white rose beds and into a forest wild. I offered him the wine and we giggled and he drank some. And we shared it.

That's how the next few minutes of my life were spent: in a church drinking my first glass of wine and eating hosts for physical—not spiritual—nourishment, hearing myself giggle, thinking that everything he said was fascinating, and being giddily happy.

He told me that he owned a pet runt chicken named Miss Raison, and that he lived in Lincolnville, and that he liked to fish. And even though the more he talked, the more I knew Miss Alice would never approve of him, for he was not lily white but mulatto and it didn't sound like his family had any wealth whatsoever—well, Sadie, the more he talked, the harder I fell.

So when he haltingly ventured to suggest that I accompany him on a picnic Saturday—the day of the cotillion I evidently would not be going to—my mannered self said, No. But my wild-hearted self, the one Miss Alice thought she'd snuffed out, said, quite clearly, into the hallowed arched air of the church, "Yes, Mr. Sammy. A picnic is a lovely idea. Thank you for asking."

Miss Alice had taught me that if a woman is to get her way in this world she sometimes has to act with stealth. That's what I did. No one asked me to the cotillion, but because I was star-struck over Mr. Sammy I no longer cared about the silly dance. Miss Alice, however, was furious. She blamed me for my dateless state. The day after I met Mr. Sammy, over a dinner of turnip soup, she told me that if I acted more like a young lady and less like "something else"—the word she wanted to hurl at me was "savage" but she managed to contain herself—the town's nice young men would take a healthy interest in me.

I looked up from my soup bowl. The steam off the broth was invisible but hot, and it caused my dark skin that she so disdained to break out in sweat. I said to her evenly and without hostility, "You are right, ma'am. I'm sorry. I will try to be better. May I be excused now?"

She did not meet my gaze and I heard her fiddling

with her rose-patterned silverware as she said, "You may."

Thus, to not let myself be engaged in any degree of argument was one of my acts of stealth. Another was to keep secret my plan to have a picnic with the boy who'd revived me in the church. This would require grace and speed and nerve. It meant that I would have to rise the next morning earlier than Miss Alice and prepare a basket of picnic foods, and to dress, and to be happy, all without her knowledge.

My plan was aided by her drowsiness. She slept longer than was her habit that Saturday morning. It may have been that she was upset with me or that she was depressed by my failure to be accepted in the ways she wished, or maybe God was conspiring with me and had sprinkled her with divine sleeping dust. Whatever the case, I was able to bake a batch of brownie cakes, prepare two cucumber sandwiches, pick a pair of the finest oranges off our tree in the back garden, place it all in a basket, take the basket to the rear gate, hide it beneath the curling vines of her Confederate jasmine—which was blooming so it looked to be studded with a million stars and which smelled like the handkerchief Mr. Sammy used to wipe my brow when I had fainted—go back into the house, walk up the stairs, and slip into the bathing chamber, all without her waking.

And still Miss Alice dozed as I took a bath infused with her rose cologne. When I finished bathing I sat before the dressing table and layered on a pale shade of makeup just exactly as she had taught me. Then I dipped Emmaline into my crystal powder jar and disappeared in a cloud of white dust, and when I reappeared I was far and away from being Sparrow but looked very, very much like Susannah.

I changed clothes four times. I didn't know what to wear. A picnic called for something casual, but for a first date a girl should wear something fancy. But if I dressed up, how would I have any fun in the middle of the woods or wherever he was taking me? I settled on a simple blue skirt and a white blouse with a lace collar, because blue looked good on me and the lace collar provided a festive air.

I think that morning I was part cat, for I prepared the picnic basket and myself in utter feline quiet. As far as I know, Miss Alice was still asleep when I slipped out the back door and down the cobbled path and retrieved the picnic basket beneath the jasmine vines.

Perhaps she was asleep even as I walked along the wheel-rutted street past the furiously chirping finches and brightly colored buntings people kept in cages attached to the outside of their homes, the picnic basket on my arm, enveloped in visions of the young man I was about to meet, remembering those beautiful green eyes that were ever so slanted and the finely boned face the color of sand, remembering his sad but kind comment about the beautiful girl he had seen a long time ago and knowing that she and I were one and the same. He was wrong. That little girl wasn't me. I would let him know that, I decided. Somehow, with wit and tact and without seeming severe, I'd inform him that he was dead wrong about me being an Injun girl.

Other than that I hadn't the faintest idea what I would talk to him about. I possessed all the symptoms of adolescent lovesickness: rapid heartbeat, clammy hands, eyes twinkling as with celestial glow, and blood so thickened with pubescent fantasies that it flowed slowly and caused my daydreams to unfold before my eyes in languid vignettes where I was in perpetual romantic distress and Mr. Sammy was perpetually saving me.

I rounded the corner at Charlotte and floated among horse carriages and people strolling through the plaza enjoying the fresh spring morning. And then I saw him. He was sitting on the cathedral steps, his runt chicken by his side, a casting net in a heap by his bare feet. He wore dungarees and a brown homespun shirt. First I felt like a fool because I was overdressed, and then I melted because he was as handsome as my fantasies had remembered him. Then I decided I couldn't go through with it. What if once he saw me without the flattering light of church candles he thought that I wasn't at all pretty and he had confused me with someone else? I was about to spin on my heels and hurry home, when, through that crowd of people who hadn't a clue as to what a fine morning this really was, because they were not love-struck, Mr. Sammy's eyes and mine locked. And he jumped up from the steps and smiled his radiant smile, and I felt my whole body from crown to toe break into a grin.

So, Sadie, that is how it all began. We were just two young people caught in the hopeless fervor of first love, the kind of love that makes you weak and strong at the same time. Weak because you're mad for the other person and strong because you believe with all your heart it can last forever. It doesn't matter that you don't know the other person very well. Because the spell is cast on the most primary level—it happens in the world of scent and sight and desire—all of it springing forth in the abundant impulse of that first glance.

Such is the nature of first loves, and even second loves if you're lucky. But what happened to Mr. Sammy and me went beyond the primal impulse. Our love demanded an exploration into our capacity for kindness or avarice. It compelled us to identify and then choose between what is just and what is unjust. This choosing, this coming to terms with the best and worst in our own souls, started on that first date.

He took me to the river, to a lush grove along the San Sebastian. Cedar hugged the shore and saw grass spread out like a fine fringed blanket all around except for a few yards in front of us, where the grass had given way to muck and sand. The sun shimmered and every so often a lone cloud passed, casting an inky shadow on the slow-moving river.

We were pleased with each other, and nervous, and alternately shy and bold. I busied myself with the picnic basket, pretending I needed to make sure the contents hadn't suffered unduly on our walk, and he stood at the water's edge, gazing down. He tossed a pebble into the river—I heard the splash—then he called to me, "Come on down here. You'll like it."

I wanted to, but I saw what I would have to trudge through. I couldn't venture into the mud in my boots and stockings. But he was so insistent, looking over his shoulder, a slight smile, a gleam in his eye that seemed to taunt, "I dare you."

So—and this, Sadie, is how wild I was—I said, "Turn around."

Then, right there by the river, in broad daylight, I unbuttoned my boots and took them off and shimmied out of my stockings. I thought I was quite the brazen one as I walked toward the shore, stockingless, laughing as the muddy earth oozed between my toes. I stood very close to him and I was quite aware that his fingers were long and slim. I said, "It's lovely here."

And he said, "One day I'm going to own a boat and I'm going to navigate all through these parts."

"What for?" I asked, and I wondered what it would feel like to touch his curls. The air smelled green, rich with the dander of fern and ivy. I dipped my toes into the river.

"Oh, Miss Susannah," he said, "there's all kinds of things out there waiting to be discovered. You ever been on a boat?"

I shook my head no. The water was cold, but I

liked it. I lifted up my skirt, not wanting it to get wet.

''When I've got my boat, I'll take you for a ride. Seeing the river from the shore just ain't the same as looking at it from the water.''

Immediately I was wild for the idea of going on a riverboat ride with him. Just the two of us. How romantic! Somehow, though, I managed not to completely swoon. I asked, sweetly, ''What's the difference?''

He closed his eyes as if he was remembering and then said, ''For one thing, the sounds of the river and the marsh just ring out, loud and clear, and you hear the way the gator or the bobcat hears, 'cept they know exactly what they are listening to, whereas it takes a man years to understand.''

A mullet jumped, and I laughed in surprise and then said, ''I have a friend at school whose father took a riverboat trip down the St. John's. He said it was filled with Yankees and they shot up everything on shore!''

Mr. Sammy turned and looked at me so directly that it was easy to believe he could see right down to my beating heart. I stared into his face and saw, yes, kindness, but also something ancient, a wisdom he didn't necessarily know he possessed.

''Miss Susannah, that's a real bad thing to be doing,'' he said, and his voice was soft but unwavering and he skimmed another stone. ''Those boatmen are taking people downriver to shoot sleeping gators and to shore trees filled with mama and papa birds and their babies. Them branches look like they are draped in snow, that's how many birds are roosting in them. And they're dressed in their birthing plumage, so they are real fine-looking. Men with their fancy rifles and pistols take aim and start firing like it's a shooting gallery. Killing all them birds 'cept the babies, who they leave alone. 'Cause their feathers aren't good enough to sell. They just leave the baby birds in the nests to die."

My swooning had given way to something far more serious. His words were pinning me down, forcing me into a stance I had long abandoned. An old memory flashed so brightly it almost knocked me off my bare feet. Most of my remembrances of that former time had been purged, but here it was: I saw clearly, from hill to horizon, a prairie littered with slaughtered buffalo. "It must smell awful," I whispered.

"It does," he said. And then we stood there, not saying anything, looking at the river and listening to far-off birds, and I had a sudden urge to dive into those black waters and swim with him. Forever.

I wanted to touch him. I wanted to know what it would be like to be held by him. To be kissed. But we were both so awkward, afraid to make the first move, fearing both rejection and acceptance, that by mutual unspoken agreement we drifted back to the basket and to Raison, who was sifting through the earth with her beak.

I had forgotten to bring a spread to sit on, so I stood there shaking out my skirt to rid it of the fiddler crabs that had scurried up the hem and trying to figure out what I was going to do. Young ladies back then just didn't sit on the ground. We needed something other than our clothes between our rear ends and the earth.

Mr. Sammy read my mind. He said, "You don't want to get those pretty clothes dirty." Right there in front of me he took off his shirt and like a prince laid it on the grass for me to sit on. I heard the river lapping gently against the shore and the wind rustling the trees, and I couldn't help noticing he had a fine chest.

I knelt down on his shirt and pulled out the plate of brownie cakes, and my eyes behaved as if they had a mind of their own, stealing glances at Mr. Sammy's naked skin. His shoulders were wide and his waist narrow, and I thought I was going to die.

I offered him a brownie cake. He took one bite and said, "My, Miss Susannah, that's the best thing I've ever tasted in my life."

The compliment, of course, pleased me no end, and I broke off a nibble for Miss Raison, and he said, "I don't want to scare you or anything, but I think you should know that Miss Raison here, she is not just your average, run-of-the-mill chicken."

I drew back my hand, thinking he meant she'd bite. "She's not?"

"Uh-uh," he said, his mouth full of brownie cake. "Oh, she won't hurt you. In fact, just the opposite." He paused before saying, "If I tell you, promise me you won't laugh."

Of course, I promised. I even crossed my heart.

He looked at me as though trying to anticipate my reaction and then blurted, "She's got the magic."

"The what?" I asked, fearful she suffered from some sort of disease.

If he thought I was stupid he didn't let on. He simply said, "Miss Susannah, there's lots of different types of magic in the world. But this here chicken, her powers come from Saint John the Conqueror. You know about him?"

"No, I don't," I answered honestly.

"He's a saint," Mr. Sammy said confidently, "and he's given Miss Raison the ability to sap the meanness right out of folks."

I looked at the chicken, with her scrawny neck and dusty mangelike feathers. She was pecking the ground and acting as dumb as any other chicken. I said, "How do you know this?"

" 'Cause I've seen it with my own eyes."

"Seen what, Mr. Sammy?"

"It's more like knowing than seeing, Miss Susannah. It's knowing that 'cause she's around, there ain't nobody gonna do me any harm. I ain't white or black or mulatto when she's around. I'm just a human that nobody wishes ill will on. That's all." He gazed out toward the river, and his face was firm, and I knew that, like me, he was stubborn by nature. "I know these things 'cause a person has to believe in something." Then he looked at me, his face happy again, and said, "Miss Susannah, would you like me to teach you how to cast this net?"

I had never, ever considered casting a net before in my life. It simply wasn't something girls thought about. But I said, "No, not today. Actually, I just want to watch you do it."

"Are you sure?"

"Yes, I believe so," and I was beginning to fear that he would insist.

"Okay. I'm gonna give it just one throw. I'll be right back," he said. He lifted the casting net, which smelled faintly of salt and mud, and asked, "You sure? I don't mind teaching you." He held out his hand to help me up, that glint of a dare lighting his eyes again.

It was then I realized I was being teased. I giggled and he walked down to the shore, saying something on the order of, "You just don't know what you're missing."

I looked around and noticed that behind me a nice stand of honeysuckle and jasmine wound through the underbrush. Red-winged blackbirds and dragonflies flitted about and just beyond the flowers grew a tangled thicket of wild blackberries.

I couldn't resist. I went over and picked a handful while Mr. Sammy fiddled with the net. In fact, I picked more than a handful. I held up my skirt so that it became a little bowl and, truthfully, I might have ended up with a couple of cups had Mr. Sammy not yelled, "Careful, snakes in them thickets."

My vision of a steaming blackberry cobbler gave way to one of a reared-up rattler. I was trying to decide whether I was going to let fear get in the way of dessert, when Mr. Sammy called, "Okay. I'm gonna cast now. You ought to watch so next time you'll know how. You've got the arms of a good caster, you know."

I laughed and then glanced down at my thin arms, which were decidedly not suitable for casting, and I was supremely happy.

So I went back to the picnic basket and sat on his shirt. I dumped the blackberries on the ground beside me and picked out three—for just a taste. I was about to place a berry on my tongue, but I paused and noticed how the sun shone with a wonderful glow all around Mr. Sammy and the river.

There he was, just beyond the shade of the trees, bare-chested, his trousers rolled up, standing ankle-deep in the water, his world awash in golden light.

He lifted his arms and I watched, entranced, as he cast that gossamer net upon the waters. Time slowed, so I saw it all in such detail: the graceful lift of his arms like a bird taking wing, the muscles in his back straining and then giving, his hands and fingers flying open as the net unfurled like fine lace against the air, and his body relaxing and waiting as the net, with a whisper, settled upon the rippling river.

I felt my soul stir. A flutter. A hint at completeness.

When he hauled in the net he called to me, "Hey, come look here. We're salty today," which meant he'd caught a lot of fish.

But I didn't want to move. I just wanted to remember him outlined in light, the net full of sky.

So I didn't say a word.

He looked up at me and smiled and then he let go of the net alive with flip-flopping mullet and walked away from the shore and sat down beside me. He said, "It's just a stupid bunch of fish anyway."

I looked at his lovely face with its odd mixture of wisdom and youth and I said, "No. It's much more than that."

He leaned over and kissed first my cheekbones, next my lips.

I began melting, melting away, and I remembered what I'd been reading the day I met him: "how much better is thy love than wine!"

As he kissed me, I clenched my fingers so hard around the three blackberries I had been planning to eat that I squashed them.

We kissed and kissed, and the world around us disappeared. There was just me and Mr. Sammy and a magic chicken. I wanted to dive underneath his skin and melt into his heart. For one brief moment I saw myself as a little girl back on that Oklahoma prairie, willing the hawk toward me. I saw her snatch me off the ground and lift me into the crisp blue heavens. In my mind her wings flapped, and for a second or two I thought I knew what absolution and majesty and love were all about.

When we quit kissing I held out my arm because blackberry juice was snaking down my wrist, slowly meandering to my elbow in beautiful purple swirls.

Mr. Sammy whispered, "Girl, you are so dirty."

And then he kissed my arm clean.

I saw Mr. Sammy at least three times a week after that first glorious day by the river. We usually went for long walks through the woods or fished or just sat by the river, talking and kissing for hours.

We even, on one of our journeys through the forest, found an old abandoned one-room shack. We took it for our own, a hideaway far removed from anyone's disapproving scowl. I hammered nails in the walls and hung seashells from them, and he stole some moss his mama had been drying for a new mattress and fixed us a moss-and-hay bed. The interior was ivy-covered and cool.

When I was with Mr. Sammy I wasn't the same girl who'd been brought up by the Widow Motherwell. I was someone who enjoyed walking barefoot and taking my hair out of its ribbons and bows and letting the earth squeeze up all around me.

Mr. Sammy gave me my first cane pole and he made me hook the worm on it myself. I squealed and made a face the entire time I had my fingers on the ugly, squirming thing, and I hardly caught any fish anyway. Mr. Sammy said I willed them away. But he never seemed to hold it against me.

Our relationship was based on exclusion and the power that gave us. People weren't willing to accept either one of us beyond the color of our skin, so we created our own society, one based upon the gratification of the flesh, the communion of our two souls, and the sweetness of secrecy.

As spring stretched into summer my lies in order to get out of the house became more artful, and the more I lied to Miss Alice, the less I respected her. People saw Mr. Sammy and me walk down the street together. They saw us disappear into the woods together. They must have told Miss Alice. But she did not confront me. Not for a while. So I triumphed in my lies.

Not only was I tripping into love, but I was falling under Raison's spell. Because I, like Mr. Sammy, witnessed things.

One lazy summer afternoon I'd been teasing him about Miss Raison and his superstitious ways. We were rolling around in the hay and moss in our abandoned house and I was saying things like, "Why don't you get yourself a real pet, like a dog? At least a dog will do tricks and stuff. This old magic chicken of yours doesn't do anything but follow you around."

At that Mr. Sammy leaned up on one arm and said, "Listen here, I want you to meet me at the west end of the plaza tomorrow evening 'round seven o'clock. Can you manage that?"

"Of course I can manage that. What are you going to do? Cast a spell?"

"I'm going to make you eat your teasing words 'bout Miss Raison. That's what." He meant it too. He seemed a little angry.

Getting out of the house that time of evening, I feared, would not be an easy task. I couldn't think of a single lie to justify it. But in fact, this momentary lapse in my ability to think up excuses aided me. After I cleared away all the supper dishes and had cleaned the kitchen spotless, I took off my apron, hung it on the hook inside the pantry, and simply walked out the back door without any attempt at permission or explanation. With my heart beating so hard it caused my fingers to tingle, I left Miss Alice sitting in her parlor doing white work by the light of a waning day and a candle.

I met Mr. Sammy, who had Miss Raison tucked in his shirt, underneath a huge oak that shadowed the widows' benches. And he took me down the south end of St. George Street, where the homes were serene and well tended, and he told me to walk ahead to a certain tall fence and find a knothole to look through. I did as he instructed, and what I saw was grotesque and upsetting. A cockfight. The men were yelling and the birds were attacking each other without mercy, and then Mr. Sammy walked up with his magic chicken and everything stopped. The fighting, the calls for blood, the money flying through the air as men placed bets. A peace settled over the crowd and the birds, and people took their money back and the two cocks were put in their cages. A bald man whose jacket was soaked through with sweat gave the winded animals water. And everyone appeared baffled as to what was going on.

Mr. Sammy said to me, "She does it every time. I've even seen her stop lynchings." Then he touched my face and said, "I know it sounds silly to you, but she keeps our love safe. That lady who raises you, she has made noises, threats. I've had people tell me. But she can't bring us harm. And neither can the ones who glare at us as we pass by. No one can hurt us. Not while Miss Raison is around. You've seen it with your own eyes now."

It's true, I had. And I would witness it on other occasions. Such as the time the two Howell boys were fighting in the plaza. Jason had taken a sharp blow on the lip and Michael had a welt over one eye. But as Mr. Sammy and Miss Raison passed, the boys fell still. And Jason said through his purple lip, "Man, what are we rassling about?" And Michael responded that fighting did seem silly, and then the two of them strolled off, laughing and backslapping each other.

Then there was the time on Cuna Street when Mrs. Tyler shrilly demanded that a Negro girl apologize for staring at her brightly feathered hat. A gauntlet of white men gathered, their full intent being to force the girl to apologize in a manner they deemed proper. But as Mr. Sammy walked by with Miss Raison, Mrs. Tyler muttered, "Oh, never mind," and she hurried off through the crowd of white men, who seemed confused, dazed.

Indeed, Miss Raison proved herself time and again to hold some sort of magic. But it was on that hot summer evening, my summer of discovering love, amid two fighting cocks gone peaceful and death delayed, that I first saw it and first believed Mr. Sammy. Our relationship was charmed. We had a chicken who could cast spells and keep us safe. We could walk down a thousand country lanes hand in hand, a gentle moon lighting our way, and nobody—not Miss Alice, not a lynching gang, not a soul sanctioned by government or hate—could do us harm.

And this is also true: Many a night after that, I would sneak out of my house and wander the streets of old St. Augustine, and unbeknownst to Mr. Sammy, I would spot him standing outside some fence, the scrawny chicken tucked up underneath his arm and the early-evening light speckling them with shadow, and from afar I would watch that humble pair, and my soul—which so often kicked and screamed and rebelled in the dark chambers of my heart, the same soul that I feared could not always perceive right from wrong—would fall silent and restful because I knew that for at least a few moments Mr. Sammy and Miss Raison were wreaking havoc with cruelty.

I FINISH the story and fall silent.

Carlos is scanning my face as if he's prepared to translate yet another torrent of words.

"There is more, *sí*?" he asks.

"No. There's not. That's my story. All of it." I feel myself hardening. I don't want to tell them any more. I know how the rest goes, how it has to go, and I know they won't like it. They didn't come here for me to spin tragedy.

Carlos is shaking his head as if he can't believe my refusal. He slaps his knee and says something to Pablo and María.

Pablo's black eyes widen and he says, "*¡No, señorita!*" He adds, "Please," but it sounds more like "peas," and then the three of them furiously confer.

The sun is strong. We're all sweating and getting sunburned, despite their Latin skin, so I decide this ride is up. We're going home. They ought to be content I told them such nice things.

Carlos turns to me. He's squinting because the sun is in his eyes and he hasn't yet gone back into hiding behind his shades. "They want more. They want to know what happens to Mr. Sammy and your Susannah."

"Yes?" I ask.

They break into a chorus of "*Sí, sí, sí,*" and their faces are insistent, like a trio of baby birds demanding their mother regurgitate for them.

"No," I say.

Carlos tilts his head and spreads open his arms, another one of his holy poses. "Sadie," he says, hanging on to the *ie.*

Their innocence begins to nauseate me. I get up and start hauling in the anchor. Carlos moves to help me, but I slap him away.

"Sadie, they are guests for me. I think you can do this. Just give them a little more. You acting like the fisherman who gives up once the hook is in." He's whispering. As if Pablo and María can understand him.

I can't believe his nerve. I wasn't trying to hook anyone with my story. It was an imposition for me to tell them as much as I did. "Listen, buster," I say, "they are your friends, not mine. But the stories belong to me. I tell them to who I want, when I want. We all had a nice time, but it's over. Got it?"

He touches my hair and I jerk back. "But Mamacita, why? They are people so nice. They like this love story. You tell it good, woman. From your heart."

"It's not a love story!" I yell. "They don't want to hear the end of it. Trust me. Just leave it alone. Miss Susannah and Mr. Sammy married and lived happily ever after. Tell them anything you want, but I don't want to go on!"

I'm so mad I can barely see. I feel trapped, both by their shocked and insistent stares and by a distant past that inexplicably haunts me. I let go of the anchor and bolt past them and into the safety of my cabin, only mildly aware of how childishly I'm behaving, leaving them on deck to sort through my outburst on their own.

I flop down on my bunk and I realize I'm crying, and that makes me even madder. I hear the motor sputter and then kick in. Carlos is taking us home. Good for him.

It is hot down here, and even though I'm not at all prone to seasickness I feel woozy. But I can't go back up there and face them, not after throwing a fit. So I'm stuck. Damn Carlos! He should have left well enough alone. He brought two old, fragile, loving people aboard and I told them the good part. I gave them a time when my grandmother was kind and gentle, before Miss Alice drove the knife in, a time when Mr. Sammy still had courage.

I try to stretch out all the way. I want to lie as still as possible, hoping that will calm my stomach, but my foot keeps hitting something. I sit up to see what's in my way. The coffin. Carlos set it at the end of my bed and tossed the quilt on top. I lean forward and pull the box toward me. Despite what Carlos claimed when he fished it from the sea, the coffin is heavy, as if it contains a boulder and not a dead baby.

I run my hand along the finely carved lid. But all I dare do is touch the wood, and wonder. Because I don't want to see the child inside. Yet I can't help thinking about him. What draws Carlos to him and what repels me? What secrets does he hold? Before he died, did he gaze into a gathering of faces and know who his parents were? If I took him to the authorities and he ended up being displayed in a museum, would onlookers marvel as though they were seeing a talisman, or would he be reduced to the status of a curiosity, some muslin-wrapped brown thing that schoolchildren would shriek at and adults would ignore?

I hear the three of them laughing and Carlos talking loudly, as if he's enjoying himself. I push away the coffin and reach for my pot box—a small ebony container I bought downtown years ago at a craft show. It holds two perfectly rolled joints, side by side. I light one, a cure for nausea, and my evil nature enjoys the fact that the fragrance will waft skyward, past Carlos's lovely Roman nose, and he won't be able to do a damn thing about it. He can't run down here and share in it because he has to keep his friends entertained and he has to steer us home. He has to act as if he doesn't smell it. I wave the smoke toward the door. Just for good measure.

But as I near the end of the joint and as my bad attitude slowly melts off my bones, my thoughts turn less caustic. I think that it would be fun to have a kitten around, a shipmate, as it were, some furry little creature to cuddle with after I've pissed off the rest of the world. I hope Carlos's friends don't think I'm nuts. They seem too nice to think I'm nuts—that's what I muse as I wander off into random thoughts and then something akin to sleep, but not quite.

I'M DISTURBED by the scent of lemon and garlic and by the clatter of pots. I open one eye and there's Carlos, in shorts so baggy I can't believe they are staying on his hips and an old torn and stained Sloppy Joe's T-shirt, playing chef. They are not the same clothes he had on earlier.

"Mmmm, smells good," I say as I gaze at him brazenly—the way men do at women, and I'm getting by with it because his back is to me. I love the color of his skin, a hue between copper and topaz.

"Yellowtail," he offers, without turning from his work. "I caught them when you sleep."

"Yeah, down at the fish market," I say, and I get out of bed. He ignores my smart mouth and with a flourish sprinkles fresh parsley over the fillets.

From behind I wrap my arms around him. He looks over his shoulder at me. "You okay?" he asks.

"Yes, everything's fine." I answer as if I hadn't, just hours earlier, shown my butt.

He faces me and holds me by the shoulders. "I'm sorry for today, my friends, all that."

I shake my head and touch my finger to his lips. "No, no, Carlos. It's my fault. I shouldn't have acted that way. Were Pablo and María okay when they left? Do they think I ought to be committed?"

He hugs me close. It's like being wrapped in a cocoon. I feel his heart beating, steadily, surely, some sort of confirmation. "Ahh, just another *gringa loca,*" he says, and kisses the top of my head, his lips betraying not a hint of grudge but simply acceptance and a sort of graceful strength that I've perceived in people who allow themselves to be shaped a bit by the world rather than broken by it.

That is Carlos, I decide—polished by time and private heartache. Where does such a person come from? Someone who so easily forgives, someone who insists on being part of my life even after I've demonstrated time and again that I am, at best, unreliable. And someone who gets carried away with far-flung superstitious thoughts about a child centuries dead.

For now, for this moment, I decide not to fight it. I decide that no matter how hard it might be, I should gaze into his bony, tanned face and accept us as two ordinary people who mean no harm.

We eat in the cramped quarters of my cabin, and it is a good meal of fish and salad and bread. A bottle of cheap wine. We talk about things that don't matter: his landlord's new truck, a yacht we saw on our way out that morning, the influx of foreign tourists—especially Germans.

Then he tells me how much he enjoyed listening to my tale and leans across the table and holds my hand and says, "But it takes some sad twists, eh?"

"Yes, it takes sad twists," I admit. And then we fall silent. I remember that he brought the mummy with him and that this morning my plan was to steal the poor thing. What a stupid idea! It's not the fact of the mummy that haunts us. It's the idea, what he represents. Until we come to grips with that, we're stuck. I stare past Carlos, at the galley and then out its three small windows. I can see a bit of deck and a patch of sky.

Oh, what the hell. I put his hand, his big, callused, thick hand, to my face, and then I begin telling him more of the story, even though it's not any of his business. But it feels good to say the words, as if they are full of weight I need to unload.

I tell him that Mr. Sammy and my grandmother virtually set up house in that little forest shanty, and they ventured out there as often as possible, except when the weather was bad. On gray rainy days Mima would sit in her lovely mansion by the bay and Mr. Sammy in his riverside shack, and although their surroundings suggested two people who were worlds apart, the two lovers were of the same mind as in unison they sulked and moped, sulked and moped.

Miss Alice, who knew full well what was going on but must have been hoping it would burn itself out before she had to take drastic measures, probably prayed daily for bad weather. And then she formulated a plan based on fresh blood. It dawned on her that the Hotel Ponce de León, a vast and vulgar palace for the rich built a few years back by an oilman turned railroad magnate, was full of visitors who knew nothing of her daughter's past and who might not be as predisposed to avoiding dark-skinned girls as the local boys were.

So, not underestimating the power of vanity, she mail-ordered three or four fabulous gowns and all the goop that went with them. She presented them to my grandmama with one stipulation: She could keep her new wardrobe if she, in search of new friends with breeding and manners, began to frequent the art teas held weekly by the hotel.

Mima, under Miss Alice's tutelage and wearing one of her finest silk dresses, marched herself down to a tea, where she met an artist-in-residence named Ellis Elijah LaCour, from Natchez, Mississippi, who lived in one of the bungalows built especially for artists at the back of the hotel. And while she had huffed and rolled her eyes when she first heard Miss Alice's plan, once in the hotel she was utterly smitten. Mima said she wasn't so taken with Mr. LaCour, however, as with the glamour and the chitchat.

Years later, even when she was so old she often forgot in midsentence what she was talking about, she never missed a beat, not a single detail, concerning those teas:

She would enter the hotel's main courtyard and walk past palms and citrus trees and tropical plants, past the fountain with whimsical frogs spewing water in an ever-flowing arc, through a massive doorway framed in mosaic and then into the lobby with its hardwood columns sculpted into pregnant goddesses, and she walked carefully because she was transformed with so much makeup and silk that she imagined herself to be very much like her porcelain half-doll and was afraid that if she tripped on the marble stairs she might shatter.

Mima told me the wealthy Yankee tourists, mainly friends of the oilman owner, who traveled days by train, would pause from their self-absorption for a moment and, even after all the lushness they had witnessed in their big-city lives, would gasp at the beauty of this place.

Thrilled and terrified, there she was in her alabaster shoulders walking among wealthy ladies with parasols draped over thin wrists and men with mustaches and golden watch fobs. This, she realized, was what Miss Alice had raised her for, to mingle with people who smelled of things store-bought and not of the earth.

Across the exquisitely polished floor she would go, and through a doorway that led to other gardens. In those sheer gloves and kid boots and that lace-trimmed silk skirt and a corset so tight she had to keep a cobalt crystal vial of smelling salts tucked in her bosom, she was someone far removed from a life of simple joys and rather a creature who demanded luxury.

Out that far doorway and past magnolias and palms and orange trees, she would finally arrive at the bungalows. Invariably she was the only person from St. Augustine to go to the teas, because the townspeople tended to have better things to do than hang out with a bunch of funny-talking snobs. But Mima's circumstances were special. She was trying to fulfill Miss Alice's dream of her. So she would enter the bungalow of whatever artist was hosting the tea that week and she'd smile graciously at the other guests and listen as they issued their comments on the colors or the form of this and that, and act as if she agreed or at least not give away that she didn't know what in the hell they were talking about. And in contrast to how she was treated by her fellow citizens, she became something of a celebrity when these Yankee visitors discovered that she was "a real live local."

Mima was enthralled with it all. The pale gardenias rising out of silver bud vases. The phonographs playing opera music. The songbird cages turreted and domed like exotic, faraway castles. The cut-crystal goblets brimming with sherry. The mahogany sideboards stuffed with silver and linen that no one in the whole world really needed. And she was entranced with a sound that rang softly underneath the laughter and chatter, like a mantra of the rich recited again and again: the tinkling of teacups being settled onto thin bone-china saucers edged in gold.

She loved it that no one knew or cared who Alice Motherwell was and that nobody had the slightest hint that the hideous fort had at one time been her jail. So she commenced upon a balancing act, tiptoeing along a high wire of her own making, bobbling first toward the earth and Mr. Sammy and then toward that aria-filled bungalow and the man who held the key, Mr. LaCour.

She continued to sneak out and see Mr. Sammy because she was in love with him. He catered to her ancient self, someone who believed in magic chickens and earth cures.

But then the other part of her, the one Miss Alice nurtured and bribed, began to blossom. In the quietest part of her heart, Mima quit scoffing at Miss Alice's hopes and dreams for her.

Miss Alice must have had to adjust her vision of her daughter's future when Mr. LaCour, a slow-moving Cajun boy who during the teas would sit himself in a corner and watch his guests rather than mingle with them, took a liking to Mima. He wasn't exactly what Miss Alice had been hoping for. She had her sights set on a rich man, not someone who simply served their higher sensibilities. But if he could break up the romance with the mulatto, she'd take him. And she'd be happy.

My grandmother imagined herself happy as well. She imagined herself the wife of a decently successful artist, pumping out babies in the glow of Miss Alice's approval, maybe even denying and hiding the fact that she'd ever, ever had a romance with a boy from Lincolnville.

She told me she knew this Ellis fellow had strange habits, mainly that he smoked something with a pungent bittersweet smell, and that he tended to drift off, not quite waking or sleeping, but sort of floating in place.

I remember her telling Mama and me about this one day when we were fishing for tarpon in Chevelier Bay. Mama snapped in her line, inspected her silver lure, and cast again as she spurted, "Mother! You were dating an opium addict! I can't believe it. Did you know?"

Mima's old, wrinkle-scratched face turned dumb, and then she slapped her knee and laughed so hard she doubled over. When she straightened back up, her black eyes glistening with giggle-tears, she said, "My God, girl, you are right. All these years I'd thought he was just exhibiting an artistic temperament."

"Did you smoke any?" Mama asked in that superior tone she sometimes used with Mima.

"Me? Oh no. He was stingy with it. He kept it in a small tin box, small enough to fit in the palm of his hand, and over and over again he'd remove the lid and stare at it, as if he was making sure none had disappeared. I guess he thought I might steal some."

And then she collapsed into another laughing fit. And because laughter is contagious, the two of us—Mama and me—laughed right along with her, so hard our sides ached.

Our laughter died out, though, when Mima recovered enough to say, "You know, girls, I didn't love him. Not for one instant. But I decided to try to take on a husband the town and Miss Alice could live with."

She leaned over and pushed my hair off my forehead and kissed me and then said, "I didn't know whether I could leave Mr. Sammy or not. But there were pressures. I felt I had to try."

I quit blabbering for a moment and look up from my near-empty plate, and Carlos refills my wineglass. His hair is on end. He tends to pull on it when he's engrossed or agitated or intently listening.

He pulls on it again, reminding me of one of those cartoon characters who has suffered an electric shock, and I can't help but smile. He says, "What of Mr. Sammy? Please, I need to know." His voice is so quiet, almost a plea, his vulnerability shining like a meteor.

Even though I'm fuzzy-headed from the wine—but when did that ever stop me?—I take another sip and decide that I will tell him, that I will try to remember faithfully what Mama and Mima said about him. And I will hope that it's true.

I lean back in my chair. Sea gulls are crying. The *Sparrow* is gently rocking due to a mild chop. I close my eyes and for Carlos's sake I begin to concentrate on my granddaddy. I sit very still, thinking fancifully that he'll come down from heaven and put his lips to my ear and very gently, sweetly, whisper:

That next summer Miss Susannah and I loved thoroughly, which was quite a feat, given the fact that the weather turned on us. Bad. Got so hot that old people did nothing but lay in the shade, fanning themselves, drinking jugs of iced tea. Dogs could barely bark. Fish didn't bite. Young folks still went out in search of each other, but when they got together their conversations were subdued, full of long silences and liquor.

To make matters worse, a drought set in. Normally decent earth decayed into dust and coated everything. White shirts turned gray. Within minutes little children playing in the streets looked ghostly. Womens swept and swept their houses out, only to have to turn 'round and do it again. So most of them just quit, sat on their front porches and drank rum-laced tea. Even food like roasted quail and mashed potato tasted like death.

The entire town was in a bad way. Husbands and wives who never fought began to be cross with one another. Best friends argued over silly things, such as who insulted who ten years prior. There was even a poker game in the back of a shoe store on St. George that ended in a shooting.

But see here, I thought we were above it all. I thought Miss Susannah and I could survive the heat and drought and even the rumor of yellow jack that the weather inspired, 'cause not only were we blessed with Miss Raison, we were blessed with a good and true love, the kind that wakes you up in the middle of a hot night, soaked down to your drawers, and not mind 'cause come tomorrow you'll be in your sweetheart's arms.

But then this here happened: Miss Raison and I were one day, just by chance, standing in the shadows of the plaza oaks, when we saw her strutting down Cathedral like Queen Victoria herself, dressed up in clothes so fancy they must of cost a fortune, entering that white man's palace they called the Ponce de León.

I took full notice that even her hat was new, and curling out from it was a beautiful white egret plume. That, after me telling her 'bout how they got those precious plumes.

I didn't know what her business behind those fancy walls was, but I knew it wasn't anything I would like. Watching her walk in there dressed in clothes that cost more than my house, to engage in some sort of something she was keeping from me, it left a bad taste in my mouth. So I made my inquiries. I had friends who carried the gatorskin bags of the rich folks who visited there. In this way I discovered everything: that she was strutting over there to see some fellow, an artist, and that she committed this sin every Wednesday.

Firstly, my reaction was to go punch Mr. Artist out. But secondly, I decided to think it through. I decided to be big about it. I tried to convince myself that if she spent time with all those fancy folks it would help her come to terms with who she really was. That she was a natural, sweet girl who needed to feel tied to the earth, not some fake doll whose laughter was practiced. Yes, I tried to believe that me being big about it would bring her back home. For good.

But the visits continued for at least a month of Wednesdays, and in between those Wednesdays we saw each other. I stayed smooth, not letting on that I was aware of the deception. But things started unraveling, such as my sleep and my good humor. Maybe it was the weather that finally caused my patience to snap or maybe I came to my senses or maybe I was just tired of being big. I'm not sure. All I know is that finally I decided enough was enough.

Miss Susannah and I had said we'd meet at our little shack in the forest, and as I walked out of town and into the woods I made up my mind that I was going to go 'round with her about Mr. Artist.

And for relief from the heat and to steady my

nerves I brought with me a flask full of Papa's moonshine mixed with orange juice.

I almost left Miss Raison at home. I was hot and full of anxiousness and I thought, She'll get in the way so just leave that old chicken be. But as I started down the porch steps, there she was in the burnt-up grass, ready to go. So I slipped her in my shirt, and saying, "You always get your way," I headed out.

Despite the heat, I kept a steady pace, determined to reach our hideaway before Miss Susannah so I could practice what I would say. But once out there, I was so hot I drank a fair amount of the Orange Blossom. Each time I tipped back my head, bottle to lips, the brightness of the sky scattered among those pines frightened me. I decided my impending set-to was giving me a case of the bad-ass jitters.

To try to get over it and because the Orange Blossom had made me sleepy, I went on inside the cottage. I stirred up the moss and hay with a stick to make sure it was free of spiders, mice, snakes. Then I laid down and took a nap.

My sleep was deep and barren, not a single dream, and when I woke I was still alone. That sure increased my dread. I thought that maybe Miss Susannah wasn't going to come here at all. Maybe she'd never give me a chance to say, "It's me or him."

I stepped outside and the air billowed like heat from an opened oven. I slumped into an old pine chair that was in the house when we first discovered the place. "Miss Raison, what do you think?" I asked. "Miss Susannah gonna come see us today?"

The chicken just went about her business, pecking pine needles, pebbles, dirt. I dared myself to peek through the skinny trees to see if I would still feel afeared. I leaned back and studied the blue sky cast in patches. I swore I saw a cloud or two, but I said to myself, The heat must be playing tricks with your brain.

I didn't know what I'd do if Susannah didn't show up. My feelings ran wild: first I'd march over to her fancy house and confront her, then I decided I never wanted to see her again, then I thought if I never saw her again I couldn't live. Then a big old lump formed in my throat and I had to fight back them bitter tears.

All of this was for naught, because as I stared forlornly in front of me, into the woods, her sweet figure came into view. At first she was nothing more than a shimmer in the distance. But as I watched her walk through the forest, she became more and more real: a bundle of yellow and blue wildflowers in her hand, her pretty black hair loose over her shoulders, her face shaded with a wide-brimmed straw hat dotted with white flowers.

And here's how foolish I can be: The moment I saw her, any plans of telling her what-for evaporated into that blistering turquoise sky. I felt light, as if all my sorrows of the past days had been experienced by some other Samuel Abraham Lincoln Jones. Certainly the one sitting on a pine chair gazing at Miss

Susannah as she walked through the forest had no troubles.

And this thought flashed through my giddy brain: Maybe there would be no more marching down to the Ponce de León to carry on with a man who could never love her the way I did. Just like that, as if I was God almighty Hisself, I decided it was so.

I forgot about notions of unhappiness. Who was that man who had planned to tell her what-for? There was only me and Miss Susannah sharing the remaining liquor, kissing on each other, playing with Miss Raison—chasing her around and feeding her and such. We laughed easily and talked about this and that and nothing. A strand of her hair wafted 'cross her face. I reached over and touched it, and I swear it felt like it was spun from the diamonds of heaven.

I remember that at one point Miss Susannah said, "You know, I think it might rain today. It looked like clouds were building up to the west."

"Why don't we just make our own rain," I whispered into her hair. She kissed my cheek and then my lips. She smelled like roses and sweat. I could not hug her hard enough.

She jumped up and ran, yelling, "If you want me you've got to come catch me."

I chased after her and caught her by the waist. We kissed. And we twirled in circles and we cuddled under those towering pines, and I think that for those minutes something special took hold of us. We went beyond our skin. We weren't intruders in this forest but part of it, like deer playing, unaware of man-made time and fear.

I touched her face and felt so purely happy. She laughed and the sound rang out, echoing 'cross the forest, blending into the busy chattering of squirrels, the calls of wild birds.

Holding hands, we floated, like two winged gods, out of the afternoon heat—leaving the close air and seed-strewn earth to Miss Raison—and entered our ivy-scented love house.

And Miss Susannah and I, we made love in unforgettable tones. Any notions 'bout separateness dissolved like cocoa in milk as we selfishly insisted on each other, else we weren't complete.

Then, in the midst of this grand new world, them skies broke loose. There we were in our safe little house, the storm raging 'round us, making our actions seem even richer—thunder, lightning, and driving rain swirling in and out of our sighs.

It was so perfect. Completely perfect. All my doubts were washed away. Mr. Artist did not exist. I did. I was a big-deal man laying in the midst of a freshly cleansed earth, Miss Susannah in my arms. I felt with dead, calm certainty that I could protect her from any harm. I could provide her with all manner of happiness. I knew it like I knew my own damn face.

We dozed together, and when we woke, the late afternoon crowded us with shadow. The storm had passed, and as we put on our clothes, both dreamy and happy, we thought we'd be stepping out into a cooler world. I floated to the yellow door, but when I pushed it open I crashed to the earth 'cause the rainstorm had done nothing to ease the heat. Just fueled it and reminded me like a slap in the face how human my skin was. I rubbed the back of my neck and watched steam rise up from the forest floor and curl like smoke between the pine.

I said to Miss Susannah, "Girl, it looks like we'll be walking home in some thick heat, after all." She stood beside me and I put my arms around her. I kissed her head, feeling that black hair like silk against my mouth. And then, still holding on to her, I looked out into the wet, steamy heat and said, "Raison, come on, Raison. It's time to head home."

Then a feeling swept over me, the kind seers have, sort of a slow-dawning dread that begins in your bowels and flashes all the way up to your brain, like mercury.

I stepped from the house and didn't see my Raison. I looked into the distance, the forest and the puddle-soaked earth. I walked 'round to the side of the house and I damn near tripped over that dead bird.

Miss Raison, the charm of my life, a saint dressed in animal clothes, had gotten confused in the rain and wind of that wily storm. For a split second I saw her in my mind's eye. I saw her lift her head to the sky and drink down all that rainwater till she drowned.

I heard myself cry out, but it was a holler so loud,

so distant, that I thought it was coming from somebody else's mouth. I fell to the earth and cradled Raison, and when I did I felt myself slip, slip away. It was as if that chicken as she floated off to heaven took with her my soul, my confidence. Even my youth.

And this here is the truth: As I screamed into that wet heat, I grew old. My eyesight dimmed and my joints ached and my skin wrinkled—just an iota, but it wrinkled.

I looked to Miss Susannah. She was staring at me horrified, screaming, "No, no, no!"

She raised her hands to the sky like she was trying to pull me—the young, confident, loving me—back down.

I got up from the earth, and still clutching my dead bird, I said, "Miss Susannah, I'm sorry. I'm so sorry."

But she was too shook and I think no longer knew me.

She didn't say a word in return.

That's how quickly life can change. In the time it took for a storm to transform the forest into a steam box, I lost everything. I had been a dirt-poor boy not fully belonging to any race and therefore not fully accepted by any. But then a magic bird comes along and erases all that. She, through the grace of God, gave me the confidence, the joy to stand upright like a man, to walk through my life like I was worthy of certain rights, such as loving a good woman and making a fair living. But this is how frail all those ideas are: As soon as Raison was gone, so was the man Miss Susannah had fallen in love with.

And I knew it. And she knew it. And there wasn't a damn thing to be done about it.

As I stood clutching my dead lucky chicken, I hadn't even the courage to see my good woman eye to eye. When that thread tying me to a charmed life was snipped, everything, even my Miss Susannah, went with it.

CARLOS PULLS on his hair and says something in Cuban. I think it's probably a phrase that means "Oh, my God!" or "How awful!" or "Couldn't you have told me a happier story?" I'm not sure, exactly. He looks at me, his intense black eyes scanning my face, trying to read me, and then in English he says, "It's so sad that this can happen in a life. The good magic goes away. I'm sorry, Mamacita."

"It's all right, Carlos." And then I lie because I want to knock him off balance, because he's zeroing in on me. I feel my heart turn to steel and I say, "It's just a story."

He bangs his hand down on the table and his tanned cheeks flush red. I think he's about to yell at me, but then he takes a deep breath and wipes his hand over his face as if trying to brush away his temper. He looks at me warily. He's measuring his words before he speaks. I can see it. I can peer right past those Latin eyes into his brain, that's furiously trying to figure me out. "You know, lady, that's not so. It's not just a story. You know like I do, it's the life. It's what we're given on this earth. It's just so," and then he stops as though he's filled with too much bitterness to go on, and the next thing I know, he's standing in front of me and pulling me to my feet and speaking so rapidly I'm having a hard time keeping up.

"Mamacita, you know how crazy it makes me, this dead baby, yes? But today I left my house and brought you friends, all this to make peace, to try to forget, just like your Mr. Sammy must have with his chicken, else he could not have gone on and lived his days. But Sadie, I have to know. Call me *loco,* call me the fool—I no care—I have to know if we found the baby for a reason. I have to know if the baby has power. You and I, we need to find this out. Together."

He says it all in about one second. His ability to believe life matters is overwhelming. So I say, "Carlos, what is it you want? I can't help you find the answers. I'm not capable."

"Aha!" And his eyes light up like those of a hunter who sees his trap snap shut on the rabbit's leg. "But I found out this lady. She can. This lady Miss McAlister. She sees things, Mamacita. Some guys told me. She'll be able to help us."

I didn't even see him set the trap. But there I am, my leg firmly caught. I look at his worried but faintly triumphant face and I know all the struggling and wiggling in the world won't get me out of this. And I don't have the will to gnaw my way out.

He stands before me, sweaty and focused, not allowing my eyes to waver, displaying a hunter's most precious virtue: patience infused with wiliness.

That's why I find myself walking with Carlos, who's cradling the coffin under his arm like a football, through the soft dusk of a spring evening past promenading locals and tourists, past small juke joints, each playing a different kind of music—reggae, then country and western, a tangle of Afro-Caribbean drums, a refrain or two of top forty, then salsa—the languid breeze carrying the conflicting strains into the heavens, until we are standing before a small shotgun shack in need of paint and new screens in Little Bahamia.

The yard is wild and overgrown and I hear things scuttling among the vines and the rich decaying stew of fallen leaves, twigs, and animal dung. I imagine neon-striped salamanders, armored beetles, palmetto bugs as big as my fist.

"Hello! Hello!" Carlos calls, and with his free hand knocks on the screen door with its rusted-and-once-white metal insert of a heron.

I listen for sounds of life. I don't hear anything. I decide nobody is home. Maybe I can slip the steel jaws, after all. I wait an appropriately long time—two seconds—before heading down the mossy flagstone walkway and saying, "Sorry. We missed her. Let's go home."

"Hello, Carlos Perez, I've been expecting you," I hear a woman say.

I spin around and am surprised at what I see. I assumed Carlos had uncovered some old black woman who drank chicken blood or something—those are the rumors. Instead, standing out in full contrast behind the torn screen is a woman, maybe in her mid-thirties, who is as albino as the day is long.

Spectral and thin and strangely sexy, she has white waist-long hair, and as I come back up the steps I notice that her blue eyes are focused on Carlos as if she can't get enough of him.

"Come in, Carlos Perez," she says. And then, still not looking at me, "You too."

That's nice of her. "Thank you so much," I say, and Carlos hums, as a warning, "Sadie."

She holds open the door. As we step out of the evening and into her house, I shoot him an I'm-never-going-to-let-you-live-this-one-down glare.

I'm expecting crystals, pyramids, incense, but what I get is postwar Florida: vintage rattan and big tropical prints and crazy, confetti-flecked vases and tabletops. The walls are lined with bookshelves, but there aren't any books on them, just junk. Literally. Pieces of broken glass, pebbles, broken-off parts of things: a Barbie's arm, a wheel from a baby carriage, a bent fork, a scrap of crimson cloth.

"Yes, I do. I collect found objects," she answers as if we'd asked. She surveys the odd assortment and scratches her head so intently I think: lice. "Objects that give off energy, that speak to me.'' Her voice is high, nearly a squeak.

Something curls around my legs and I jump and then feel foolish because it's only a cat. No, not a black one but a big orange guy who flicks his tail royally through the air, showing it off.

''Meatloaf. That's the cat's name,'' she says, and smiles. Her teeth are amazingly small. ''He's one of Hemingway's cats. I mean, descended from. Most cats are. The island cats, of course.''

I start to agree with her, but before I can she sticks her face just inches away from Carlos's and then mine. I'm overwhelmed by garlic-laced breath.

''What are you doing?'' I ask, not so politely.

She steps back and grins like a saleslady who just goosed her client. ''I'm sorry. I should have explained. I have terrible eyesight. I have to be near things to see them. I wanted to know what you and this man look like.''

And then, even though she's shorter than Carlos and about my height, and even though she is half blind, she manages to stare down at us. It's some kind of control thing she's perfected.

This is all too weird for me. I decide it's time to turn around and go home, but Carlos is keeping one hand on my arm. He's not about to let me escape now.

''Tell me,'' she says, squinting at us, ''what are we here for?''

''For the baby,'' Carlos says as though he's visiting a doctor with his newborn. He lets go of me and holds out the coffin.

Miss McAlister's entire slim body shrinks in on itself. It seems we've just placed an unbearable burden on her shoulders. She's no longer sexy. Meatloaf, all blubber and fur, darts down the dark hallway. Miss McAlister shuts her weak eyes and seems to be listening to someone. But no one is speaking. She ought to be in the movies, I think, with an act like this. Then her eyes blaze open and she orders, "This way."

We fall in line behind her and I pinch Carlos's ribs and he screws up his eyebrows at me like, Hey, what the hell.

We follow her into her kitchen, which is spotless but nevertheless bizarre. The cupboards have glass doors, so I can see all her food products. Boxes of dried dog food. Towers and towers of canned cat food. Glass canisters, some filled with birdseed and others with green and brown pellets, I guess rabbit or rat food. I don't know. But I don't see anything a human should consume. Nothing at all.

She sits down at her kitchen table that reeks 1950s with its turquoise-and-gray laminate top—not a crystal ball in sight—and says, "I like to feed animals."

Obviously.

Carlos, looking so serious I can't believe it, sets the coffin on the table and pushes it in her direction.

"Sit," she orders.

I pull out my chair, but before settling into it I

brush off a smattering of what I presume is cat fur. It's black, not Meatloaf's color.

She starts to touch the coffin but stops. "Water? Would you like water?" she asks.

"No, thank you. We're fine," I answer for us.

Miss McAlister leans into Carlos, those mostly blind eyes scanning his face. "You I like," she chirps, leaving me noticeably out. "Let's get to work."

She runs her hands over the coffin, as though she's picking up vibrations, and then struggles to open it, but neither of us moves to help her. I think we'd be disturbing her. So we let her fiddle until she figures it out on her own.

She lifts the baby from the coffin and holds him about an inch in front of her nose. "What a pretty child," she says, just as if people normally stop by with mummies.

From my vantage point, her face is eclipsed by the body. I hear her whispering, but I can't make out the words.

With her eyes closed and her face tilted toward the ceiling, she cradles him and rocks back and forth. Her right hand is cupped over his chest and she moves her fingers like a doctor searching for a heartbeat.

"Where did you find him?" she asks.

Carlos explains briefly and she's nodding, and I think she's listening not to Carlos but to something else.

"Yes. Yes," she says.

Then she sets the baby back in the coffin and gazes at him, adoringly, her bunting-blue eyes glistening, and I want to know what she sees. She strokes his stony cheek.

Softly, like a parent talking in front of a sleeping infant, she says, "He's very, very special. His people knew it. And they grew afraid. That's why they killed him. But as humans often do, after they murdered the baby they turned him into a martyr, a symbol, thus the mummification. And they would not allow him to rest. They would not let go of the child they killed. They named the dead baby king and demanded he live forever. His soul suffered from it. He needs to rest."

She cocks her head at me and then at Carlos and says, "He can help you."

Abruptly she closes the lid and stands and raises her arm as if inviting us to leave. "That's all. I don't know any more." She is sexy again. The burden is gone.

Carlos jumps up and rummages through his pockets. He looks stricken and I know we're in for trouble. This was a big mistake, coming here. "Money," Carlos says. "We need to pay you."

"Just bring me food. For the animals. You can leave it outside the gate." Then she smiles, her small teeth adding to the paleness of her face, and says, "We will know who it's from."

I WENT BACK with Carlos to his apartment. That was an even bigger mistake. Because the albino witch had only fueled his superstitious nature. He kept insisting we had to help the baby.

I kept insisting that you can't help the dead, short of reburying them.

Carlos couldn't shake the woman's words, and even though I thought she was full of crap, her whispered voodoo bothered me as well.

So we drank, trying to burn ourselves away.

We sat on his couch, the coffin on the coffee table next to a full bottle of tequila and two water tumblers. We drank without benefit of orange juice or grenadine or ice but downed the clear liquid with only bitter lemons in a ritual of sorrow, a communion celebrating not the blood and body of Christ but a granite corpse.

I can't remember whether it was his suggestion that we keep the child forever or his request that we get married that set me off most.

I told him that I wasn't made for marriage, or even companionship, and that if he didn't get rid of the dead thing I was finally going to tell the sheriff.

He didn't believe me.

He just popped in a Robert Johnson tape and started howling with that long-dead voice. He sucked on his liquor and pulled on his hair and wailed about some evil-hearted woman out to do him no good.

"Jesus, Carlos," I said. "You must have some black blood in those veins, to sing like that."

He poured more liquor and sang another refrain, and for a moment, through the alcohol-shrouded mist, I thought I saw us.

He was a man needing love and mystery. He needed to believe that there was a woman on earth who could give herself over to him fully, without reservation, and that there was a god or a saint or two who would look over them and protect them.

Me, I was a woman just wanting to live out her days as unencumbered as possible. I wanted to stop missing the dead and at the same time I wanted to believe in them.

I stood up and said, "I've got to get out of here."

Carlos paused from his song. "Please, please, Mamacita, don't leave tonight." He said, "We have to figure things out. We are buried people, Mamacita, but this baby has answers. That witch lady said it: 'He can help you.' "

His words stung, but I didn't want him to know that, so I sniped, "Carlos, you're talking crap. Enough is enough. I'm headed home."

He looked at the coffin and then back at me and then he shut his eyes. I knew he was feeling responsible. He didn't know what to do with the dead baby and he believed without question the albino lady's mumbo jumbo. He must have feared that any action he might take regarding the child would turn the universe on end and his entire cosmology of saints and virgins and magical dead children would rain down upon us like stones.

I thought, That's what religion and superstition do for you. I took one last swallow. And then I said, "Listen, Carlos, I simply can't do this. And you should forget about everything. Forget about the mummy. And the witch lady. And Saint Christopher. And your family in Cuba. And for tonight, forget about me. Because I'm out of here."

He shot me that down-the-nose sneer of his, but his eyes were dulled by too much tequila and sadness, and he said, "You, Mamacita, know like me: There's no way to forget."

Fuck him. That one hit home. But it wasn't enough to make me stay. I threw open the door. "Don't ever call me Mamacita again," I said, and I walked out, leaving him and his depressing music and his need for truth.

Now I'm threading my way back to the *Sparrow* and I'm trying to concentrate on the undulating sidewalk—I hit the tequila wall, the one that causes inanimate objects to shimmy, the one that if you can get past it and keep drinking you might have visions—and I am trying like hell to forget the hurt look in Carlos's sweet eyes. His hurt is rarely visible. Most folks probably never discern it, because he masks it in poetry and Latin bravado, but it's there, all right, with my name all over it. Yet I can't seem to stop hurting him. It's a compulsion: hurt Carlos, hurt Sadie, hurt Carlos, hurt Sadie. Yep, I'm stuck on one long fucked-up ride.

Then, not so much because I'm drunk as because the sidewalk has buckled from the root system of a jacaranda that overhangs the street, I trip, landing on my knees and palms in a carpet of fallen petals.

I'm scraped and cut. The wounds sting. I'm as drunk as upset, so I just sit there and sob. I want Mama to come pick me up and hold me to her breast and tell me, "Hush, hush, baby, don't cry."

But of course that doesn't happen. I'm a grown woman. What in Jesus's name is wrong with me?

I pick myself up and wipe off my face, and even though my skinned knees and hands burn, I continue on. I make the turn down by the docks. Occasionally a car drives past, but mainly I am alone, just hobbling along. If not for the lights left on in the Island Grocery, I would have stepped right on it. A mass of dark blue feathers and two skinny legs with webbed toes. A heron. It must have tried to fly across the street to the dockside, but these birds often glide so low that oncoming cars don't have any choice. By the time they see the big birds, it's too late.

I kneel down and I say, "Oh, shit," because the bird is not dead. The bastards who hit her could have at least stopped. They could have called the wildlife-care folks. Or they could have shot her so she didn't die slowly.

She was hit on her right side, the side she is lying on, and her yellow eye is staring at me, fearfully, helplessly.

What am I going to do? I know she's hurt too badly to recover, but I don't want stray dogs to get her. And I don't want her to die alone. I scan the fluorescent-lit night. There's nobody around. It's just me and this dying bird.

So I do the only moral thing: I lie down beside her. In the dirt and dust. I think that if I were dying underneath a cloudy, moonless sky, I would want someone to lie down beside me. And hold me.

I slip my arm underneath her matted feathers and cradle her, like a lover. She cries a single long note, a mournful, hollow song of loss. It is a song I know well. She falls silent. I rest my hand on her breast. I feel her heart beat faintly beneath her crumpled shoulder. Very softly, I sing, "Hush, little baby, don't you cry. . . . Mama's gonna buy you . . . a looking glass."

And then her heartbeat stops.

The only sound now is the wind rustling through the tropical canopy. I shut my eyes, and as I did when I was a child, I make a wish with all my soul. I wish that her heart would start beating again. Why is that so impossible? Why can't whatever it is we call God revive a stilled heart? I wish so hard that my breathing becomes shallow, and I imagine my own heart breaking, shattering, and then dispersing among the hidden stars of this dark night.

I whisper, "I name you Lazarus."

But it does no good. There are no revived hearts in this party. Not the bird's. Not mine. I am not God, and the divinity of this bird is beyond me.

Here I am, foolish and drunk and without miracles. At this moment I know only one thing: I intensely need to be back aboard the *Sparrow*.

So I pull myself up from the earth. And because I cannot in good conscience leave the heron on the side of the road as if she's just so much trash, I scoop her up in my arms.

With her graceful neck hanging over my shoulder, she gazes blankly at where we came from. I take her home.

I HAVE LOST track of time. I'm not sure when I left port. I just know that once I boarded the *Sparrow* and set the heron on the deck, a notion overcame me and it hasn't let up: Return to the islands of your youth. Because I need, more than anything, to be alone. I need to sit on some desolate shore and stumble through my thoughts and try to make sense of them. And those islands where Mama, Mima, and I spent our lives together provide more solitude than most folks can stand.

There are no stars. And the moonlight is at best intermittent, so I feel as if I'm traveling not through Gulf waters but through space. My good sense tells me to stop now. I am no longer familiar with the shoals and shallow passages of the islands. But I can't help myself. I have to get there. So I continue on, sipping from a pint of tequila I retrieved from my freezer and relying solely on my intuition and faded memory to guide me to some built-up mound of earth in the middle of nowhere.

I'm to the north of Cape Sable and Florida Bay but still well south of Chokoloskee. I don't plan to go that far, actually. I don't want to go back to the place where my women died. Back in 1960, Hurricane Donna took out the Crocodile Saloon, but I know the plot of ground where it sat. The sheared-off cypress posts are probably still in the ground, gray and weathered and taken over by prickly pear. No, I don't need to go back there and see that. Not when my mind's eye sees those two women so clearly. Like right now. There they are, in my thoughts, suspended forever in the joy of that last dance. So it won't be Chokoloskee for me. I just want to find a key with a bit of beach so I can sit my butt down and think.

Everything—the sky, the water, the mangrove—it's all black. I'm using my searchlight to help navigate. I do not want to run up on a shoal and get stuck out here. I don't have any charts for this area, so I'm more or less navigating by the seat of my pants. But coming up on my starboard bow is a huge island. I think I'm near or at Lostmans River. I'm almost sure of it. Just south of the island is a small key at the mouth of a bay leading into the river. That would be South Lostmans. I'm amazed that I can remember this area at all. Sometimes I think memories are like tattoos—you might be able to hide them, but they don't ever go away.

I get in as close to the island's shore as I dare. I don't moor the *Sparrow* on the bank because sometimes I'm not strong enough to shove her off. I hate asking for help. And out here I might not find any. Unless I run into a park ranger—this area is all federal preserve, and I'm supposed to have a permit—but I don't think anyone will find me tonight.

I throw the anchor, and as I do I feel strangely in control, as if I know what I'm doing. I tuck the pint of tequila in my back pocket. I take the quilt off my bunk and place the heron on top of it. Then, hoping that I don't run into any gators, I jump into the hip-deep water and wade to the shore, keeping the bird and quilt well out of reach of the warm sea.

The ringlet of white shoreline is the only thing visible, and I head straight for it, as quickly as possible, trying not to think about what might be in the water.

As I come ashore, I stumble over a horseshoe crab and almost fall. "God damn it," I cuss. The sand is littered with broken conch shells and abandoned horseshoe armor. I stake out my territory, kicking the marine skeletons aside, and then sit down. The mosquitoes are bad, so I lay the bird on the sand and wrap the quilt around me, head and all.

But once I'm completely cocooned, I realize I can't just leave the heron lying on the sand. I need to bury her. I look around. I don't dare take her into the woods—even I'm a bit wary of what might be in there—so I throw off the quilt and get down on all fours, and with my hands I dig and dig until I've created a bowl deep enough to be a proper grave.

I start to make this a fairly simple affair. But something comes over me, something so strong that I ignore the mosquitoes. I run my hand across the bird's gorgeous wings. They are soft. But powerful. I decide I want them, as if they hold magic that might save me, as if I just have to have them. I take the tequila out of my back pocket and then the Swiss army knife that I always carry—a toolbox that fits in the palm of your hand. Feeling my way along the bird's shoulder, I cut through skin, cartilage, tendon, removing first one wing and then the other.

I set them aside and place the bird in the grave and turn her so that she is facing east, toward the Everglades and the sunrise. "You can rest now," I say.

When I'm finished, I sit back down and rewrap myself in the quilt. Thoughts scuttle through my mind like windblown trash. I'm somewhat happy that maybe the bird is at peace and that I'm sitting on a deserted island with nothing but a bunch of bugs for company.

I sip my tequila and pray for visions. I try to focus my thoughts. I entertain the notion that it's too damn bad I'll never be able to break down my own walls and be as good to Carlos and myself as I should. But in my case, I decide as I slap a mosquito, I guess it's, Like grandmother, like granddaughter.

The night sky is so dark it weighs me down. I imagine myself Atlas, but unlike the god, I can't handle the load. Sometimes the silliest things set me off—Carlos touching me when I don't want to be touched, a rainy day when I was counting on sun, running out of coffee first thing in the morning so that I have to go up to the corner, sleepy-eyed, and buy some. Jesus, what would I do if something really bad happened? Like, what if by mistake I got on a boat headed out of America and could never return home? I'm sure I wouldn't be as stoic about it as Carlos.

Or what if I were in Mima's shoes when she was a young woman struggling between worlds and cultures? She told me that, given her social concerns and her desire to please the woman who had raised her, the thought of marrying someone Miss Alice would never approve of—namely, Mr. Sammy—truly scared her. She told me it broke her heart: Mr. Sammy turning old and spineless. But she said she decided to believe again what the white people had taught her. She said she decided once and for all to be one of them. She said, "Sadie, a young woman named Susannah Motherwell made that decision. But Susannah Motherwell wasn't real."

That's the word she used: "real." She said she hardened beyond recognition. She said she had to if she was going to do what was expected.

This island is far more full of life than I had thought. Animals I cannot name are beginning to make themselves known. I hear twigs snap, and cries filter now and again from woods to sky. I wrap up tighter and try to concentrate on Mama and Mima. I think about that day Mr. Sammy decided he had turned old. His sudden despair and Miss Raison's drowning weren't the only life-changing events in the forest hideaway that stormy afternoon. Mima conceived my mother in the middle of all that lightning and rain. But she decided Mr. Sammy would never know. She decided she had Mr. Artist hooked pretty well and that her way out of the entire mess was to reel in Mr. Artist and make him think the baby was his.

Her plan was to keep her pregnancy a secret until she got him to the altar. But her belly popped out too soon, too proudly. She couldn't, especially in those silk dresses, disguise her condition. And Mr. LaCour, regardless of his opium-shaded state, noticed that fertile curve and got the hell out of town.

Maybe she should have just gone to Mr. Sammy and made her peace. But she couldn't. I think that by the time Ellis Elijah LaCour left, too many lies had been told and she was too confused about which world—the Indian or the white or the in-between—she was supposed to live in.

So Miss Alice, completely fed up and unwilling to have anything else to do with Susannah Motherwell and her fatherless baby, bought a clapboard house in West Augustine. She furnished it with a secondhand couch and bed. Then she told Mima, "Pack up your clothes and get out of my house. I don't ever want to see you again."

And that was it. My grandmother was alone in the world with a belly full of baby. She wouldn't admit to anyone whose child it was. I remember we were roaming through Florida Bay and she held both my little white hands in her big brown ones and said, "I decided the baby was mine. No other person would lay claim. And I decided to live my life completely independent from anyone or anything. Because as far as I could tell, getting one's life snapped up inside somebody else's only caused heartache."

Of course, Mr. Sammy, he may not have been the rooster of his dead youth, but he still had a brain. And all through Mima's pregnancy he steadily insisted on being a presence. There was no more romance. But he stuck around and put up with her harsh words and actions, and he helped her get a smoked-mullet business going, and he became, though at the time she would not admit to this, her one and only friend.

I brush a mosquito off my face and drink more, in the ridiculous hope that the liquor will still my spinning head. I tuck the wings under my feet. Their scent might draw critters out from the brush, so I reach around and gather in stones, shells, sticks. I'm going to sit here until daybreak, I decide. I'm going to drink and muse and maybe cry. I'm going to wander the dark passages of my brain until I feel better.

The quilt enforces the darkness of the night sky. It is a shroud warm and comforting. I wonder what it would have been like to be a little girl able to climb up in her granddaddy's lap. I hope he would have loved me. He loved Mama. He sure did.

I listen to Lostmans River gently lapping at the

white necklace of sand. I listen closely, filtering out the forest sounds: a gentle roll, a sudden slap, the liquid cadence of the water's ebb and flow, and then, finally, a murmur amid the oyster shells and limestone, a murmur that builds and becomes clear. As my granddaddy speaks, I balance the night's weight more easily:

AFTER MISS RAISON DIED, I was a different kind of man. The sort who let Susannah slip through his fingers, the sort who didn't, anywhere but in his dreams, fight for her.

It's not that I didn't try. I struggled with myself. I turned over leaf after leaf in an attempt to figure out where I'd gone. I searched the day and the night, but all I ever came up with was a man suddenly old who stood in the shadows and watched his woman take up with another man.

Don't be mistaken: The end of our love was a happening I suspect we both fought against. Surely, Miss Susannah must have had moments when she stared at her reflection in the looking glass and couldn't stand what was happening. Didn't she see herself in all those stuffy clothes and social ties and feel suffocated? Didn't she ever close her eyes and see us as we had been: two barefoot lovers kissing each other into existence?

But it all turned into this: a man without enough imagination to figure out a way to stop what was happening to Susannah. And a girl who went fully over to the other side, thinking that white folks were once again gonna save her.

Fate has a funny way of messing with both the finest and vilest of plans. Miss Susannah found herself in the family way, and once that happened, Mr. Artist hightailed it out of town with all the speed of a horse thief. I have to admit I was a happy man when I found out her marriage plan was thwarted.

But if you're thinking that opened the door for my return, then you're thinking wrong. 'Cause what it did was only harden Miss Susannah's heart even more. She'd been twisted thisaway and thataway too many times. Like a woman bent on unhappiness, she locked up her heart full of thorns in some forgotten drawer and decided love was not for her.

So there was no opportunity to be her lover.

But I did weasel in as her friend. She would probably describe it as an irritant. But I was an irritant who saved her life.

Let me tell you what I did, 'bout how I knew her heart was wounded, not dead.

I decided I needed to act selflessly. And provide protection. But my reasons were not just that my love for the mean woman ran so deep and helpless. I woke up one morning and stared at my reflection in the mirror Old Mama had nailed over my bed. She nailed it there with some no-nonsense pounding and said, "There you go, son. Now look in that mirror every day till you find yourself."

And that's what I did. I stared and stared at that strange reflection, and as I studied my new wrinkles and my hair with its hint of gray, I stumbled upon this: Maybe the baby was mine. Just maybe. And just maybe I ought to take some precautions for its welfare, since odds probably were in my favor.

So I got my butt out of bed and journeyed into the woods as far as I dared. I could not bring myself to go to our shack. I couldn't face the memories of Raison. And I sure as hell could not face the memories of me and Susannah in love, 'cause that was another time. A place of youth and love lost. So I didn't go to the shack, but I did go to the woods.

And I cut me down a fair-sized pine tree, and from it I fashioned one long board. Old Papa always told me haunts hated brand-spanking-new Holy Boards. They drive spirits out and prevent new ones from getting in. So I sawed a board four feet long and then snuck a pint of holy water out of the church and sprinkled the entire knotty surface.

Then I bundled up my energy and courage, put on Old Papa's brown hat, and marched over to Miss Susannah's new house. I did all this not only so I could act as Protector but because, of course, I wanted to see Miss Susannah. And I wanted to know if I could pinpoint anything about the child.

The house was an older place, had a huge porch in front, but you could tell that beyond the porch, where the windows looked out like dead man's eyes, this piece of real estate was potentially crawling with if not haunts at least bad memories.

I was standing with the Holy Board under my arm in the shade of a huge live oak—the house had that going for it, a fine, fine yard—and I'm thinking I had not seen this woman since the day I turned old. And I'm thinking I might not have the courage to see her now, when damned if she doesn't open her front screen door and walk out on her porch and look at me with not a stitch of joy on her face. She just says, "Mr. Sammy."

And I say, "Miss Susannah." And then there was about an eternity of silence, and then 'cause I didn't know what else to say I offered the obvious: "I brought you a housewarming present." I held up the board. "This here, Miss Susannah, is what you call a Holy Board. It will keep you and your family safe. Got any nails?"

Her hair was covered with a blue scarf. The puffy white sleeves of her blouse were rolled up past her elbows. She held a cleaning rag in her left hand. If she was surprised at my reference to her family, she did not let on. She simply pointed at a tin bucket by the front stoop. "There are some nails in there. Really, you shouldn't have bothered," she said, eyeing the Holy Board.

"It's no bother, Miss Susannah." Then I ventured, "We can be friends, after all, can't we?"

She didn't say a word but fiddled with that scarf on her head. I guessed I shouldn't of said that.

We were both standing there, just looking awkward, so I went to work, nailing the board over her front door. And while I was hammering I noticed that the ceiling and corners were fairly thick with spiderwebs. I stepped back and admired my handiwork, all the while trying to pin myself down, trying to figure out exactly what role to play in this woman's life. I looked at her straight-on. I was going to offer to clean off the webs. Even if she'd thought of doing it herself, she was a short woman and there was no way she could reach all of them.

But I never got the chance, 'cause this here is what happened. I shot her a look and she shot one back and damned if our eyes did not lock. And damned if her sour face didn't turn gentle. And everything—her hardness, my old age, her stubbornness, my waning courage—it all shook and almost disappeared.

I wanted so bad to reach out and touch her. I think I did reach. I mean, I think I put out my hand and nearly caressed her cheek. But she looked away—fast like a little fly. I didn't see a trace of meanness, though, in her eyes or her set jaw. We stood there trapped in a million unspoken what-could-have-beens. The wind whistled through the trees and a horse clip-clopped by.

Then Miss Susannah looked down toward the old porch planks painted white, but her gaze wasn't on the ground, it was on that rising belly of hers, and she said, "Mr. Sammy, you can't ever come back here."

Her voice didn't have an ounce of conviction, but it was thick with fear. That's sure true.

And I don't know where it came from, but I managed to speak to the point. I said, "Woman, you and me have been through a lot. And we both know you're in a bit of trouble. And we both know you ain't exactly got a lot of friends in this town. But don't worry about it. I'll take care of you. Best way I know how."

She looked up from her belly, and her once sweet and gentle face was just snapping with anger. But she couldn't get a single mean word to roll off her tongue. And those black eyes of hers revealed not only a scared heart but a lonely one.

A heart capable of that much feeling, one capable of turning black eyes into fiery coals, is not dead. It's simply in need of a steady hand.

I decided that I would be that hand and that the only way to do it without burning myself up in the process was to ignore the possiblity that it was my seed in her womb and concentrate on seeing her through the birth.

That's how it all happened, how I wasn't dumped from her life.

It's a damn good thing I took charge too, 'cause the baby in her belly was making the woman sick. Her pretty brown skin went bad—white splotches all over her face. And from her cheeks to her toes she bloated up. She should have been thankful that I'd paid a mindful eye to my mama when she used to take care of pregnant womens, 'cause I knew what to do. Miss Susannah needed greens cooked without any salt, any pork. She needed at least three glasses of orange juice every day. She needed a healthy pot of lavender set by her bed. She needed to take her feet out of those hoity-toity white girl's shoes she loved to wear and instead put on her oldest pair of socks and keep them on. And then, right about when it was time to push the baby into the world, she needed a big old glass of milk and honey spiked with St. Augustine holly for strength and attitude.

To make sure all this was happening proper, I went by every day, twice a day. She wasn't very friendly, but she didn't send me away either. She was crabby, and we took to not looking fully in each other's eyes, like we did on the Holy Board day, lest we stumble upon an emotion too wild for us to hold on to. We wandered through life behaving like we didn't share a past, behaving like youth and happiness were far removed from our domain. Some days I felt like we were puppets and our master had changed the script on us in midplay, pulling our strings and making us behave in a manner we would not before have dreamed possible.

I had friends tell me, "Sammy, you stuck in a sacrifice syndrome. Take off from that woman."

But I listened to no one.

While she was pregnant I cooked for her. I mopped her floors. I made sure her sheets were clean and her bed smelled fresh. I sprinkled the mattress with crushed orange blossoms. I made her cut out the lemon balls, a habit she started in her Mr.

Artist days. 'Cause they could make that baby more sour than sweet.

Now, she never told me to go away. But she never, for instance, reached over and touched my hand or relaxed the snotty tilt of her head and said, "Mr. Sammy, it's late. Why don't you just sleep here tonight?" She never smiled and said, "Thank you."

Yes, sometimes I wanted her to. Sometimes I wished for just a glimmer of a kind word, a sweet action. But nothing. The woman sure as hell had turned to stone. And you know, a stone gives the lizard a place to sun hisself but doesn't give him any food, any water. Gives him no fern or moss. For that the lizard has got to go somewhere else. But not me. I just loved her so much. Maybe too much. Day after day I went taking care of the woman and the baby inside her, hoping that the lizard in me wasn't going to decide to move off the stone too late, thinking maybe he'd scurry away before he got burnt up in the sun.

I had done my calculations, and I had studied Miss Susannah's belly rising like a full moon. And one day when she was in her front yard looking up at a cackling crow perched in the oak branches, yelling at him to "stop that stupid racket," I saw her belly drop. And I know she felt it, 'cause she quit yelling and went inside the house, banging the screen door behind her.

And my birthing calculations told me this: I was

probably the papa. But I wasn't celebrating, because I weren't a gambling man.

Then, late on a Thursday afternoon in mid-April, when the air was bursting with new scents such as blossoming jasmine and honeysuckle and wisteria, and the yard was full of the sounds of new life—baby wrens and jays and cardinals and buntings—I handed Miss Susannah, who was sitting at her broad oak kitchen table, a cup of freshly brewed blackberry tea, and what I saw made my heart soar. She looked at me and said in a harsh voice 'cause she couldn't help herself, "That tea smells good." I smiled so wide she must of thought I was crazy, but I had good reason, 'cause this is what I saw: yellow sparks flickering in her dark eyes, the sparks of life, a signal that the child was ready for birthing.

But I didn't let on to her what I knew. I just got up from the table and fixed us a dinner of greens and liver, and while I did I told her old family stories, like 'bout my ancestors being part gator. Then I warmed some milk and sweetened it with hibiscus blossom. The sun had gone down and the air had turned cold, and I could see she was chilled from the way she folded her arms in front of her.

I said, "Susannah, I don't want you to argue with me. You need to get some rest. Don't sit up late tonight knitting or reading or whatever it is you do."

For once she didn't sass back. She just nodded and took her milk and waddled down the hall to bed.

I closed up her house and as I was leaving I paused

on the front stoop and looked around. The night was truly beautiful. The sky was indigo and the moon was still low on the horizon. Night-blooming jasmine lay thick in the air. An idle man could have been made drunk by the scent and the beauty. But not me. 'Cause as I walked home my mind was furious in its planning. I was for certain that by tomorrow evening there'd be a second set of lungs in Miss Susannah's house, breathing in, breathing out. And those lungs might belong to a human being I helped create. And if the child wasn't mine, it would not matter. Because it would still be a person in need of love. It was my job, then, to make sure the air was free of haunts, full of dreams, full of hope.

When I got home, Old Mama and Papa, they was waiting for me on our front porch, slowly rocking in their respective chairs. They spoke softly to each other, on and on. In all my days I never knew what it was they was saying to each other. It was as if their life together had been a long whisper, one that no one else had been privy to.

I stepped up on the porch and said, "Evening." See here, when I came to a certain age, say twelve or thirteen years, I didn't ever talk with them 'bout my personal affairs. The name Susannah Motherwell had never once been uttered to them by me in our house.

But there they were, after dark, rocking, waiting, ancient as hell, full of conspiracy. Old Mama and Papa had, in time, grown to look identical. Except Old Mama still had all her silver hair and Old Papa had done lost most his. But their wrinkles ran the same way, the same depth, and their hands were twinly callused, as if neither set of long brown fingers had ever once taken an action independent of the other. That's sure the way they were, always of the same mind. And as they got closer and closer to that old graveyard, they was getting more and more of the same body.

Like I spoke, we had never had a what-for 'bout my affairs with Miss Susannah, but I had not so much as gotten both my weary feet on the first porch step before Old Papa says, "Don't you forget to sprinkle garlic root 'round that house tomorrow. And you've got to mix up a strong quantity of M-and-H, and attire her in the right birth clothes."

"Yes, sir. I'll be sure to do those things," I said.

And then Old Mama smiled at me as if I'd made her a grandma, and she said, "Son, I guess we'll be going to bed now. You get a good night's sleep. You hear me?" Then my parents stood up and shuffled inside, and though there wasn't much spring in their gait and their elbows looked creaky, they seemed completely satisfied, just as if they'd solved the world.

But right before the door slapped shut, Old Mama turned to me and says, "Son, I sure hope you won't need it, but remember, cold water shocks."

I had no idea what that meant, but I said, "Yes, ma'am, I'll remember."

I didn't have any notion as to how my parents were such know-it-alls. But their advice fueled my wish that Miss Susannah and I had created a bond that could never be denied. No matter what. I went on to bed. And I'd be lying if I said I wasn't thinking this: A new life in our lives might kindle new hope.

Maybe that's why my sleep was filled with such vivid dreams. They ran all night long, like mullet after bait fish. In dream after dream, Susannah and I were giving birth to a baby. Sometimes it wasn't just a baby but a beautiful fish with heaven-blue scales and soft lemony eyes. And in every damn one of those dreams we was just proud as Pete to be giving birth to a fish!

I'd given birth so many times during the night I was sort of exhausted come morning.

But the day's promise wouldn't allow me to dawdle. So I got busy right off at gathering the need-bes. I grated garlic root until my right hand started to bleed. I visited Moses Lars 'cause he grew the sweetest orange blossom honey 'round these parts, and I bought a quart jar full. I emptied the entire contents of a good-luck conjure ball into my tub and took the hottest bath I could stand. And I didn't eat anything, but I did drink some orange juice.

Finally, I headed to Miss Susannah's. In my left hand I carried the honey jar and in my right hand I carried the milk jar. And I thought I was just the smartest man under the April sun, until I got to the railroad tracks. As I stood waiting for the train to go by I realized I was bareheaded. I had left my hat, that brown one that belonged to Old Papa until I wore it so much it belonged to me, sitting in the pine side chair right next to the screen door. Miss Susannah had to have the hat. She had to wear it, no getting 'round that, 'cause such an item would be sure to ease her pains. Sitting atop her head would be all my strength and all my papa's strength, and all our good wishes and hope-fors. So I turned myself 'round and walked all the way back home for it.

This put me at her door later than I wanted. It was deep into the afternoon, and the spring air was gentle. Bees hovered over the lavender wisteria, and the grass, having overcome last year's drought, looked so green and tender that if I'd been a grasshopper I would have eaten it too.

I went right to work. Didn't even bother to say hello to Miss Susannah. I hurried with my garlic sprinkling, all around the front door, 'cause sometimes when a baby is born, it's just like fresh fruit for flies. Haunts want to mess with those newborn souls. But the dead hate garlic. Makes them stay where they belong: in the grave, in the past. So I hurried with the sprinkling.

I knew time was working against me. I put on my fiercest face and I flapped my arms and made all manner of noise, for just in case something had already visited the house who shouldn't be there. I was doing a high-stepping, arm-flapping number and honking like a crow when I ran into Miss Susannah 'round back.

She was sitting in her cypress yard chair wearing her old socks just like I had told her to. I do believe she was approaching scared, due to the racket I'd been making, 'cause when she saw me a look of relief and anger swept over her plump face.

''What in the world do you think you're doing, Mr. Sammy? You about scared the dickens out of me with all that noise. You and your silly superstitions!'' She looked at me, her pretty features gnarled with stubbornness, and I just ignored her mean words 'cause it's what I usually did and also 'cause of this: I saw the unmistakable—the sparks that were in her eyes the night before had grown bolder. Truly, yellow flames blazed. That child sure was looking out at the world through the eyes of its mama.

I said to myself, Mr. Sammy, you have shown up right in the nick of time. To Miss Susannah I said, ''Come on, girl, let's get you up out of that chair and into bed.''

''Bed! I'm perfectly fine. I don't need to go to bed.'' She tried to stare me down but couldn't manage it, since she wasn't the only one gazing out. She looked away and, despite herself, started crying.

''Let's go,'' I coaxed. ''Everything is going to be okay.'' I helped her out of the yard chair and she held on to me as we headed into the house. She had some real trouble with the back porch steps. All that weight in front of her had thrown her bearings cockeyed. But we managed, we sure did, even though that baby was taking over.

As we walked I started my prayers, out-loud soothing prayers: ''Such a grand little world you going to come into. Don't be scared. Leave all that fear over there on the other side. Just slip on off that far riverbank, 'cause the waters are cool, sweet as honey. Just swim, swim, swim. Land ain't far now. Ain't far at all."

I must have whispered this to the child three hundred, maybe four hundred times. I know that these days all the rage is to have the child born in a hospital with glaring, mean lights, and nobody there who loves it, and no sweet words, just science words. Ain't no mystery the children are born without any belief or wonder or magic. 'Cause these big-butt medical doctors with their cold, harsh gadgets can't instill nothing but sterilized air.

Now, once I got Miss Susannah in the bed, first thing I did was plant my hat on her head. This eased her some, plus it gave that baby strength and a notion of who I was. Then I opened the white lace bedroom curtains and said, "Just look at them pretty flowers and trees. Smell that luscious spring air."

And Miss Susannah did, she turned her head and gazed out that window. The child must have been thinking it was an awfully nice world. An afternoon shower started up. But not a thunderstorm, just a soft spring rain.

I went to the kitchen and began mixing the birth nectar: milk and honey and a pinch of St. Augustine holly. A fingernail full of this wild holly was magic—it took the mind to a softer place. But too much could be deadly. The holly was not medicine a know-nothing could fool with. But I understood the portions. I knew a pinch would be all she needed to glide her through this birth.

It took close to a half-hour for her to drink the spiked M-and-H—not because it wasn't sweet, good-tasting, but because her physical self was in stress. She would lift her head off her pillow and look at me like she was the most miserable creature on the face of the earth, and she'd say, "I can't do it."

And I'd say, "Yes you can."

I'd put the glass to her lips and she'd down a little bit more. Sip by sip, complaint by complaint, she finally drank it all.

The pains began just before nightfall. I lit a lamp and sat it on the side table next to the lavender plant. I worked hard at keeping my composure. I tried to make my face calm and sweet-looking, 'cause Miss Susannah didn't need to know that inside I was shaking like a leaf in the wind.

As events progressed, there was some screaming and also some moaning. But overall, between the holly, and me talking to the child about the cool river and wonderful world, the labor wasn't too bad as I understand labors go. We went at it maybe four, five hours. I worked hard too. I kept on massaging her belly, her arms, her thighs glistening with sweat, urging her to relax. She'd slap my hands off and tell me to go away, and I behaved as if her hands and words did not sting me. I continued trying to ease her.

I don't know that it did any good.

Oh, every once in a while she'd fall silent for a second or so, and then I'd get in my prayer real quick. "Just swim, swim, swim," I'd urge.

And Miss Susannah would growl, "Shut up, you son of a bitch."

As things got tenser and as she cussed more thoroughly and as the rain fell harder, I saw in my mind's eye Miss Raison flapping her wings and lifting her face to the water-filled sky.

"Go away, Raison," I said. "Not now. I can't deal with your memory right now."

I looked up to the heavens for help and then back down at Miss Susannah, and it was then that I saw salvation: a little black-haired head crowning out from between her legs.

I was so excited I almost cried. I told myself, Stay calm, Mr. Sammy, stay calm. You've got to finish the job.

But as she pushed one last time and let out with a scream so brutal I can hear it to this day, I wished with all my soul I'd gone and gotten a doctor. Because she produced a baby, all right, but it was a baby made of stone.

That's the God's honest truth. It weren't moving. It weren't crying. It weren't breathing. It weren't nothing but a rock.

I said, "Oh, my dear God!"

And Susannah went wild in a fevered delirium, groping at me, screaming, "My baby, where's my baby?"

I had no idea what to do. I was about to take the little stony child and run into the streets hollering for help when Mama's words came back to me: "Remember, cold water shocks."

I bundled the child into Miss Susannah's top bureau drawer. I ran into the kitchen and pulled a block of ice out of the icebox. I put it in a copper washtub she kept on the back porch and then I rushed to the pump in the backyard. I pumped so hard I 'bout near threw my shoulder out. When it was deep enough to dunk a soul, I ran the tub, water sloshing over the sides, back inside the house and into the bedroom.

Miss Susannah was crying from fever and, I thought, madness.

I took the little stone baby in my hands and I said, "Please, dear God, make this work."

I plunged that unmoving body into the ice bath. I realized then, as I gazed into the water, that I was holding a baby girl and that she was hard and brittle, slick as a river rock, and I was scared that if I brought her out of the water I might drop her and she would splinter into a million pieces.

So, carefully, I brought her to the surface. But still no breath, no movement.

Again, I plunged her into the water and, again, nothing.

I must have looked like a monster as I dipped her head below the surface for the third time and kept her there, down, down, down, trying to drown life into her.

I looked at her watery features and saw how perfect her face was, with her tightly shut eyes and her upturned nose. I looked at her beautiful hands held in front of her in two tiny defiant fists. I saw how completely unmoving all her precious fingers and lips and toes were.

How could anything so beautiful be so dead? At that moment I decided there was no God, no hope. I decided to release the little rock baby. She's dead, Mr. Sammy, I said to myself, she's dead.

Then I felt something. A tug, a pull, an attempt at struggle, a small fish wiggling. In my mind, Miss Raison was still drinking rain and flapping her wings in warning or agitation. Miss Susannah was moaning and grabbing at me like a crazy woman.

I lifted the baby out of the water, this little stone angel, and her blue face flushed rosy and her death mask cracked, and her silence was broken by the sweetest, angriest demand for life I have ever heard.

She opened her perfect mouth and, I swear to God, I saw the intake of breath and then the rain stopped and the sky filled with her beautiful, beautiful hollering.

The three of our living souls were awash in moonlight. A gentle wind scented with spring rolled over us. I held the screaming, wet baby and I began to bawl. But I was celebrating between my tears. I was so happy and so proud because I knew that tiny, wrinkled baby girl who was trying out her lungs for the whole world to hear was my daughter. No doubt 'bout it. She was my flesh and blood.

How do I know? The same way folks know to have faith, the way they know the wind exists even if it hasn't blown in a good long time. I know because of the memory mixed in our blood. I know because my soul and my bones and my skin seemed suddenly and completely unimportant.

I floated in my daughter's screams and in the birth glow of Miss Susannah's face.

I know because of this: When I put the child in Susannah's arms, the three of us hugged and cuddled, and for a few minutes everything—the moon, the stars, the breeze, our fingers and arms touching, our love—seemed just right.

THE COON is a forward little bastard. He's sitting right where the woods begin, staring at me like he thinks he might come over here and find food. I'm an empty bucket, so he'd best quit looking at me.

I hold up the bottle to the moon, but there is no moon, so I can't tell how much liquor I have left. I lift it to my ear and swish the elixir around. Just a couple of good draws, by the sound of it. I drink the rest down, and because the coon spooks me I throw the bottle at him. I miss. But he moves deeper into the woods. The little fucker is probably staring at me through the palmetto, licking his little coon lips, imagining I taste good.

Most men can't believe the way I drink when I set my mind to it. A few have made the mistake of challenging me. Guess who ends up under the table?

Despite the quilt, the mosquitoes are getting to me. But I don't care. The tequila has stolen my ability to hurt. At least physically.

I hear something large rushing through the brush. I twirl around and yell, "Go away!" and then there is a guttural squeal and birds clacking their beaks in warning. I am an intruder here, someone who doesn't fit into their natural order, and I fear them. Foolishly. My heart is pounding so hard that I am completely aware of it. This is not good. People are not supposed to be aware of their internal organs.

I need to calm down. I can't return to the *Sparrow* because the water isn't cool and inviting. It reminds me of a tomb, a place where I bury the dead. So I am going to have to sit here through the night and survive whatever foe lingers in this island's dense brush.

I try to concentrate on Mima and Mr. Sammy and not my fear. I try to ignore the strange sounds of the night and immerse myself in Mima's sins. But they are so many. Or are they? Where do I place the blame this time? Is producing a baby made of stone a sin? I think not. An act of the deepest despair, perhaps. But not a sin.

What she did after the birth, though, was most definitely sinful. She refused Mr. Sammy any rights as a father. I mean, any spoken or legal rights. Sure, she let Mr. Sammy baby-sit and change diapers and feed my mama orange pudding and sing lullabies to her, and as Mama got older Mima even let Mr. Sammy offer all sorts of advice a young girl growing up might need, like, Stay away from boys.

But she never allowed the word "Daddy" to be spoken. She never admitted to him he was the father, and when he pushed her on it she told him he was nuts.

The darkness is beginning to spin, and as I whirl, unable to make it go away, I hear Mima, but she's telling an unfamiliar story. I yell into the night, "What? What is it you want?"

The tequila finally does what I've been hoping for. I look into the surrounding darkness and I see with the eyes of the dead. For I believe it is the dead and not the living who have visions.

I see her in the distance, out over the river, shimmering. A young, beautiful Mima who is lamenting motherhood, whose eyes have hardened into stone like the child she gave birth to, preventing her from seeing the folly of her ways.

"No, Mima, no," I cry. In my vision she is far younger than when I knew her, but she is sad beyond her years, and when she speaks it is to her newborn child, yet her words sound futile, like those of a woman who has looked into the dark oval of her soul and found nothing. No fluttering wing. No gasp of light:

BABY GIRL, born of stone but immersed in the secret of water, listen closely and try to understand. This is the core of my sadness: I do not know what to do with you. You are a stranger in my hands. You are a creature love created, but it is a love I must deny. I deny it for your sake. And for mine. Because we can never admit what we really are. I have been instructed in the discipline of denial for so many years that I am no longer sure who I once was, or what remains of her. Yet when I look at you, I begin to remember.

On the day of your birth, Oneida, you looked a million years old. This is my theory: With your first intake of breath you wrinkled your face in order to crack the stone, and from your scalp even down to your toes, you stayed that way. Wrinkled.

So every morning and every evening I lovingly rub unsalted butter all over you, yes! As though you are a suckling pig! The butter has worked wonders. Your wrinkles, one by one, are fading, and a sweet-faced baby is taking the place of the wizened mermaid I gave birth to. I have heard people say that all babies look alike. This is not so. You are my proof.

I will tell you now who you look like. The reflections of my people are there—in your staunch, high cheekbones, and the greenness of your eyes, and the dusty blush of your skin. I tell you this now, but it will be the last time. For I am making a conscious decision to remove from your life everything about mine that has caused such pain.

You look like a woman who gave birth to me on the prairie. I do not remember her name, nor can I re-create the sound of her voice. But she is there, in your cheekbones. And it haunts me.

When I run my finger along your mouth I am reminded of my father. For like his lips, yours are full and lively, as though all your emotions are concentrated in those two fleshy petals. I love your ability to go from grimace to grin in one breath, but I must find a way not to think of him each time you do.

And then, of course, there are your eyes, the eyes of your father. But you will not know him as your father, because he is a love I should never have let myself indulge in. He is a man who touched areas of my soul that I once thought had been removed, a little pocket of my heart capable of believing in magic, capable of not caring about the dictates of white society. This is a part of me you cannot know, or ever see, because a child born of an Indian and a mulatto will be a child without promise. I have learned that lesson well. So I will deny you your father and your heritage. And I will replace them with lies. But at least they will be lies you can live with:

Mr. Sammy is a well-meaning man I have hired to help around the house. Your father died at sea before you were born, a yachting accident. We are of Castilian blood, perhaps even royal blood. Never, never are we to be confused with Minorcans, for they are common in St. Augustine.

If anyone ever tells you an ounce of the truth, I will deny it as self-righteously and vigorously as Saint Joan herself.

Oneida, I have so very many dreams for you. And they are sweet dreams, without malice, even if they are fueled by lies. I dream you will be so outstanding and forthright that, even though you are a little tan doll, you will be popular among your classmates, and you will be invited to birthday parties, and when the time comes for your first cotillion, your only problem will be deciding which young man's invitation to accept.

You will not be like me, for I hold on to a hardness that is impenetrable. But you, my little girl, you will remain soft and unhurt.

Indeed, I have more dreams for you than I can ever convey. But child, here are a few that I will make sure come true: You will be smart and poised and dutiful and you will love me with such singular clarity that you will feel not the slightest longing for a father.

Oneida, I do not act upon these lies and spin such dreams carelessly. I sit by the light of a candle and stare down into your face with its ability to haunt me, and I consider each lie, each dream, as if it is an individual jewel, holding it up to the flame to test for strength and beauty.

But as I do, I become aware of a deep silence. I hear no birds, no wind, no children in the shell road playing. It is a bereft silence, born of deception.

In this moment, amid the deadly quiet, with you in my lap and a nettled but sincere love flooding my veins, I ask God right out loud, "Don't I deserve anything for trying to be a good mother?"

But I never get an answer.

As day descends into night, and day again, I ask the same question, but the hours tick by, silently.

It is possible such stillness is caused by my not knowing whose god I am trying to talk to.

But you, baby girl, will not have such confusion. The lies I instill in your soul will breed in you what I have never had: the myopic happiness of certainty.

"MIMA!" I scream into the darkness. She's out there, her face youthful and sad. I want to tell her, the young, hard her, how years of sorrow can be erased. Just tell your daughter who you really are. Tell her who Mr. Sammy is. Tell him you do love him.

I yell these things into the darkness, but she does not hear me. The past cannot be rewritten. It is what it is, and as much as I want to, I can't reinvent her life for her. And it doesn't matter anyway, because she is no longer there. One quick glance down and everything returns to normal. How easily these visions come and go.

The animal sounds are louder now. And it's true, my fear is growing. I can no longer distinguish the high whine of the bat from the warning cry of a bobcat or panther. Even if the water didn't remind me of a graveyard, I could not head back to the *Sparrow* and away from the animals, because I am blinded by liquor and darkness and I cannot find my way.

I think I should never have removed the heron's wings. That's what they're after. That's what they are coming out of the woods for. I grab the wings and hug them to my chest. I'm not giving them up. I don't care. I feel, for some reason, that they are mine.

And then, added to the growing sounds of animals trying to take back the wings, are Mama and Mima and Mr. Sammy talking to me all at once, pleading their cases, justifying their sadness and selfishness and inaction. I cry out for them to shut up.

But Mima with her stubbornness wins. She's saying, "I lost myself. Can't you see? It wasn't me bringing up a child and denying her truthful knowledge of her father and people. It was somebody they created. Them, out there. The intolerant ones. The ones who called me savage."

I want to shake her. I want to yell at her that she too is responsible. In fact, the three of them created a triangle of lies.

Mama, at some point, knew that what she'd been told about her father wasn't true, and at some point she must have at least suspected Mr. Sammy was her blood daddy. But no one would challenge Mima. She was too tough, with a wicked tongue that could cut down even the hardiest, not to mention the meek.

So she and my mother did nothing but avoid the truth. Because they couldn't speak to each other honestly they argued about things that did not matter, such as each other's hairstyle and taste in fashion. Mima was constantly telling my mother she wasn't good enough, at anything, until finally my mother moved out of her home and quit speaking to my grandma.

And Mr. Sammy, they say his descent into old age accelerated and he drifted into a fantasy world—one spun from the stories his papa had told about their being gator people—and when Mima saw him, which wasn't very often, he talked to her about searching for a white gator with sapphire eyes. He told her that the mythic creature was for sure out there, somewhere in the Florida swamp, and he aimed to find him because such a monster was said to be a bearer of good luck, an animal that could wipe away the sorrow of all your days.

As for Mima, she told me things began to change for her after my mother married. Mama hitched her star to a rascal named John Looney, who wandered south out of Georgia and played bass in a dance band.

Mima refused to go to the wedding. And when my mother got pregnant with her first child and

Mima could not find it in herself to feel any happiness about it whatsoever, Mima said she despised what she had become but didn't know how to change.

My grandmama would sit, alone in her dark house, cursing her unhappiness and rigidity and dreaming of the way she once was: sassy and free and loving Mr. Sammy. But she said it was like thinking about someone else, a stranger capable of feelings that were beyond her.

So Mima went to the river and hunted for that person she used to be. She thought that if she found her she would discover someone who would love and be good to a grandbaby. She walked past the blackberry thicket and jasmine, down to the cedar grove and marsh grass. She took off her shoes and walked in the muck to the exact spot where she had stood with Mr. Sammy so many years before. She looked out over the water and tried to remember him throwing the net. She searched the far shore and the deep sky. She shut her eyes and listened.

But there was nothing.

Not one image of Mr. Sammy or the sound of one heron crying. No egret or wood stork spiraling toward heaven or earth. She recalled Mr. Sammy's concern that the birds might one day be shot out, lost to plume hunters. My grandmama said that as she stood alone by the river she realized she had nothing left. No images of a young Mr. Sammy. No comfort of seeing a bird take wing. No remnant of the soul she'd been born with. She said she opened her eyes and stared bleakly into the river, desperately saddened by the loss of the birds and her soul and Mr. Sammy and her daughter, and then she caught her breath.

She told me it was a fresh spring day and she was a middle-aged woman rushing headlong into old age and loneliness, and she searched that river. She said she knelt down to it and let her face linger over it. The sun was high and glimmered white-hot, unfiltered by clouds. But it didn't matter, for try as she might, she couldn't cast a shadow. She said to me, "The skinning was complete."

It was then, as she stared down into those calm waters and saw the potential for all manner of life bar her own, that she knew what she had to do.

She hurried back home, making sure she didn't pause to speak to anyone along her way, because she feared that they might notice she was shadowless.

Once there, she opened her chifforobe and pulled out all the gorgeous silk dresses that she'd never been able to throw away, the ones Miss Motherwell had given her to help her seduce the rich crowd at the Ponce de León, and she began cutting them into squares of garnet, emerald, and gold. When she was finished, she put them in her sewing basket with a bountiful supply of needle and thread.

Then she pulled her suitcase out from under her bed. She packed three workaday skirts and blouses, some toiletries, and makeup. She packed a framed picture of my mama that she'd snapped herself with a borrowed camera on her daughter's fifteenth birthday.

She retrieved from the back of her chifforobe a catchall box that she'd bought at a secondhand shop right after my mother was born. It was a hard, dark wood with primitive, childlike fishes carved all over it. It held a lock of Oneida's hair, a fragile skeleton of a fiddler crab she'd found in her skirt that first day by the river, the half-doll Emmaline, her head and one arm broken off. Underneath the broken pieces of the doll lay the checkered hankie Mr. Sammy had offered her when he picked her up off the church floor after she'd fainted. She said it still smelled of him and jasmine.

She shut the lid and tucked the box and all its contents into her suitcase.

Then she got her hatbox off the top shelf of her pantry—it's where she hid her cash. She'd never made much money smoking mullet and selling it to the restaurants downtown, but she had managed to save three hundred dollars. She slipped one hundred into her purse.

After that she sat down at her kitchen table with a blank piece of paper and tried to compose a note, something Oneida would understand. She wanted to ask her daughter not to hate her. She wanted to ask her to lobby for Mr. Sammy's forgiveness. She wanted to write something gracious, something that made sense.

She sat there staring into the crisp cool whiteness, hoping that the perfection, the geometry, of the paper would cause her to think up the proper apologies. But it never did. In the end, she wrote all that she was capable of: *See you later.*

She placed the two hundred dollars next to the note. Then she retrieved her sewing basket full of freshly cut silk the color of jewels and her one small suitcase, and she walked out the front door where Mr. Sammy had so kindly nailed up a Holy Board that never worked, out of the darkness of her house, out of her beloved yard, and into the soft light of a spring afternoon.

The sky, she told me, was wildly blue.

I am surrounded by animals and relatives mythic, dead, real, and unreal. A bull rat lingers at the wood's edge and every now and again I hear the low hiss of a gator. I ought to get back to the *Sparrow.* But I cannot move. I'm afraid of venturing into the river. I'm afraid that it will swallow me up, that Mama and Mima will pull me down with them and not allow me to return.

It is a chance I cannot take. I want to live. I don't want to linger with the dead and determined in harsh currents that lead westward to the sea.

So I stay put. The quilt is my armor, and the wings I cling to are my breastplate. I need to stay awake, because if I sleep, surely I will become prey. But to what? To the animals pressing the edge of the woods and my imagination? To my fears of man, woman, and God? To the knowledge that I have cultivated in myself a stubborn refusal to give or love equal to or exceeding that of my grandmother? Isn't that why she left? So she could discover herself and maybe return and make things right with the people she had hurt? Why haven't I learned? Why haven't I taken the knowledge of the past and sculpted it into something that can fly?

The bull rat is inching closer and a fox has come out of the woods and is testing the air, deciding if he can challenge me. I'm so tired I don't know if I can fight them. They smell my fear. I pick up handfuls of sand and throw wildly. I hear them thunder deeper into the darkness, and the sky echoes their noise. I can't protect myself any longer. I have tried too hard and for too long.

I lie belly-down on the beach, the wings against my chest, and I attempt one by one to distinguish the calls and cries and threats of the wild. Which one the cicada? Which one the fox? Which one the gator or heron?

But exhaustion and confusion conspire to make me want to stop this silly game. Do I really care what lovely fluted song rises from which throat? What does it matter?

In fact, I begin to believe they are all the same voice, simply crying out in different pitches. I love this thought. I love that at least for the moment I am not concerned with assigning meaning, but content to listen. I love that I am lying in the sand without protection. This is new to me.

I am open and vulnerable, and as I feel the wind whip over my body, carrying with it the verdant scent of the gator, I am happy.

It is not the whispering of the dark waters upon the shore that wakes me but the soft yellow laser of the sun dawning behind my closed lids. Slowly I shake off the quilt and sit up. The wings are stuck to my chest. Quill by quill, so as not to do further harm, I remove them.

I look out at the river and see egret and ibis and heron fishing. I look to the woods that so frightened me in my drunken stupor and I laugh out loud into the clear morning air, because the trees are a rookery, laden to the point that the branches are bending under the weight of new life. Much of the evening's noise must have come from babes and mothers at the nest, cautiously figuring out the night. Vines of moonflowers snake into the woods, their white petals firmly closed. They open only for their namesake.

The sand around me is trail-covered. Nosy critters must have ventured near. I see the sharp-clawed tracks of the coon and then, far more frightening, a wide swath in the sand, and I think gator and then I say, It couldn't be. There are depressions in the sand, so I guess creatures I cannot name nested through the night near me. But all such signs are disappearing because the wind is softly shifting the sand, and fiddler crabs are popping their helmeted selves out into the new day.

I gaze all around. The sun is silvering sea, sky, and land, and even though I'm suffering from a tequila-inspired headache and I'm so thirsty I'm tempted to drink the brackish water lapping at my feet, I know that I am standing in a sacred place, a place where the laws of nature haven't yet been skewed by the vagaries of the human heart and mind.

I may be a wild-ass of a sort, but I'm not so stupid that I could go through last night and think my world is fine. Things need to change. Fast.

I fold my quilt and set the wings on top of it. I'm mosquito-bit from head to toe and I smell like a goat. I place three cockleshells on the heron's grave. I don't know why. A need to mark the passing, I guess.

Then, balancing my quilt and wings, I wade back into the river and head for the *Sparrow.* She is gently and surely afloat, a few yards out, beckoning me.

Chokoloskee is beyond my sight, somewhere to the north. I could go there. I could stand in the spot where Mama and Mima danced their last dance. But I decide, No. It's time to go home—with my memories and my heron wings and my quilt. Because I need to see Carlos. I just need to.

I idle out of Lostmans River and through a narrow, mangrove-lined pass, and then speed almost full throttle into the open Gulf.

I'm embarrassed by the way I've been behaving, especially toward Carlos. If my mama and Mima were alive today, they'd probably say, "Girl, march yourself over to his place this instant and talk to him. Work it out." And I hope Mima would say this to me: "Don't do to Carlos what I did to Mr. Sammy."

My eyes well up—I tend to cry when I'm tired and hung over—and I say into the wind, "Mima, I'm going to try not to. I'm going to try to make things work."

There is so much I need to do that I can't figure out where to begin. I know I have to treat Carlos better. I know I'm going to have to say something disgusting, like, "I'm sorry." And then I'm going to have to back it up with my actions, or else finally call it quits.

And Carlos and I have got to come to terms with that dead baby. We cannot cart a mummy around and continue to be paralyzed by its ghostly presence. We must find a way to stop questioning my dead people. But how do we believe in it all, how do we swallow each detail—the sordid and the celebratory—and find the strength to go on? Do we just decide to? That seems far too simple.

In the deepest regions of my memory I hear my granddaddy. He is saying, "Have faith, girl. Believe in the stories, and believe in those two sweet women, with all the fervor your soul can muster. Believe in them the way I did.''

Even though I never knew the man, on this boat I feel close to him. *Sparrow,* modest vessel that she is, is the only home I've ever known. Suddenly, I'm sentimental about this rickety but watertight trawler he built with his own two hands. Mama and Mima said he toiled over it for years. They said building the boat was what kept him going.

I imagine his sweat and his labor and his dream. Isn't it wonderful, I muse, that he constructed this baby far ahead of a world fueled by the microchip and compressed time. Maybe I've been lucky to have been able to grow up on this boat. Maybe there's nothing sad about it.

I hear my granddaddy, out there in the infinity of this deep sky. He says, ''It took me years.''

As I fly through a world of a million blues toward an anchor of green, I say to the sun and the sleeping stars, ''Talk to me. I want to know'':

FOLKS SAID I was a fool. Said I'd never get her built. Said if I did she'd never float.

I knew otherwise. 'Cause I listened to the wood: live oak yellow pine cypress. I studied which way the grain ran, looking for strength weakness beauty. I smelled the timber fresh-cut and knew which pieces might rot and go wormy and which ones wouldn't. I touched every single plank over and over as the wood whispered, "Live oak will be her ribs, yellow pine her cabin, cypress her skin."

I had never seen such beauty since the time I was a young pup with a naked Miss Susannah in my arms. My boat would be no substitute but maybe some solace. She and I would be a single ribbon threading through a cradle of clouds and water.

No, building my boat weren't an act of a crazy man. In fact, it kept me sane. It kept my dreams alive. As long as I was able to turn a notion that existed only in my head into something physical, something I could touch, I was able to believe that somewhere in the blue yonder Miss Susannah was alive. I was able to believe in her possibilities.

Yes, I dreamed of her return, I dreamed of telling my daughter the truth, I dreamed of finding the white gator, for I knew he would give me the wisdom to accept with dignity the pain of my days.

Ever since the day Miss Susannah went away, I waited for a card, a letter, a homecoming. I dreamed of seeing her old face peering at me through my screen door. I dreamed of sitting 'cross a table from her and talking about little things—the weather, our health, what might be for supper. And I dreamed that when we finally told Miss Oneida the truth about me being her blood daddy she'd not be bitter at the deception but happier than a mud hog at the honesty, however late.

I know most folks would disagree. People with good sense don't remain true to a mean no-good woman and they don't hold back from claiming what is rightfully theirs. Yes, I have heard these arguments. I have actually listened to them in my own head upon occasion. I could be doing anything—fishing, bathing, sitting on my front porch ruminating—and that argument rises up my spine all puff and wind but then cowers and slinks back to the sewer it came from.

I don't forget Miss Susannah and I don't tell my daughter the truth, because I have to have faith that the woman is going to return and we, together, will make all things right again. I will be patient, I will wait for her to find and gather up her strength, and I will honor her request that I remain silent about my daughter until my woman cultivates enough courage to face Oneida with me. I have to believe that this will happen. I have to believe that she will not remain lost forever.

I will be the one person who will not forsake her.

'Cause see here, a certain memory is always with me—the first time I ever saw Miss Susannah, when Old Mama and Papa and I mistook her and all the others for ghost spirits. I peer through my mind's peephole and I see that horrible look in Susannah's eyes when she tried to chill me into stone.

But now, as an old man, I realize that she weren't glowering at me with hate that moonless, jasmine-smelling night. What was looking at me dead in the face was loss. Susannah might not of been nothing but a knee-high girl, but she'd already lost a life. And any recollection of it, any good feelings about it, were wiped out by righteous white folks who told her to be like them or die.

Through the years of loneliness and regret I have come to understand that what she lost back there on the prairie was her soul.

That's why, every day and every night of her absence, I pray that she is roaming the blue yonder searching for it. I pray that she will find it.

And you know, I also pray this: that I'll still be alive when she does. I can't stand thinking she might return and I'll already be six feet under. In many ways I owe my longevity to that woman, for despite my poor eyesight and my aches and pains and my elbows and shoulders that don't do well no more in wet weather, I am determined to stay on this earth till I see her again.

I'm so close to finishing my boat. In fact, there are just a few final touches to be done in the cabin and then I'm going to paint her pearly white, all over, like she is somehow worthy of sailing through the gates of heaven.

I'm finishing her none too soon, that's a fact, 'cause after years of wondering when that old white gator was gonna start teasing me the way he'd teased all the other men in my family, it has finally happened. Twice in the past week he has hunted me down in my dreams. Both times I was deeply asleep and suddenly I am at the river's edge, surrounded by palmetto and pin oak. I look out at the marsh and there's Miss Susannah floating above the water. Shimmering green scales cover her skin and she's got a fin as splendid and flashy as the prettiest fish you ever did see. Miss Raison is on her left shoulder, no longer a scrawny dirtwater chicken but a gal in full bloom. And Susannah's calling to me. She's saying, "Mr. Sammy, the water is warm and safe. You'll never drown if you're with me."

I start to go to her, but I pause 'cause I am overwhelmed by a sudden smell, a stink so ungodly awful that I know it's coming from a creature who has lived many a lifetime, who has taken part in many a miracle and sin alike. I say, "You. It's you."

I know his sapphire eyes are staring out at me from the dense brush and I search all around, but I do not find him. He's just beyond my fingertips, just out of sight, but then there's Miss Susannah, looking like a flying fish, and Miss Raison trying her wings. Susannah, calling me to join her in the warm water.

Then I wake up.

Don't know what Mr. Gator is trying to tell me. Don't know why he won't show hisself and make things easy for an old man. But I have determined this—he ain't no freshwater monster, but a briny boy. This will make my search easier. In fact, I think he's somewhere in *my* river, right under *my* nose. And I can't shake the hope that once I find him, there will I discover anew my Miss Susannah.

Then, after all these thoughts run through my weary brain, I pull my blankets up 'round my neck more securely and I try to lull myself back into a gentle sleep. In the morning there is work to do—a boat to finish, day journeys to take while I wait for Susannah's return, and more dreams to conjure.

Yes, I tell myself, you got to get your sleep, 'cause you may not ever find the gator and Susannah may stay forever gone, but at least if your sleep is filled with dreams, you've put Mr. Death off for one more night.

I have washed myself from head to toe and I am combing my hair and trying to look the slightest bit sweet for Carlos, because my plan is to go over to his apartment and actually say to him, "I'm sorry for being such a bitch."

I have to start somewhere, and I guess that's it.

But then I hear someone boarding and I know instinctively who it is and immediately I'm pissed off because he's ruining my plans. Why couldn't he have just stayed put and let me make the cordial gesture of visiting him at his place? Besides, now if we get into a tangle I can't just storm out. I live here, and even though I know it's not healing behavior, I'll feel compelled to tell him to leave, and I hate doing that. It makes me look rude.

This is the rant I'm having with myself when he sticks his head into my cabin and says, "Mamacita, hello."

I'm fixing to fly off the handle. I told him to never call me that again. I turn and face him, but my rant stops. It just evaporates off my brain. He's dressed in new jeans and a white collared shirt with fine tailoring and he looks so handsome in white and he's staring at me, gobbling me up, not crassly but with a romantic air, as if we are surrounded by a small army of gondoliers who are about to serenade us while we sail away.

"Hi," I say, and push my hair off my face. And I think that perhaps Mamacita isn't such a bad name, after all.

He walks over to me and takes my hands in his and kisses them, staring at me so intently that I make a wish. I wish I would disappear.

It's my usual reaction to kindness or love. And I know I need to stop it. I need to find a way to stare back at a person full of good intentions and say, "Okay. I'll try this out. Here's my heart. I trust you with it."

But I can't yet say those words. However, the thought of them provokes my crying reflex. I feel the wet surge behind my eyes. The floodgates aren't actually open—it's just that foreboding pressure. If I busy myself with something, maybe I can prevent even one tear from trickling down my face. So I turn away and start brewing a pot of coffee.

"We need to talk, Sadie," he says.

I keep my back turned and I fight to maintain a level tone of voice. "Sure. Okay. We can talk," I answer. But my thoughts reel. I'm afraid he's going to ask something of me I can't do. Like move in with him. Or agree to keep the dead baby. Or marry him. Or leave him alone. Oh, God!

I pour the coffee before it's finished brewing. I put as much milk as coffee into his cup, which is the way he likes it, and then throw in a couple of teaspoons of sugar. Me, I like mine black and bitter as can be.

I hand Carlos his and then sit across from him. I eye him over the edge of my cup. I think, Who but a saintly soul could put up with my pendulum moods and actions? Maybe that's why he's here. To tell me he's tired of being Saint Carlos.

He sets his cup down and takes hold of my hands again. He's formulating his words, choosing them carefully. I know that look. Then he says, "Listen, Sadie, I am not a stupid man like maybe you think. I have known many women in my days. One or two I loved. The others, we had sex and thin friendship and maybe we were trying not to be lonely. But you, Sadie, you have touched my soul. And I want us to make it. I believe in us, woman. I know we have our troubles, but I have this idea."

I think I might run out of here right now, before he can say anything that will hurt us or suggest an action I know I can't go through with. I open my mouth to speak, not at all sure of what I'm going to say, but he touches my face, interrupting my impulse: "No. Just listen. Don't fight me until at least you hear this thing I have to ask you."

And I do. I shut my mouth and I look over his head and out the window and I try to concentrate on the sky, and he says, "Let's take the boat and go north, Sadie. You and me. I want to take you back to your women, to St. Augustine. Not where they died. Where they lived, Sadie. I've looked at the map. We just shoot up the Atlantic side, but on the river. That, how you say, Intracoastal. We'll just go straight north to that town. You'll learn things, Mamacita. And we'll take the dead baby with us. We'll find answers. Together."

I look at him, at his faint freckles, and his worried brow, and his deep, wide eyes that are boring a hole through me, and I think to myself, I never, never expected this. That town where they lived—Mama, Mima, and Mr. Sammy—has been a place hidden in my dreams, a place I've been so scared to go to for fear of what I would find, for fear I would discover that their stories were spun from ether and not flesh.

I'm working hard at remaining calm—or at least appearing so—and I manage to spit out, "I don't think we can do it. We don't have enough money, and besides, we'll probably kill each other after a few days of being cooped up on this boat."

He squeezes my hands and then shoots me his just-on-the-brink-of-arrogance glower, and he says, "So. If we die, we die. But at least we die trying to figure out something. You know"—and his voice is rising in pitch and vigor—"we live our lives running away. Let's try running to something, woman. I dare you. No! I dare us. I dare us to run to each other. And to know some happiness about it!"

I can't believe it. He's flipping his lid—and in English, no less. I get up from the table and go over to the stove. I grab my rag and start wiping down surfaces. It doesn't matter what surfaces, it just matters that I keep my back turned, because if I look at him I might shout. Or drown.

But he's on his feet. I hear the chair scrape, a pause, and then, "Okay, Mamacita. I have tried. But I don't know. I don't think I try no more."

Dear God, I can't let this happen. I spin around. "No, no, Carlos, please don't go. It's just—I'm scared."

"Of what? Of me? Of your dead people? Of what?"

Before I can think up an excuse to run out of here, I answer him. And I talk quickly, so that I can't formulate any lies. "What if we find nothing, Carlos? What if none of their stories ring true at all once we're there? Then what will I have?"

He's as serious as I've ever seen him. And I know I'm in danger of losing him. "Either way, woman, you'll be free. Free because you know they lied. Or free because they spoke the truth." His big scarred hands are on his hips, and his hair is long enough that it just touches his collar, and he looks determined, as if he really isn't going to put up with my childishness anymore.

So I actually, in a flash, make a decision. Like I'm an adult or something. I decide I'm not going to fuck this up.

Suddenly I'm shaking, and I hear words tumbling from my mouth, but they are of a nature I'm not used to. I'm saying, "When we get there, will you walk with me and hold my hand, and if the shadows scare me will you push them away until I can deal with them?"

He takes me in his arms and I press my head against his chest. I hear his heart beating like crazy and I know mine is doing the same, as though they are marching together toward something, maybe a future we can live with. Even though we're standing still, I feel that I'm swirling. But I don't miss out on what he says. I hear him clearly, above the sound of our hearts and my swirling head, I hear him whisper, "*Sí,* sweet woman, you know I will."

THE TRIP through Hawk Channel is effortless. The water on the Atlantic side is deeper than what I'm used to in the Gulf, so I am confident as we head north, riding the Intracoastal, that series of interconnected rivers that snakes between Florida's buffer islands and the mainland. A gentle southerly breeze has prevailed at our backs since we left Key West early this morning. So we have made fair time.

The dead baby, we decided, would stay in the cabin, and Carlos has promised that he won't take him out of the coffin and worry over him. We've decided that we'll try to come to terms gently with whatever haunts us about him.

I have the heron wings too. For good luck. They're in the freezer.

And Carlos and I, we are being kind to each other. This is easy for Carlos. Me, I have to work at me. He asked me to keep my wide-brimmed straw hat on to protect my face from the strengthening April sun. He ran his finger down my long straight nose and counted its spattering of freckles. He said he loved them.

And I didn't pull away. Or say anything wise-assed. In fact, even though I'm too old for such things, and far too mean, I felt myself blush. The most I can hope for is that it was the kind of blush you feel in your bones, where it stays, never quite venturing up to your skin to give you away.

This is all new to me, being nice, accepting kind gestures. I don't know if I can keep it up. But I know I have to try. Because, out of nowhere, I've become petrified at the thought of growing old alone. Mima always said, It's never too late. It didn't matter what we were talking about doing. Pondering what to fix for supper, cruising the bay or the islands, going for a swim. She'd sit like a massive short rock, her legs spread wide under the folds of her cotton skirt, and she'd say, "Well. It's never too late."

She had to believe that. After the life she'd led and the amends she'd made when she was an old woman, she had to believe it.

But God, what a price she paid. Years alone. Years wandering. Years that could have been spent with Mr. Sammy and her daughter and her grand-babies. I was the only grandbaby she ever knew. The others were lost to her, grown and gone before she could hold them. Yet I never heard her say she regretted her life. She simply recited the facts, sometimes quietly but other times raucously, in a voice that split open the night.

Flipping over on my stomach, I shade my eyes and peer at Carlos. He is so tan he's almost black. His Saint Christopher medal glints brightly off his chest, like a third eye. He knows I'm looking at him, but he pretends he's oblivious, just watching the waterway like a good captain.

I have been known to be stingy with the *Sparrow,* usually not allowing anyone but me to navigate her. Unless I have no choice, as on the afternoon I threw a fit in front of Pablo and María. But today I enjoy being a passenger. I like letting Carlos take charge. I almost feel as if I'm on vacation, although that's a concept I'm not too familiar with. I've always thought vacations are for Yankees.

On my back again, I place the hat over my face. The oval of dark shade feels good and so does the sun. The insistent hum of the motor and the rhythmic motion of the *Sparrow* as she cuts through the channel lull me into an easy, slumberlike state. My mind drifts, and then Carlos shouts, "Sea turtle! Starboard bow!"

By the time I lean up and scan the water, it's gone, swimming through depths we cannot see. I look back over my shoulder, and Carlos is smiling as if he has won a prize.

"Big guy," he shouts. I'm disappointed I missed it. It's not that I've never seen one, but the sight of those massive prehistoric bodies shadowing past always thrills me.

I close my eyes against the brightness of the sun and see Mima. In a sparse, humble room in Oklahoma, gathering her belongings, accepting the fact that she knows all she will ever know about who the people she came from and how she went from being Sparrow to Susannah and then, as an old woman, back to Sparrow.

She used to tell me about her train ride west. That's what she did the bright spring day she left her home and daughter and onetime lover. She caught a train back to the prairie.

She told me about sitting in the cramped seat with a map in front of her. She said she traced her finger along a pencil-thin black line and paused at each dot, saying the name of the town attached to the dot as if it was a sound faintly holy. She repeated the names over and over until she had them memorized.

She made me memorize them too. In the bright sunshine in a world vast with water and salt prairies, we'd play the game of singing the funny-sounding words. Even now, I hold them dear. Sallisaw. Checotah. Choctaw. Weleetka. Wetumka. Okemah. Konawa. Sasakwa. Shawnee. Wewoka. Kiowa. Tiny towns, before they were towns, where she, as a child named Sparrow, chased after that cloud of pin-sized prairie-colored birds; the place where she made images in the grass for eagles.

As Carlos speeds us toward St. Augustine, I see her in her small apartment right before she walks out the door. I imagine her chopped-off blunt gray hair. And her heavy footsteps, for she is no longer lithe but carries the weight of age and time like an old prizefighter whose fires of youth have taken their toll.

But as she prepares to leave, I do not feel sorrow for her. There is joy in her old face. As I listen to her and watch her, I know she has turned regret on its ear:

I HAVE BEEN DREAMING of the sea of late, and longing for Mr. Sammy as if I were a wild teenager again. I have been missing my daughter to the point that in the middle of the day, even when nothing bad has happened, I begin to cry. I never meant to stay away for so long. I never dreamed my silence would stretch on into so many years that I'm no longer sure when I left.

My time in Oklahoma, however, has not been wasted, for I have learned things. Not the least of which is that getting back to your own heart, knowing it when you see it, welcoming it rather than running from it, can be arduous, full of pitfalls, a feat that doesn't happen overnight.

I settled down near Tulsa just because it felt right.

The flatness of the earth, the color of the prairie grass, they were familiar. Without much effort, I found a job. I went to work for a Mexican couple who owned the Martinez Family Market. Eight hours every day I punched the cash register, adding up the tariff on people's onions, tomatoes, peppers, dry goods. I would say thank you and they would say thank you and then they would leave with their bundles of groceries and I would wonder if anybody in their family had ever known anyone in mine. I wondered if it would even matter to them. If I blurted, "I had family here once. Do you think you know anything of them?" would they simply shake their heads and walk off muttering that I must be deranged?

At night I would crawl into my bed in my rented apartment and I would hear the sound of the register—ca-ching! ca-ching! ca-ching!—and I would imagine it was adding up my sins.

Despite my occasional impulse to ask strangers about my family, overall I pursued my past gingerly. My fear of what I might find outweighed my need to know. I didn't try to make friends with anyone, Indian or otherwise. And when the people I worked with asked intrusive questions, I would tell them that I was a widow and had no children. Instead of aging and acquiring a longer past, I simply aged and had more to forget. Indeed, time magnified my hateful actions, causing them to burgeon far beyond my capacity to withstand their awful weight.

But then came the ice storm. It blew in from the

west and immobilized the town. Trees, sidewalks, cars, streets, everything was sheathed in crystal. Businesses shut down, including the Martinez market. It was too cold and slippery to venture outside, so I was stuck in my apartment, feeling a bit like a prisoner. But my discomfort was to be heightened tenfold because the apartment building's boiler went out, leaving the tenants without heat.

In an effort to keep warm I turned on my oven and opened its door. I put on two layers of socks and my gloves and then fixed myself a cup of coffee. I wrapped up in some blankets and sat in a chair next to the window that overlooked the street. I sat there for hours, drinking my coffee, staring out at that frigid world, watching the day's shadows grow longer and longer, and suddenly something in my mind snapped. I wasn't sitting in a chair by a window pretending to be a woman without a past or a family. I was a small girl walking across the frozen earth, holding my mother's hand, hoping that the soldiers didn't shoot me. It's odd how a memory can be as painful as a blow to the head. But this one sure was. In fact, it knocked the wind out of me and it gave rise to the emptiest of ideas: I could put out the oven's pilot light and simply drift off to sleep, never to wake, never to confront these demons. I decided it would be so easy. Why hadn't it occurred to me before? I think I was setting down my coffee cup and removing my blankets, my intentions centered on the pilot light and the silent gas, when the wailing started. At first I mistook it for the memory of my mother howling as the soldiers tried to separate her from her husband. And then I decided it was that dream-filtered wail which haunted me as a child growing up in Miss Alice's house. But then I heard pounding at my door, and the wailing stopped, and I recovered enough to say, "Yes? Who is it?"

"Mrs. Motherwell, are you okay? Is that you screaming?" Mrs. Campbell, my landlady, asked through my closed door.

"Everything is fine, Mrs. Campbell. Thank you," I answered. I listened to her walk down the hallway and it was as if she was carrying my suicidal thoughts with her, carrying them away to a safe place, safe because I couldn't get to them.

As quickly as that, a person acting out of innocent concern unknowingly prevented me from committing the most selfish act of my life. Even in my distraught frame of mind, standing in my socks in my cold-to-the-bone apartment, I knew I'd been given something special, something I wasn't sure I deserved: a second chance.

That is how I was able to summon the courage to turn intention into action and why, after the ice melted, I began nosing around, asking questions of longtime residents about the area's Indian population. I didn't want to talk to lots of people. I wanted to locate one or two individuals I could trust.

I decided to ask my boss's wife if she could recommend anyone to speak to. This round-faced Mexican woman, who had birthed six children and seemed to have an infinite supply of love for each one, knew virtually everybody, and I liked her. So one day at work I tentatively broached the subject. I said, "I think I might have some distant family ties out here. My mother told me we had Indian blood in us, and I've always been sort of curious. I'd like to find out. Do you know of someone I might speak to, you know, just about what it was like before the reservations and all that?"

She was putting price stickers on some canned goods, but she paused and seemed to be considering my inquiry carefully, and then she said, "Yes. I do. You ought to talk to Paul Oldfeather. He's the caller at the bingo hall. He's been around here for years, in fact was born here. He knows a lot of the history about this place, stuff they don't teach in school."

And so I began going to the bingo hall every Wednesday night. I didn't feel I could just walk in and say, "Mr. Oldfeather, my name is Susannah Motherwell, but my parents called me Sparrow Hunter, and I'd like to know if you have ever heard of them." I probably should have, but I proceeded slowly, carefully, because I was beginning to feel fragile.

Paul Oldfeather sat at the front of the hall, a cowboy hat pulled down so firmly on his head it scraped his ears. In a steady voice that suggested a man who'd dealt with life head-on, he called, "B nine, N twenty-seven, O fifty-three . . ." for hours on end. There was something reassuring in that random coupling of number and letter spoken precisely, as if, even in the midst of chaos and chance, there was order.

I never got to shout "Bingo!" but finally, after three or four evenings of this, I did gather up enough nerve to approach him. He was so wrinkled it looked as though his face had been balled up and then flattened back out, but his black eyes were alert, and when he stared at me I got the odd impression that I was being looked at by a bird, those huge, curious eyes that see more than humans do. I offered to buy him a cup of coffee at the diner down the road.

He drank three cups of black coffee and had a slice of cherry pie. He listened as I explained I was trying to find out something about my parents, but I couldn't recall their names and I wasn't even sure they had come back out here after being released from the fort.

He chewed a mouthful of pie as if it was leather, and then he asked, "Why do you want to know?"

My temper flared fast as a match strike. He didn't need to question me. I was the one needing information, not him. I almost got up and left then and there. But something pulled me back down. I tried to snuff out my anger. I looked around the diner, with its red-and-white-checkered curtains and the chalkboard with the day's special scrawled on it—beef stew with fried potatoes—and the big green malt mixer and Indian men sitting at the counter dressed like cowboys, and I snapped, "Because I don't know who I am anymore and I don't think I'll find out unless I understand what or who I come from. I'm never going to stop hurting people until I find out."

He drank some coffee. He took another bite of pie. And then he casually said, "Nightwater."

"Excuse me?" I wasn't sure what he meant.

He shot me that direct stare again, like he was half hawk, and said, "Nightwater. I think that was your mother's name. You were the only child who went east when the government took our men. And you were the only one who didn't return. When your parents came back, there was lots of talk about how the white people had kept you for their own. 'Sparrow Hunter has flown the coop,' the reservation children used to sing. I sang it. Plenty of times. Until your father shook me so hard I thought my teeth would fall out. He was a gentle man, but he couldn't stand that song. 'Sparrow Hunter has flown the coop.' His name was Billy. He was a good man, Sparrow."

Nightwater? Billy? How could I know whether he was telling the truth? The names didn't feel familiar. They felt horrible. Because they only opened the door to more questions, only made me feel more like a stranger in my own skin. I gathered up my purse and jacket. "I have to go."

"I understand," he said, returning to his pie.

And I walked out of the diner and into the night, blind.

So that was the beginning of my education, of regaining my memory, of growing amazed that despite my having left this place as a child and growing up in the ways of another culture, I had not been forgotten.

In these years I have gone from rejecting Sparrow to remembering my youth and the wild prairie, and my parents' hopeful faces, and their voices . . . *There she goes, our little Sparrow Hunter*. Now, as an old woman, I feel good about Sparrow. She was a decent little girl, a bit hardheaded, but decent.

No, I didn't reclaim all the details of my past. But I did learn that I was never a savage. I learned that the government was wrong to take us away from here, and that even though I told my parents I didn't want them anymore, they never stopped loving me. I finally understood that I came from a people who were as vital and worthy as any other on this earth, that despite what I had been taught, there was no reason for me to be ashamed.

But I also know that I am different. I don't completely fit in here. I am still a woman from back east. I hold notions considered more white than Indian. I am the woman who flew the coop, here *and* there.

Well, I am about to do it again. I've decided I cannot die without looking at my daughter's face and touching her and saying, "Forgive me." And I cannot die without seeing Mr. Sammy once more and trying to set my awful actions straight. I do not know if they will accept me. I do not even know if they are dead or alive, although my instincts say neither one has gone over to the other side yet. It's true, I have instincts again.

My decision to return home has not been easy, and it certainly wasn't quick. There was no sudden moment when I said, "Aha! I'm whole again. I must return home." Every day upon waking, before allowing myself to get out of bed, I would stare up at my ceiling and imagine them—Mr. Sammy and Oneida—and I'd whisper into the faint light of dawn, "I will see you again."

Then I'd throw back my covers and go about my day, quietly struggling to pick up the pieces of my scattered past.

This is the way I've come to think of my solitary life in a town far from the sea, peopled by both adults and children who look like me but who are so different from what I became: A child doesn't mature overnight, and neither does a stubborn adult who has to figure out where the lines in her face come from, who has to sit herself down and trace them back through time and decide whom they are connected to. I am a grown woman who had to force herself to sit on a blanket in the open prairie and try to hear the way the coyote hears, the way she could as a tiny girl, before she ever saw the sea.

So there wasn't that single glittering moment of revelation. Rather, I have undergone a slow, often painful, and always lonely process of letting the stone wear down until I could discover my buried heart.

I have my train tickets. I have cleaned my apartment so thoroughly that I know Mrs. Campbell will come in here tomorrow expecting to have to scrub and instead she'll say, "She was a good tenant."

And my travel bag is packed. It contains a few skirts and blouses, simple cotton affairs that I have taken a liking to. It holds my box of treasures: Mr. Sammy's handkerchief and my picture of Oneida. But the splintered pieces of Emmaline are gone.

I caught a taxi one day out to a place that Paul Oldfeather had told me was Ghost Prairie. It was nothing but an area of undisturbed grassland surrounded by melon farms on all sides. I buried her there. And as I did, as I dug up a patch of tall grass, I remembered Sparrow's childhood game, her flat grass angels. I lay down in the grass and moved my arms and legs, and I found myself giggling as I flew in place like a giant crow. It felt so good to get rid of Emmaline. And to fly.

Also in my bag is the quilt I finally finished piecing together, made from those horrible gaudy dresses Miss Alice bought me. The quilt is plain—just jeweled squares stitched in the early morning and in the middle of the night—but quite pretty. It will be my gift to Oneida. At the reservation shop I bought a tourist trinket for Mr. Sammy. A peace pipe. That should give him a laugh.

It is eight forty-five. My train leaves in two hours. I want to be at the station early. I don't want anything to go wrong. Before I leave, however, I stop and take a last-minute look at myself in the full-length mirror nailed to the closet door. My hair, once long and black, is now short and gray. I'm dark and wrinkled, and my face is clean.

I gave up all that makeup. I am what I am. The face in the mirror reflects not just me; I see my own mother, and more important, I see Oneida. I have so much to tell her. So much forgiveness to ask for and so many stories to tell.

As I walk away from the mirror and out of my room, I realize that I may not be the person Alice Motherwell wanted me to be, but I sure do have good features.

THE JOURNEY UPRIVER has so far been uneventful. Except for one fight. I wanted to keep going our first night so that by our third morning we would be sailing through Miami. I wanted to see for myself what all the fuss was about. Even though I'm a born-and-bred Floridian, I've never been to Miami. It is part of the self-righteous disdain that I have been cultivating my entire life. I have a jillion reasons—as in: too many people, too many buildings, too many encroachments on the Everglades. I've decided there is simply not enough land to support the population, even if the developers filled in what's left of the 'Glades. So I've consciously avoided Miami as if it's cholera-ridden. But here's my fickle heart: Now that I have to ride straight up its watery spine, I want to see it in the full benefit of daylight.

Carlos, firmly and without any sign of budging, said no.

The sun was setting and the clouds appeared to be fire-tinged. "Why not?" I demanded.

As he aimed us toward a shallow west of the channel, he said, "It's a maniac town. Everybody speaking at once and nobody listening. And too many boats. We go through Miami at night."

Even as he set the anchor, I argued with him. My voice turned shrill, the way it does when I'm working up to one of my furies. In my head I damned myself for agreeing to this trip.

But then my new emerging self said, Sadie, shut the hell up. Maybe he knows what he's talking about.

I felt as if my head might burst from trying not to be stubborn. So I turned away from him and looked up at the bright orange glow splashed across the sky as though God had Her own private Crayola box, and I whispered, "Damn. Damn. Damn," as hard as I could. Then I took a deep breath and in a pleasant, unfamiliar voice suggested, "How about us fixing those yellowtail we caught today."

I fired up my grill on the deck, and Carlos seasoned the fish with lemon and olive oil. So that was supper, yellowtail and mangoes Carlos's next-door neighbor had given him. Carlos ate with abandon, as if the river inspired in him a fit of gluttony. In addition to two pieces of fish and part of mine, he consumed three mangoes, the juice dribbling down his chin. But me, I tried to be polite about it. I don't know why. I just felt, even in our primitive circumstance, that I wanted to be attractive.

He reached over and touched my hair once, gumping it up with mango slop. I said, "We're going to have to go for a swim."

After supper we skinny-dipped in the twilight waters, but we barely spoke. I think we were both exhausted, and I enjoyed listening to the quiet night, and also I didn't know what to say to him. Even though I was swimming around naked with a man I'd had sex with so many times I'd lost count, I felt foolish, as if he'd never seen my white butt before.

So when we got out of the water I put a towel around myself and said, "I need to wash down with some fresh water." And I touched my wet, salty hair, and I sort of wished that through the years I hadn't let the sun and salt and wind turn it to straw.

The sun was almost gone and the three-quarter moon hung low but bright on the horizon. Carlos brought up some fresh water. He opened a jug and held it over his head and doused himself. He shook his head with such force, causing the water to fly, that he reminded me of an old hound dog caught in the rain. He said, "Sadie, lean over the rail, please. I'll wash your hair."

I know that my face gave me away. I know that for a second or two it hardened into its usual stubborn defiance. But Carlos waited me out. He smoothed back his wet hair and reminded me of a 1940s leading man, hair slick and heart cavalier.

"Okay, I guess I'll let you," I said, surprising myself that I surrendered so easily. I sat down and leaned my head out over the river. I watched the evening star suddenly pierce the sky as Carlos poured the sweet water over my hair. I closed my eyes and I felt myself breathe out. An involuntary exhaling of stubbornness, that's what I thought.

I let him wash me. We were silent as he wiped the sponge across my face, down the bridge of my nose, to my neck with its many dirt beads strung like pearls across my skin, over my breasts and belly, down my thighs and knobby knees, all the way to my toes. He spread my thighs apart gently and knelt between them like a good Catholic and ventured between my legs, cleaning my feminine rolls and tucks with such tenderness that I didn't fight the vulnerability of that moment, not for one second. He wiped away the day's salt and grime, leaving me so clean I imagined the moon would squeak against my skin if only I could touch it.

When we lay down on my bed, Carlos kissed my lids shut and held my hand. He whispered against my skin, "Mamacita, I want you to believe that you're a good woman."

I touched his face, which in the dim light seemed to be made of angles and shadows. "I'm trying, Carlos. It's not easy."

"Your women, they believed in you," he said.

His words were simple, but they went through

me, all the way to my hidden core, for they amounted to the nicest thing anybody had ever, ever whispered to me.

We didn't speak again that night. We held each other as we listened to the shrimp feed on the *Sparrow*'s hull. And I fought back my tears until I drifted into a deep sleep. Just me and Carlos, intertwined and at rest beneath the lovely orbit of an oval moon.

I'M SO GLAD I let Carlos have his way. Even at night, Miami is like nothing I've ever seen. The river is busy, and those high-speed cigarette boats jet past us as if they own the damn place. Twice we've almost been run over. Carlos is cussing in Cuban and I tell him to be careful. "I don't know what you're saying, but they probably do," I nag. "Besides, everybody here is armed."

"So"—he looks over my head—"we are too."

I can't argue with that. My .38 is down in the cabin next to the silverware. But from what I understand, Miamians tote Uzis.

It's taking forever to thread our way through this mess. The waterway is seawalled, lined by towering condos and homes that look sterile and perfect on their pesticide-green lawns. Even at night I can see the pollutants floating on the water's surface like bacon grease.

I slip my hand inside Carlos's and say, "This is terrible."

"This is money," he says.

I decide I can't stand it. I decide to close my eyes and pretend we're meandering through Miami the way it used to be, say pre-1920. Behind my shut lids—as I concentrate so hard my scalp thickens—I re-create it, bit by bit, a wild land the Indians once called Tekesta. I see it now, the Miami River, a slow-winding yawn of water cutting through the heart of a tropical jungle. Live oaks, banyans, sabal palms, silver palms, gumbo-limbos, mastics, and more rise toward a moth-white sun forming a canopy of cool shade for the feather-leafed ferns carpeting the jungle floor. Miami is not a city that is asphalt-hot but a triumphant, unhindered garden where the tropical sun is disarmed by sea breezes and endless trees. Butterflies and lizards, air plants and vines flourish here. And in the crown of the canopy I hear the Carolina parakeet—America's only indigenous parakeet. The last place it was seen on earth was Miami in the 1920s, that final flash of bright green winging through the branches just before the jungle came tumbling down.

The sounds of city traffic interlope on my daydream, but I push the racket out of my mind. I'm going to keep my eyes closed and continue imagining that the used-to-be world is not all gone. I'm going to pretend that the homes are tucked up under the vast green lace of native trees and that they face a river that gently curves within its natural borders of saw-grass marsh, home to egrets and herons, bitterns and limpkins. I'm going to pretend that oyster beds still thrive here.

"Sadie?"

Carlos is interrupting my fantasy.

"What?" I respond, not hiding my irritation.

"You okay? What are you doing?"

With my eyes closed, I explain. "Pretending. I don't want to see this mess."

Even with my lids shut, I know he's coming toward me. I can smell him. He brought the Old Spice with him. I feel his hands on my shoulders, and then he kisses my eyelids. He whispers, "I told you."

I open my eyes. He's smiling at me as if my behavior amuses the bejesus out of him.

"So you did," I say. "Now"—and I lightly kiss his lips—"let's get the fuck out of here."

He tweaks my nose. "Okay, lady. The captain will take care of it."

And he tries, but no matter what we do or how much I will it, our progress is slow. There are bridges that must be opened for boats far larger than mine, sailboats with towering masts and then yachts outfitted like Christmas Day journeying back to home ports of cold climates in Maine, Massachusetts, Maryland. I want to shoot right past them, but Carlos is a careful sailor and the waterway is narrow. "Too many fast boats, too many chances for pile-ups," he explains.

There's not a whole lot I can do about it, so I flip on the radio. Cuban music blares, which causes Carlos to smile. But then his eyes darken and he says softly, almost to himself, ''You know, I have a relative here.''

''You do?'' It could only be José, his infamous second cousin, the person who is sort of responsible for Carlos's being in America. ''Do you want to see him?'' I ask out of obligation, praying the answer is no.

''Just a distant relative. No big deal,'' he says. And he sighs heavily, exhaling the memory of his family, I think.

I get us a couple of beers and prepare to go slow. Forever. I sit in the chair beside Carlos and stare glumly at a new high-rise that has a banner draped across it: EFFICIENCY CONDOS READY NOW! Efficiency condo—I suppose that means a recently painted closet with a microwave stuck in it.

Because there is nothing else happening and because the big city is irritating me, I bring up a touchy subject. ''Carlos, what are we going to do with the dead thing?''

He pats his chest, and I know he's making sure his Saint Christopher medal is still around his neck. ''It's not 'the dead thing.' It's a baby,'' he says crossly.

''Okay. What are we going to do with the dead baby?''

He rubs his eyes as if the question has made him tired and then says, ''Whatever we do, Sadie, we decide between us. Right? Not just you. Not me. Us.''

"I hope that—" I start, but then shut up.

"Hope? Hope what?" Carlos leans across the humid space between us and holds my face in his big hand. "Hope what, Mamacita?"

"I hope that the baby didn't suffer," I say. "I hope, if there's anything such as consciousness beyond death, even if it's only in our minds and not in his dead tissue, that he's at peace."

Carlos hugs me, and through the clutter of the radio, and people laughing and partying on a speedboat behind us, and impatient folks on land honking their car horns, I hear him whisper, "He will be."

IT HAS TAKEN us two full days to get out of the madness of south Florida. I am beginning to think we've made a mistake. If the entire coast is nothing but seawalled, condo-lined canyons, I'm going to turn around and go home.

We stopped and talked to an old-timer who was sailing to the islands. I can't remember if we spoke to him yesterday or the day before; time has become as monotonous as the waterway—the Big Ditch, some call it—but he insisted everything gets better north of here. "Once you've made Hobe Sound, things begin to improve," he said, running his tanned-to-leather hand over his bald head. "And when you reach Sebastian Inlet and Mosquito Lagoon you'll see snatches of old Florida. It's worth it. Hang in there.'' I believed him when he said it. But I'm no longer sure.

Carlos smells my discontent. So he's been singing a lot. Trying to calm me. But we are not behaving like lovers. There are no moonlit swims or natural vistas to take our breath away. The air is close and the skyline cluttered. I don't want to make love here. I want to go on, and wait until we reach the place the old man spoke of, and see if then we can't find joy in the sight of one another's nakedness, and feel that it's okay to be vulnerable, not on your guard, to say to hell with the afternoon and spend at least a part of it melting into each other's arms.

My caginess is being helped along by insomnia. I won't rest until we're out of condo-land. But it's nightfall, and Carlos, the voice of reason, is insisting we stop. However, there's no place to pull over and gunkhole. ''We'll have to tie up at a marina,'' I tell him. ''They are probably very expensive here.''

''That's A-okay. I'll pay for it,'' he grumbles.

I know this won't be possible. We're almost to Palm Beach. We can't stay there. I won't do it. It's against my principles and I don't want to spend the money. Besides, I'm sure there are no out-of-the-way docks in Palm Beach but only yacht clubs that won't allow a thirty-foot wooden tub like this one to defile its ritzy marina-that-crime-built. ''Go below and get in bed. I'll take it till morning.''

He's so tired he doesn't argue with me. He kisses my forehead and then holds me by the shoulders and says, "If you need me for anything, wake me. Don't be too brave. Just come and get me."

I raise my head to try to meet his gaze. "Carlos," I say, "I have taken care of myself for this long. I think I can manage to live through the night."

He mumbles some words I don't understand and pats me on the rear as he goes past.

We are not at all a good match, I bitch to myself. How in the hell do I get myself in such fixes? You would think that Mama and Mima raised an idiot, for me to get mixed up with some man who actually thinks his role is to take care of me. God damn it!

And then I stop. I hear that voice, the new one I've been trying to cultivate, speaking in one of those housewives-on-TV-joyously-doing-the-laundry lilts: "Tirades won't do you a bit of good. All he's doing is being kind."

Hell, that's probably true. I look skyward. It's a cloudy night. The big moon lights the clouds from behind so they shine with a deep lavender glow. A misty rain begins to fall. Mama and Mima probably would have liked Carlos. They would have thought he was cute. They would probably tell me to grow up and behave. That's probably exactly what they'd say.

As I push the *Sparrow* north, trying like hell to get us out of south Florida, I think what it must have been like for Mima to return after all those years. I think it took guts to walk back into the lions' den. It took guts and perseverance to walk up to her daughter and say, "Listen here, I'm sorry as hell for the trouble I caused you, and for leaving, but I love you and always have and I'm here to talk about it.''

And Mama, for all her stubbornness and discontent, must have loved Mima too. I mean always, even after she ran off and didn't write or anything. It's funny. Usually the children run away from home. But not my clan. With us, it's the adults who run, who wake up one morning and look at themselves in the mirror and don't see a damn thing, or at least nobody they recognize. And then they scurry off like spring hares.

I know that when Mima returned, Mama threw a fit. Refused to let her in the house, even though it was Mima's, technically. She called her all kinds of names, and the two of them screamed and hollered and cried. Mama yelled out the screen door for all the neighbors to hear, ''I raised up two sons all by myself and you've never laid eyes on either one of them. And it's too late. 'Cause they are both gone and wild and don't want much to do with me, let alone their grandmama, who never so much as even sent them a piece of dirt. Get out of here, old woman.''

I don't know how long it took for them to stop yelling at each other. Mama said weeks, but Mima thought it was just a few days. Mima went by daily, for however long it was, and asked her daughter to let her in the house, and my mother staunchly and self-righteously refused.

However, they agreed on what finally broke their stalemate. Mima stood in her front yard, which was all overgrown and gnarled and wonderful, and she started reciting, as loud as her voice could manage, a litany denouncing her lies. "I have always loved you," she shouted. "You are not Spanish and your daddy wasn't some yacht-owning white man. We don't have any kind of royal blood floating through our veins, as I said. I didn't leave because I hated you. I left because I hated myself so much I couldn't see our line continued. I was scared of how I would react once you had your baby. I hated myself, what I had become, Oneida. Mr. Sammy was never just some old half-colored hired hand. Your daddy is that dear mulatto man whom we have both always loved, even when I denied him. Oneida, girl, you are a Plains Indian and you are black and you are white and you are the fruit of an affair I had with Mr. Sammy when we were young and wild for each other."

Mama was peering from behind her venetian blinds as Mima poured her heart out under the shade of the live oak. Mama said she looked tiny compared with the tree, and very old. She said she always knew Mr. Sammy was her daddy but decided that if everybody was going to deny it, she would too. But suddenly, on a lovely April morning when the sycamore was full of green shoots and the azaleas were blossom-covered, the lies were out there, shining under the branch-laced sun, showing themselves for what they really were, no longer cloaked in secrecy or a polite two-step of half-truths.

Mama walked over to the screen door and opened it. "Come on in," she said.

My women claimed there was an instant familiarity, but also an uneasiness. For there was so much for each to learn about the other. And so many instances when the words "I'm sorry" would just have to do.

But then there is Mr. Sammy. Oh, how I wish I'd been standing on the porch the day of their reunion. Oh, how I wish.

As I cut through the Palm Beach night, I am surrounded by multimillion-dollar mansions and riverfront high-rises that are home to investment brokers and attorneys and bankers and all the other professionals needed by the rich. But in my heart I fly ahead of the *Sparrow,* pushing time against my new wings, lighting for a moment upon the worn planks of Mr. Sammy's front stoop, watching that old woman walk with the heavy but determined gait of a person who knows she is about to be reacquainted with destiny:

I approached the old shack slowly, clutching the peace pipe to my breast with both hands.

It's not easy to describe what seeing him again felt like. But I will try.

It was midmorning, a lovely April day. He'd

planted a vegetable garden in his front yard. I'm sure he had put in tomatoes, and probably beans. Bees hovered and then disappeared deeply into the fragrant butter-colored petals of his yellow jasmine, which trumpeted this way and that all over his porch rail.

And there, in an old pine rocker, sat Mr. Sammy, sound asleep, his chin resting on his chest, cushioned by a beautiful long gray beard. The beard was full and framed his face like a gathering of clouds, but the bottom half was braided. One single tail. It quite suited him.

I didn't know what to expect when he opened his eyes. I was prepared for him not to recognize me. I'd been back for two days, attempting to make peace with my daughter but not succeeding. I'd wanted to do that first, above all else. But I feared time was short, and she was as stubborn as I was, so that's why I was standing in front of him by myself, without the support of Oneida. And I was fully expecting that once I told him who I was he'd try throwing me off the porch. But I'd come too far not to stand my ground and have my say.

I walked up on the porch and politely coughed. But it did no good. He was deep into dreamland. So I took the mouth end of the peace pipe and poked him in the chest.

He came to, bobbing his head and sputtering, and then he opened his eyes, which were still spooky-green after all those years, and their sleepy veil gave way to recognition and surprise as he said, "My

God, woman. It's you, ain't it?'' And he rubbed his eyes as if he couldn't trust them.

''You recognize me,'' I said, and I looked down at my feet, quickly. I thought I might cry. But no. My heart bucked. And my soul soared. But I didn't cry. Perhaps tears were beyond me.

He said very simply, ''Welcome home.''

I couldn't speak. I was afraid of my voice, afraid it would give my emotions away. I just nodded and offered him the peace pipe.

He looked at it, puzzled, and then took it from me, running his hands up and down its brightly colored length. ''It's a pretty thing,'' he said.

''It's a peace pipe,'' I explained.

He did not appear to be fighting to overcome his emotions the way I was. In fact, I was about to think old age had stolen his wits, when he finally chuckled and then reached for my hand and said, ''Susannah, it's good to see you.''

I looked at him directly. ''I'm not Susannah. Not anymore,'' I told him. ''I am Sparrow. Sparrow Hunter. And I'm most pleased about it.''

He said nothing, just scanned my face.

''Can we go inside and sit down?'' I asked. ''My legs aren't what they used to be.''

''Okay. We can do that,'' he agreed, and he raised himself out of the rocker and I heard his bones crack and I followed him into his simple, sparse house, and I was trying to decide whether his attitude was fed by happiness, sadness, shock, or indifference.

We sat at his kitchen table and he put a bottle of bourbon and two jelly jars between us. "This deserves a celebration," he offered quietly, but he might as well have said, "This is too damn bad."

As he poured us a drink, I thought about how I had prepared for this visit, how I had gone over the words again and again in my head. But now that I was here, I could barely engage in small talk. With the morning sun filtering through his back screen door, we sat drinking bourbon and shifting in our chairs and avoiding shooting any arrows that might stick in the heart. After all, what does one say, how does one chat, after a lifetime of bad behavior?

But we tried.

He went first. "Been building a boat," he said.

"Oh, yes?" I looked down at my hands so I would quit staring at him. "You always wanted one of your own."

He was as wrinkled as I was, but I detected that somewhere inside him the young man I once knew, the young man who flew away the day Miss Raison died, had flown back home and was turning him spry. I could see it, a light beneath his skin and a directness in his gaze that I didn't remember from before. I said, "Mr. Sammy, what's going on with you?"

"Nothing." And then, "I've just got to finish painting the boat and then I'm headed out. I've got a date with a gator."

"You're still on that? After all these years? You really believe there's a sacred gator out there for you to find?"

"Yes," he said, and then he squinted at me as though daring me to say otherwise.

We fell silent again. He hadn't even asked me where I'd been all those years or why I was home or what I wanted. He simply poured us a second drink, and I listened to birds singing and I heard some children playing tag in the street and the fragrant wind shaking the tree limbs, and I asked, "When did you grow that beard?"

"Years ago," and even though he spoke in a neutral tone, his response only pointed out my most obvious embarrassment: my unforgivable absence. But he wasn't asking for explanations.

I tossed down the whiskey and took a deep breath, and I looked at him straight-on and said what I needed to: "I am very sorry, Samuel Abraham Lincoln Jones. I treated you in a reprehensible manner. For years. I kept you from your daughter, and your grandchildren, and I denied my love for you. I behaved most regrettably. And I am back not to ask your forgiveness, because considering what I've put you through that would be arrogant and presumptuous on my part. But I am here to say I'm sorry."

I looked at the pool of sunlight splashed on his kitchen floor. Maybe it was the bourbon, or maybe it was just age, but I swear I saw dots, and I decided they were small black fish darting in and out of my past and future. In fact, I was beginning to feel as if our conversation wasn't purely set in the present but was happening outside the boundaries of time. I thought, Maybe if you go on too long without saying what you need to, then intentions never turn into actions but simply drown in a vacuous pool of wistful dreams. I didn't want to drown. I had traveled a long and tortuous road and my journey had been painful. I looked up from the floor. "And I am here," I continued, "to set things straight with Oneida and to tell you that, even in my cruelest moments, I loved you. The part of me that I'd stuffed into a dark corner of my bony heart never, ever stopped loving you."

Mr. Sammy contemplated his jelly jar and its amber liquid. His bones were still fine, and his fingers, though callused and scarred, were still graceful. Very quietly, with a firmness only a fool would have been stupid enough to argue with, he said, "There ain't going to be any amends until she knows."

I shut my eyes, but even behind my closed lids I saw the darting fish. "I am trying, Mr. Sammy. But she won't let me in the house. She just hurls accusations at me from behind her screen door. And even though much of what she says is true, she's effectively preventing me from telling her about you. About us."

Without giving an inch, this stubborn old man whom I longed to lie down and take a sweet nap with said, "Then march yourself over there and stand in the front yard and shout the truth at her. And don't you give a second thought if folks for miles around hear your carrying on. 'Cause the truth is the truth no matter how it's delivered."

I stood up and walked over to the back door and peered out. He certainly had been building a boat. With a cabin and a helm and everything. From where I stood, it looked like he'd done some fine work. He'd built her close to the river's edge, as though he was getting her used to the water right from the start. "She's a handsome boat," I said. "How about a kitchen? Does she have a kitchen?"

"Yes, Sparrow, but it's called a galley." He got up and walked over to the sink. He tossed out what was left in his glass and rinsed it.

"Okay. That's good," I said, feeling lost. He kept his back turned to me and I feared that my entire notion of a homecoming had been a mistake. Maybe I should have stayed out west and never told the truth to anyone. I was sad to the point of despair. I was such a fool to think I could return after so many years and expect anyone to give me an ounce of time or consideration. This was all a big mistake. He looked frail and old and oddly resolute standing there with his back to me. I decided there was nothing left for me to do, no way for me to break through and undo the past. I unlatched the screen door and said, "Mr. Sammy, I suppose I'll be going now."

He turned around and nodded. He tucked his hands in his pockets. I loved that braid. "You can go out the front, Sparrow."

"No, that's all right. I've learned you can't ever go out the same way you came in."

I stepped out of his house and into the full sun. As

I left his yard, I thought I heard him call, "Welcome back, honey," but when I turned to wave, to acknowledge him, there wasn't anything there but sunlight and a closed door.

I AM GROWING so tired that I am afraid I might fall asleep at the helm. The rain has stopped, but the clouds have not blown off. With Carlos asleep, I feel very alone and afraid. I know this is irrational. I'm the tough woman who has spent a lifetime navigating Florida Bay and the waters of the Ten Thousand Islands and the Gulf since I could walk. So why am I scared now? There is a dock coming up on my right, extending out from the seawall of a home that costs more than all the money I'll ever see in my whole life. But it is boatless. The owners are probably gone for the season. They probably won't ever know I docked here for the night. I'll tie her up and get just a few hours of shut-eye and be on my way again before even Carlos knows what I've done.

It's easy as silk. I barely nudge the dock. I'm real good.

I go below. Carlos is sleeping like a baby. As I retrieve my quilt from the foot of the bunk, I stub my toe on the coffin but manage not to cuss so loud I wake Carlos. Then I hobble back up and lie on the deck, quilt-covered.

As I close my sleep-starved lids, I think about Mr. Sammy and Mima. I think that it is good that he put his foot down about Mama. He'd never really told Mima what-for when they were young. He never exposed Mima's silence or lies. Maybe it wasn't right. Maybe after Mima took off he should have betrayed her. But who's to say? Maybe the fact that he remained true to her all the way to the end inspired both women to love him even more.

I fix them, the three of them, in my mind's eye. I arrange them around a supper table and they are eating and drinking and laughing together. It makes me feel not so alone. It makes me feel that I have a family. Seabirds cry in the distance and the scent of grass freshly cut permeates the air as I concentrate on that sweet image, the three of them unbroken and hearts glittering.

CARLOS AND I were sound asleep—he below and me still on deck—when, out of nowhere, I couldn't breathe and an immense weight came down on me. I opened my eyes, and while I couldn't focus, I heard an unfamiliar voice, a male voice, growling, "Give it to me, bitch, now."

I tried to scream, but his hand was over my mouth. It smelled like stale beer and oil. I thought he was going to rape me. He took his hand off my mouth and shook me by the shoulders. I felt my neck snap as he ordered, "Do it, before I hurt you!"

I couldn't get out any words that made sense. I was just kind of moaning and trying to steel my thoughts. I looked at this angry face staring down at me. He was a teenager, a white boy, and his eyes were dead. Crack cocaine dead.

I was preparing to organize my voice into a blood-curdling scream so Carlos would run up here and save my ass, but before I could I heard the safety being snapped off and the trigger being cocked and then I heard Carlos. In perfect, Latin-spiced English, he said, "Time to go."

The boy's dull eyes widened. Then hardened into slits. He got off me, and with Carlos pointing the gun at the base of his skull, he stood up and jumped from the *Sparrow,* ran down the dock, and disappeared into the maze of neat, trim Palm Beach landscaping.

I started crying and Carlos held me. "It's okay, Mamacita. It's okay."

"He tried to rape me," I cried.

"Shhh," Carlos whispered. "No, baby, he was after drugs. He thought we were a drug boat."

I pressed my face into Carlos's chest, and as I slowly calmed down I realized he was right. The little punk wanted drugs. The shit-ass. I should have spit in his face. I felt like chasing him down and pummeling him.

But instead, I let myself be held. And comforted.

And when we started once more upriver, the sun

beginning to break over our shoulders, Carlos did not once admonish me, not once did he say we should have docked at a marina or that we could have been arrested for trespassing or that I should have woken him up and he would have taken the helm.

We stood side by side, steering the *Sparrow* together, and he kept his hand on mine, and he sang very softly some Cuban song, and I didn't understand one moment of it, not even one, but it was sweet and soothing and I liked it good.

That was yesterday.

Today the old man's promise of a better journey is at hand. We've gone through Hobe Sound and up along Hutchinson Island, a surreal place of natural beauty and nuclear cooling towers. We drifted slowly, for the manatees had gathered to frolic in the water warmed by the nuclear plant. A cow and her baby floated past us like a pair of gentle, graceful underwater zeppelins. I counted. We saw half a dozen manatees, and while I was thrilled to see them I was also deeply saddened, because all of them—just like the ones at home—with the exception of the baby, had propeller-inflicted scars.

The coast now becomes a crazy hopscotch of areas pristine and undeveloped sandwiched between condos and commerce. But it's still better than what we saw south of us. And I know we can both feel it, the easing up of tension as the river, in more and more instances, flows within marshy banks and not walls of concrete.

We are both tanned to a crisp and we're dirty as

hell, but it feels wonderful. Carlos hasn't shaved in days, and there is something very sexy in this new, unkempt look of his.

I'm beginning to feel the way I did when it was Mama, Mima, and me just wandering around, not giving a hoot for the type of responsibility that inlanders subscribe to. I'm at the helm and we have stopped two times because Carlos has seen some solid runs of red and sheepshead. He didn't catch any red, but it's sheepshead for dinner. He looks so fine, his shocking black hair uncombed and wild, and his torn T-shirt. Now if I could only get him to change those plaid swimming shorts he has on. I've never seen them, and the sight of him wearing them causes me to laugh every time I look.

"Where'd you get the plaid?" I asked when he appeared on deck. "You roll a yuppie or something?"

Even with his tan, he turned scarlet. So to try to make him feel better, I said, "No, really, they look nice." But then I couldn't help myself. I burst out laughing.

In an obviously sarcastic tone, he sputtered something in Cuban. His language is his last resort. If we're at an impasse, humorous or otherwise, he relies on that old weapon called the native tongue.

But I have to admit that something strange has happened on our journey. Each day we're out here together, just the two of us, it seems that his English is getting better. Or maybe I'm just bothering to listen to him more closely. I don't know.

We've decided to stop for the night near Fort Pierce. There we can take on fuel and provisions, go for a swim and maybe act like lovers later on. It wouldn't be a bad thing, I decide as I watch him gazing out at the shore. I could pretend I don't mind commitment. I can try to act as if he doesn't scare me, as if the thought of loving someone back doesn't send me overboard. "Remember Mima," I say right out loud.

"What?" Carlos asks.

"Nothing. Just talking to myself."

At Fort Pierce, where the Intracoastal is called the Indian River, the waterway is wide and lovely and islet-dotted, so I feel at home. Dusk is beginning to sprinkle the sky with suggestions of gray. There are lots of seabirds here. Most are fishing in the shallows, but we've seen osprey, and as I radio the marina, Carlos starts shouting. I stick my head up from the cabin and I see him, a bald eagle gliding high, with a movement that suggests he's all muscle and no bone. Like an idiot, like someone trying to make contact with another world, I wave at the bird. But he's gone, ascended into the twilight shadows.

The marina is simple and basic. As is often the case, the sign proclaiming the sailor's holy trinity—BEER BAIT ICE—is bigger than the marina's name. The dockhand, a boy with a shaved head—except for the top, where the hair is long and blond and hangs down in his eyes like a sheepdog's—says, "What kind of boat is this?"

He looks at the *Sparrow* as if he can't imagine people actually embarrassing themselves enough to be seen in it. "It's my house," I say.

"Oh," he deadpans, and I don't know if he's bored, or trying to keep his disdain to himself, or if this laconic behavior is only a symptom of adolescence. "There's one slip left," he says accusingly, as though our presence here is offensive. But I'm smart enough to know it isn't our old boat and our disheveled selves that bother him. He simply wants to go back to the air-conditioning and watch TV or play video games or whatever it is teenagers do.

Kids are running up and down the dock. Boat dogs are barking. Anonymous voices laugh and argue and agree, and some folks have their radios tuned to top-forty stations, and others to country and western, and it's all too loud for my taste.

Carlos and I exchange glances. We're in sync on this one. I nod at him, and Carlos says to the boy, "Not us. We're just going to do fuel tonight. Then"—and Carlos makes a zipping sound and jabs his arm forward to indicate our intention—"we're out of here."

The boy nods glumly and then does the rest of his job in silence. Our tank was near empty, so it takes forever, and I'm worried about what it will cost. Diesel isn't cheap. But when it comes time to pay, Carlos hands him a credit card.

"Plastic! When did you get that? More important, how did you get that?" I can't believe it.

"Mamacita," he says, as though I'm really stupid, "I'm a good credit risk."

That explains that. Jesus. Yuppie plaid shorts and a credit card. As we head out, I say, "You're not a Republican now, are you?"

He shrugs and puts his credit-card-containing wallet in his waistband. "I no vote," he says.

I look at him closer, demanding a better answer.

He stares over my head. "Republican, Libertarian, Communist. No difference."

I start laughing. "Carlos, you need a civics lesson."

He puts his arms around me. "No, Carlos needs love."

Oh, God. We're getting slaphappy. "Listen, help me find a place to stop. What we need is to sleep and eat."

"Okay," he says amiably, and he stands behind me, but he keeps his arms around my shoulders, and after we've puttered north maybe five miles, he whispers, "There. Right there."

He's pointing to the east. I look, and yes, a nice little cutoff. A lagoon, actually, surrounded by hammock. It looks unowned. Maybe it's a state park, or a cul-de-sac of shore and river nobody has had time to take a bulldozer to.

I'm so looking forward to this. A night under the stars. No honking horns or visual mess of a big city. Just a nice, calm night.

I nestle us into a picture-perfect spot. The black waters of the lagoon are still and lovely. I taste the water. It's brackish. The mucky shore leads to scrub and then hammock, and I venture that we're in a perfect setting for water moccasins. Maybe I'll go for a swim some other time.

But the place is idyllic. I look to the color-streaked sky. Tonight's is a gentle sunset, soft purples and oranges not quite red. Then, coming in from feeding in the marshes are egrets. They look so graceful shooting through the darkening canopy, but as they land to roost for the night in a huge oak near the shore, they stick out their skinny, toothpick legs and sort of skid to a stop. If this were a cartoon, you would hear the *eeeeeee* as their splayed feet act as brakes, settling them into the moss-tossed branches.

I set the anchor and shut off the motor. The lagoon is noisy with nature's cacophonous jazz. We're standing on deck so close that we're touching, just enjoying this speck of heaven we've been lucky enough to find, when they hit us. This is not a mosquito swarm. This is a herd. A thundering herd. A furious, wing-splattered tornado of stinging, buzzing pestilence. The air around me turns black.

I scream. They are all over my face, including my eyes. They've got Carlos trapped too. We're squealing and panicking, slapping ourselves like Shiites on a holy day. Carlos points to the water, and because they've stung out my brains, I agree with him. We jump overboard, and we stay underwater for as long as we possibly can. I pop to the surface first. Carlos is close behind.

"What are we going to do?" I ask, spitting water.

Carlos starts to say something, but I tell him to hush. We both listen. I hear that unmistakable low hiss. Gator. I say, "They don't want to eat us. We don't taste good. Don't they just want to stay away from humans?"

And then we hear the hollow splash, a large animal moving into the water.

I think we fly back aboard the *Sparrow*. In fact, I'm sure of it. It is a vertical leap out and a horizontal run through the air until we land.

But the mosquitoes are still there, in their dense stinging clouds, so we run for the cabin and I start to shut the door and then curse myself because its hinges, which I had been meaning to replace but never got around to, are rusted frozen. The door won't budge.

I look around for something to block the doorway.

Carlos grabs the quilt. "Use this."

"No, no, I can't," I say. But a swarm heads toward the door. I haven't any choice. There's nothing else heavy enough.

I hold the quilt over the doorway and Carlos finds my mayonnaise jar full of nails and pounds the quilt to the doorframe. And I'm crying as he does it, because I know that with each hammer blow a hole is being put in my mama's and grandmama's creation. It's like driving nails straight down into their hearts. Little rips in the silk that I can never mend.

By the time he's finished, I'm sobbing uncontrollably. He sets down the hammer and holds me. "Mamacita. Mamacita. No, no cry. What is this?"

Between my tear heaves I manage to say, "Because they hurt so much when they were alive. And now I feel like I've hurt them again. Like I've somehow harmed them by driving holes into their quilt."

"Ahh, Sadie." He presses my head against his chest. "We both have to learn."

I try to stop my foolish whimpering and calm down. "Learn what?" I ask.

He sighs, and even without looking at him, I know his eyes are closed. "Sometimes, you and me, we give too much to things of the past. You, so haunted with these women of yours. Me, lost and sad because he never visited me again."

"Carlos," I gently chide, "you grew up is all. Saint Christopher or whatever you saw was part of your childhood, part of the magic of growing up. Nothing more."

He hugs me tight and says, "No, it wasn't just age. Once they stopped, Sadie, the visits, I felt like maybe God no more loved me. That's why the dead baby is shaking me so bad. I was hoping it was him, Saint Christopher, coming to tell me I was still okay, that Mama forgives me for leaving, that I'm not just some guy who doesn't matter, whose family no more wants him."

I pull back and stare into his faintly bearded face that looks acne-pocked, though I know the angry red marks are mosquito bites, and I say, "Oh, Carlos, you are far more than okay. You are the loveliest man I have ever known. And I've known plenty in my day. And mothers don't stop loving their sons. They just don't."

It feels good to say those words—clean, honest words intended to heal, words that define how you feel about someone else. Perhaps, I venture, I ought to try it more often.

So tonight, in my cramped cabin, shut off from the outside world by a dear old quilt, I set out a candle and we eat Carlos's black-and-silver-striped fish in the flickering light, and then I fill my tin bucket with fresh water and we take off our clothes, and as if we're handling something precious, like a dew-spun web that might break at the touch, we cleanse each other's wounds.

I even get out my first aid kit with its calamine lotion and we paint each other. We whisper and giggle and kiss as we smear on the pale pink liquid. We look funny, but the lotion soothes our skin.

The laughter and sweet touching, of course, ease us right down to our bones.

It is the middle of the night and I awake to Carlos kissing me. I moan as I come up through slumbering layers of consciousness.

"Mamacita."

"What is it, Carlos? I was sound asleep."

"Tell me what happened to Mr. Sammy and your ladies."

It is hot. The quilt-covered doorway is preventing

any air from circulating. Carlos has thrown off even the sheet. The calamine causes us to glow faintly.

"It's the middle of the night," I bitch.

"Ahh, Sadie," he says in his endearing he-always-gets-his-way tone, "your lover needs a bedtime story." He kisses my forehead, which must feel like crackled paint thanks to the dried lotion. "Please?"

"Okay." I huff as if it's a horrible imposition. "But light the candle. The dark scares me."

The dancing flame throws wild shadows across the cabin, and I think back to the night they died, to their dancing and the walls reflecting their movement in broad, crazy strokes. Proof, I decide, that Mima most definitely regained her soul and shadow while she was away from home.

So I tell Carlos all about it. I fluff up my pillow and I let him hold my hand and I tell him that in the years of my grandmother's absence my mother developed very sticky fingers.

They said the entire house was filled with cheap glass trinkets she'd stolen from shops downtown. She set them on her windowsills, and when the sun shone just right, it reflected through the blues and greens and yellows of the glass animals and sprayed her house with rays of colored light. Like a rainbow.

Oneida said she stole to feel better. She said she felt as if everything and everyone she'd ever loved had been taken from her. Her mother ran away, her father wouldn't admit to being so, her husband walked out of the house one frigid February morning and never returned, her children—the two boys—

left home the second they got a chance. She said her older boy, who was quiet and shy, joined the service as soon as he was of age, and the younger one, who had inherited musical talent from his wayward father, was wild and defiant from the day he was conceived. She said her first-born did as he was told but remained oddly detached, and her second-born did nothing he was told and that she and he fought anytime they were in the same room.

Mama would clasp my hands and hug me close and say, "I know your brothers loved me, but my wild Charles, he also always resented me. I think he thought I drove your daddy away. It's not true and I told him that. But still, we just never got along. I don't think I was ever good enough for him."

Her big green eyes would turn dark, like the color of the sea before a storm, and I knew she was imagining a different life for herself, one in which her children loved her good and so did her husband. But then she would smile and bring her face close to mine and she'd say, "You'll meet them one day. I'm sure they will love you."

I know she wrote to Charles. I saw the letter. And I heard her fret that she couldn't write to John Wesley because she had no idea what part of the earth he was on. So she wrote Charles to tell him about her new life with Mima and me and the *Sparrow*. And to ask the whereabouts of John Wesley. She told him about Mr. Sammy. She read the letter right out loud to Mima and me one summer day as the sun was setting, and she was crying as she read.

Then she put it in an envelope, which she let me lick and seal shut, and we sailed to Fort Myers and we mailed it. The three of us marched into the post office and Mama looked at the postmaster with enough intensity to knock him right over and she said, "Make sure it gets there."

Soon after they died, the letter came back, stamped RETURN TO SENDER. Unopened. I saw it peeking out of Whitey's jacket pocket one day. I felt like I'd been stabbed. Did my brother get the letter and refuse to read it? Was he dead? Did he live in a different town? Even though I was a kid, I suspected my brothers were two people I'd never meet.

I don't know what happened to the letter. I slipped it back into Whitey's pocket so he wouldn't know I'd been snooping. He never mentioned it to me. When I got older I searched and searched the *Sparrow* for it, but it's not here. It's as if I dreamed it all. As if maybe none of it really happened.

But that's the sad part. There were happy times. Mima came back, of course, and Mama finally allowed her into the house, and while I'm sure things were tense and uneasy, they began to talk.

And Mr. Sammy, now feeling he could claim what was his and not betray the love of his life, entered their lives with new vigor. He fixed them supper. He puttered around the house. He took to wearing a bow tie, which was silly since his beard mostly hid it. And he would hold Mama's hand and tell her how proud he was that she was his daughter. And he talked to them a lot about the white gator. Mima said she told him, "Now, Mr. Sammy, maybe you should reconsider all this talk of a magic gator."

They say he looked at her real closely, just studied her face like he wanted to remember it forever, and then he said, "Why, Sparrow, you know I never give up, not on anybody."

One night he fixed them a supper of fried mullet and grits and datil pepper sauce and sweet corn bread. Mama and Mima said they felt uncomfortable the way he watched their every move, listened too closely to their every utterance. And, they said, while at least they were speaking, still they were distant with each other, as if they were scared to get reacquainted. As if Mama might not like the woman Mima had become and vice versa.

But Mr. Sammy, he kept saying, "Talk, girls, talk! Don't mind me any."

It was at that dinner, after the dishes had been stacked on the counter and as the three of them sat politely drinking Mr. Sammy's strong black coffee, that he made the suggestion. He looked at the two women as though he had them perfectly pegged and he said, "I know what's needed."

"Oh?" Mima used a high tone with him.

"A journey," he said, matter-of-factly. "My boat's maiden voyage. She needs you two on it. It will make for a right nice trip."

Mama and Mima said they rejected his suggestion out of hand at first. The thought of being in such close quarters with each other, after so many years of not speaking, scared them both right down to their livers.

But as the days stretched on, and as they began to feel suffocated by their inability to say anything very meaningful to each other, even though they both wanted to, they came to see—each on her own—that Mr. Sammy's idea was fine indeed.

I say to Carlos, "I think they spent about a week getting ready for the trip. They even helped Mr. Sammy with the final coat of paint. And one day Mima went over there and she walked into the backyard and started bawling like a baby. After being such a tough woman, once she was a part of Mama's and Mr. Sammy's lives she took to crying a lot. What was getting to her this time was that Mr. Sammy had painted on the bow in big bright red letters *Sparrow Hunter*."

Carlos looks so serious you'd think it was Judgment Day. He stares at the candle and says, "She is a good boat."

I let my hand rest on his chest. He has nice pecs. I have always appreciated them. He, tonight and always, seems unaware of how handsome he is. Most men have the opposite problem—they're a good fifty pounds overweight and bald and have bad breath and they think they're God's gift. I run my hand down the length of his chest, and because it's late and because I'm tired of being scared and always on guard, I go ahead and ask him what I've been wanting to since that humid ninety-eight-degree day under the banyan tree when I ran into him—literally.

"Carlos, why do you stick around? It's not like I'm some rosebud beauty. I come with baggage, lots of it. And I am not, exactly, without my moods."

"Ahh, Mamacita," he says, and cuddles me and then rolls on top of me. It feels wonderful, the full measure of his weight against my body. And then I remember the heat, and the calamine lotion, and the fact that we're both sweating.

"Carlos, if we do this for too long we're going to get stuck."

He ignores my joke and gazes into my ghostly face with his, and I wish to hell we'd not slathered this damn stuff on, and he says, "Sadie, from the moment I saw you I knew you were a woman with a heart so wild and large that every day I could spend with you would be a day of wonder and love and passion. I knew first thing that you tried to hide it in this hard package of yours. But always I have seen your spirit kicking, trying to break out, trying to tear away the hardness. And I love both the hardness and this wild heart. You, Mamacita, are a good woman. You may never be able to get rid of me."

I feel myself floating away in the cool depths of his dark eyes. "I can try," I whisper.

"You been trying," he says, and he brushes his lips against mine. "See where it's gotten you?"

He is so smart, with his rolled *r*'s and lovely words and deep eyes. But then there is the problem of our two lotion-splattered bodies. "I can't make love tonight. Not with this stuff on. It just sort of neutralizes the mood, you know?"

"Keep your eyes closed, then," he says.

"Carlos, we both feel like gator skin, like we have a fatal epidermal disease."

He huffs and rolls off me but lets his hand linger on my breasts. "Then tell me a sex story," he says.

"What!" And we both start laughing.

"Tell me a sex story," he insists between our giggles.

At first I think he's just being silly. And then I think, The son of a bitch is challenging me. Okay. I'll give him a sex story. I hunker down into my pillow. I look up at the ceiling and the wild shadows thrown by the flickering candles. I know what has to happen for the story to be complete. I know how it goes.

I fix Mr. Sammy in my mind. He is walking around his yard surveying spring: the sudden grass, the white buds that will give way to hard green balls and then inexorably ripen into blood-red fruit, the tender shoots of fresh leaves renewing all the trees.

Come hell or high water, they have survived the pall of winter and are young again:

I WAS CHECKING my tomato leaves. Checking for disease and bugs. And here she comes, walking down the dirt road like she owns it. No, she weren't graceful and light no more, not like when she was young. But still, she was a good woman to look at. And in the days since her return, we'd made some amends.

For one, she said she was sorry. For two, she talked to our daughter, and all that mess made by years of lying was slowly being cleaned up, word by painful by honest word. And me, I was feeling pretty good. Good enough to stand up straight and walk around like I belonged here.

She nodded as she came into my yard. Time had broadened her hips and had healed the stony hurt look that once dulled her eyes. Now they were black and snapping, the eyes of the little girl I first fell for.

"Hey, there," she said.

Maybe it was the sound of her voice or that she was smiling when she said it, but my heart quickened. "Afternoon, Sparrow."

"Tomatoes are looking good. Nice thick stalks."

"Yep," I said as I wiped my hands and then my forehead with my kerchief. "They're real healthy this year." And I felt silly 'cause she was staring at me like I'd suddenly grown a second head.

''Your handkerchief. Can I see it?''

''Sure,'' I said, and handed it over. But then I did a double take, because for a second she looked young. She surely did. I thought to myself, It's that old mind of yours playing tricks.

Sparrow put the kerchief to her nose and sniffed deeply. And she broke into a big grin. ''Your handkerchiefs still smell like flowers, like jasmine,'' she said. ''I still have—'' She stopped and gazed at me sheepishly, like she'd been caught with her hand in the cookie jar, and she wouldn't say any more.

''Have what?'' I straightened my beard braid.

''Nothing.'' She handed me back the kerchief. ''Thank you.''

''Anytime.'' I stuffed it into my shirt pocket. ''Old Mama had this habit, she sprinkled our drawers with dried jasmine flowers. Made everything smell good. I stopped doing it for a while.'' I studied her hair, which wasn't gorgeous anymore, but she sure had a bountiful headful. ''But I missed the smell,'' I explained.

''Me too,'' she said, which caused me no end of embarrassment.

And then we just stood there, like two gawky teenagers. I knew all my neighbors were peering out their blinds at us. I knew my friend Ulysses White, who lived next door, was probably getting the biggest kick out of this he ever enjoyed. And I knew he'd not let me live it down. Finally I said, ''Sparrow, you here for something in particular?''

More forward than I had ever known her to be,

she said, ''Yes, sir. I would like the two of us to get in that nice car of yours and I would like you to drive us out to the woods. I would like us, together, to try to find our old love shack.'' Then she smiled at me sweetly. Like she was seventeen.

I looked down at my thick carpet of grass and shook my head. ''Oh, no. I don't think that's a good idea.'' I'd not gone out there since I was a boy, not since that day I lost my youth. I didn't think I could face it. And I didn't want to grieve openly again for Miss Raison, 'cause even though I hid it, the wound was still there. ''No, honey, I can't do that.''

''Oh?'' she said. And then she reached across the blue bright space between us, and as she did, it was as though she was reaching through time, ripping away the years. She grabbed my arthritis-swollen hand and she said, ''You've got to. You and me. Mr. Sammy, it's time to close the circle.''

The afternoon stopped. Dead still in its tracks. No birds sang. I didn't hear any cars or any children playing. Didn't hear a single radio tuned up too loud, nor a single phonograph. I bet them clocks inside homes all around stopped ticking in that instant. There was just the bright sky and the virgin sap running through old trees and Miss Sparrow Hunter and me. As I stared into that face gone wild with time, I weighed the import of her words: ''time to close the circle.''

By God, as much as I hated to admit it, the woman was right.

I sighed and stared at the grass. I considered my

life, this long journey where by day and by night I had waited for her. And now she was here, and I could walk away and never face that broken moment of the past, or I could go with her and try to mend the awful memory, I could try to slip back into the skin of my last happiness.

I looked at her staunch, sweet face. "I'll get the keys," I whispered, and the wind blew and a mockingbird whistled and the clocks—I'm sure—began again their endless ticking. I was scared as I walked into that house and scared as I returned to the bright outdoors. But I'd go through with it. For Sparrow. And yes, for me too.

When we got in the car, I told her, right even before I'd cranked the motor, "Don't get your hopes up. That area out there may well have been clear-cut for timber or something. We might not recognize anything. You prepared for that?"

Her face looked solemn, but there was also a peace there, like a woman who had come to terms with the vagaries and wrong turns of life. "I am prepared, Mr. Sammy."

As we drove through neighborhoods some of which I'm sure were familiar to her and others not, I said, "What do you think of the old town? Changed much?"

"Oh yes, it's different. Some of the streets are wider, that sort of thing. But I don't know. This place is stubborn. I don't think it changes easily."

"You can say that again," I agreed.

And I asked her how things were going with

Oneida, and she said, ''Okay.'' Then she bit down on her lower lip and smoothed out her cotton skirt and said, ''No, that's not true. We are like strangers. Or worse. We're strangers holding more secrets than we can bear.''

I knew it would be tough. That's why my inspired idea of a river journey. The water and endless sky loosen the tongue. ''Once we get the *Sparrow* in the water and spend a few days meandering, you'll warm. It'll be like you never left.''

She threw back her head and laughed. It was startling, her newfound ability to laugh so freely. Hers was a joyful laughter and it celebrated all over me real good. ''When did you start laughing like that?'' I asked as we headed into the country. We were close, I figured just a mile or two now, and I was afeared that the shack would be gone and that it wouldn't.

''Oh,'' she said, ''it just happened one day. One of the girls I worked with said her husband would rather wear drawers that squeaked when he walked than ever wash them himself, and I just laughed, and I liked it so well I kept on laughing.''

''I see.'' I slowed down, scanning the trees and roadside for something familiar. ''The woods are still here,'' I said. ''But I don't know where to stop.'' I was getting confused. When I was young I knew exactly what turns to make. But now this all looked like a thick, harsh forest. It was hard to believe we once pranced through it like it was our own private garden.

"This feels right," Sparrow said. "I think we should stop here." She was leaned forward, peering through the windshield, damn near sniffing it out.

The shoulder was soft and I was afraid of getting stuck. I pulled over to firmer soil. I set the brake and looked at those tall pines and I said, "We could get lost in there and ain't nobody gonna find us."

"Nonsense. It's like riding a bike. Once we get headed in the right direction we'll just navigate as though it was yesterday."

I grumbled to myself and I got my bourbon flask from the glove compartment, and at the sight of it Sparrow lit up. "Ohhh, Mr. Sammy," she said, "you old devil. Give me some of that." I handed it to her and she tipped it up to her lips and took a polite sip just as if we were having tea.

She handed the flask back and I tucked it down my shirt, and then I went around to the trunk and pulled out my car blanket.

"We might need this," I said, "if we get lost or something. It still gets nippy at night."

"You got to take chances in life," Sparrow said like she was a know-it-all, and then she headed into the woods, betraying no fear.

The forest was dark and cool and smelled fresh, untouched. It's funny how a scent can transport you back in time. But it did. In fact, for a second I decided my face was unwrinkled and my joints were not bent with arthritis. As we walked, I filled up my lungs again and again.

Sparrow, despite her determination, trudged with

heavy steps and at one point she slipped. But I caught her. And it so shocked me I said, "I'm sorry."

She smiled gently and said, "I'd forgotten how slick a pine-needle floor can be."

So I helped her. I offered her my arm, which she accepted with a blush, and the two of us continued on, deeper and deeper into this closed, secret world, and the thought crossed my mind that if we were attacked by a rabid bobcat or a bear I would protect this woman to the death.

After a while, we stopped to rest, sharing the liquor, and she put some of my fear into words. "Maybe this isn't right. I don't remember it being this far."

She looked so sad and, I mean, really old. The two of us even smelled old, as if the devil had sprinkled us with death dust, making our skin go dry and offer up a hint of what was to come.

As much as I feared returning to the scene of Raison's death, I didn't want to let Sparrow down. I said, "Let's give it a little more. And if we don't find it soon we'll turn around."

So we started again even though our legs ached. I kept whispering in my head, "Please let us be traveling in the proper direction, please be it." But after a long time wandering through woods that only got thicker, I leaned over and rested my hands on my wobbly knees and gave up. I said, "I'm sorry, but I don't think we've chosen the proper path."

I heard her cry out and I raised my head, and there she was, a woman with at least her little toe touching the grave, but she was running. Not full tilt or anything, but it was a definite run. And I thought I heard her. I thought her words lingered in the air like dollops of sun: "I see it. It's right there."

I picked up my pace as best I could, and goodness she was right. Our lean-to love shack still standing in a world of fat-trunked pines and giant ferns, a place that only occasionally saw the likes of humankind. I was aware of the hollow sad cry of a whippoorwill and the stubborn, rapid thump-thumpthumpthump! of the woodpecker, and in a flash I remembered the rain and our love cries and then the awful visage of my dead bird. It was like running into a brick wall. The pain was so sudden and sharp I moaned.

Sparrow caught me by the waist. "Are you okay?"

But I couldn't respond. I just kept my old bleary eyes shut and tried to kill the remembrance. I had put all my hopes and dreams into that magic chicken, and out of selfishness I had let her die.

I felt Sparrow's hands on my face. She shook it. Shook it hard. I opened my eyes and she was looking at me like she thought I might get away, and she said, "Listen to me, Mr. Sammy, you are not responsible for that bird's death. It's just something that happened. And any powers of magic she had were powers you gave her. You just stopped believing once she was gone. That's all. I want you to believe again. It's your dear heart that pumps out the magic. Not that poor chicken."

She kept her hands on my beard and I gazed at her face, measuring this woman's words, measuring them carefully, as if they were gold dust and I was still steady. From the day of Raison's death to the day of Sparrow's return I had done nothing but lament myself and my failed love affair. I had behaved as if I was unworthy of life, not fit for the fruits that came to others: a good woman, a family, a life filled with purpose and goals instead of regrets. I lifted my hands to hers and held them and kissed them, first her left and then her right, and then I said, "How could we have let it happen?"

"We all have our journeys to take, Mr. Sammy. There are lessons to learn, and memories of love to cherish and make new. We can renew our love, Mr. Sammy. I know we can." When she said this her eyes were steady and bright, without one flicker of doubt. She reached up and softly kissed my cheek. "I'm here now. And I know I'm not thin and soft and lovely anymore. But I'm a better woman than I was back then. And I am full of love for you." Her black eyes filled with tears. I hugged her close.

I whispered into her hair, "You're wrong. You are still soft."

She pulled away from me and said, "Come on, old man. Let's see what kind of shape our house is in."

I touched her lips and then her face, and then together we entered the house. The door, its yellow paint nearly all worn off, creaked open with a rusty moan. It was dark and about damn near impossible to see.

"If I remember right, we left an old oil lamp out here. Let me think. Yes. Probably in that corner over there." I fiddled in my dungaree pockets and pulled out a book of matches. I lit one. Its faint light revealed the lamp and the musty walls.

"It's like stepping back in time," I said.

"Look! Even my seashells are still on the walls," she marveled.

And we, at the same time, looked at the hay nest and it quite embarrassed me and she didn't help any, 'cause she said, "Oooh, what we did there!"

And then she tucked one hand in mine and with the other pulled on my beard braid, and she said, "You know what, Mr. Sammy—I have come to believe it's never too late. Why don't we give it a try?"

"Woman, you're crazy! We are way too old." I was immediately filled with dread. I couldn't perform no more. She must have left some of her marbles out on that prairie.

"You're not scared, are you?"

"Of course I'm not scared. But we're both liable to have heart attacks, and besides, the hay ain't fresh. You know it's full of vermin."

She set her hands on her beautiful broad hips, and she said, "That's what the blanket is for."

I studied her full. And she studied me back. The scent from the lamp was doing a good job of filtering out the musty smell and I became aware that ivy still covered two of the walls. Finally I said, ''I'll lay down with you, Sparrow, but I ain't making any promises.''

I set the lamp back down on the pine table and together we spread the blanket out on the dirt floor, and I just couldn't believe what I was agreeing to try.

Then I said, ''Wait a second.'' I went outside and peed, and when I returned, damned if she didn't already have her shirt off.

She stood there smiling at me just like it was Christmas Day.

She said, ''Do you mind?'' and she turned her back to me.

I said, ''Mind what?''

''My brassiere. I could use an extra hand.''

Leaning back as far as I could so as to see, I fumbled with the hooks for way too long. But eventually I figured it out, and as the straps fell down her shoulders, she said, ''Ahh, I would like to live to see the day we don't have to wear these awful things.''

I put my hands on her naked arms. Her skin was warm. And no, it did not feel young. It felt like a body that had done its job, that was well lived-in, and I said, ''Please, turn around.''

Slowly she spun to face me, and the sight of her full breasts, no longer pert, no longer firm with youthful want, made me a very happy man.

I said, ''Sparrow dear, you are still a beautiful woman.''

She said, "Take off your clothes, old man. I want to see you."

She helped me with my buttons and snaps and I with hers, and when we were both as naked as birthing day, I said, "Ain't we a hell of a sight!"

"I sure love that beard of yours. You should have grown it sooner," she said.

Then we helped each other lay down, which was most comical, because our joints and muscles were no longer limber, and we both made cracking noises as we settled onto the earth.

We snuggled in each other's arms, and I know we both smelled the devil's death dust, but we chose to ignore it. She rubbed my belly and asked, "Mr. Sammy, how many women have you been with?"

"A few. I may have lost my youth but I was still a man," I explained. I let my hand find her breast and then her nipple grown large.

"Why didn't you marry any of them?"

"Because, Sparrow"—and I let my hands fiddle more—"I knew you'd be back. And even though I felt lost and angry and hurt, every single day I looked up at the sky and I said I loved you. And I did, and I still do. What about you?" My hand wandered.

"Me what?"

"Other men, woman."

"Never. Not one time, you old coot. I had what some might call my opportunities, but I always considered them more like wrong turns. Besides, I was too busy being mean, to myself and everyone else."

She ran her hands down my thighs. It felt good, so

easy. I wondered if she was telling me the truth or just something she thought I wanted to hear, and then I decided it didn't matter.

"Listen here, I love you too," she said, and I felt her sigh. It was a sweet feeling against my skin.

Just as if this was natural, what two people near the end of their lives were supposed to do, we faced each other and we kissed and we kissed and we fiddled with one another's most precious, most private parts. And we made our apologies, for we were not what we were in our youth. I could not get to full staff and she was not completely whatever it is women do, but this here happened: We enjoyed our time together.

And even though we weren't physical specimens no more, I felt myself become a part of this old gal, and when we moaned it was together, and when we touched and kissed and explored the nooks and crannies of our two bodies, it was as if we were exploring one body, a new, gentle person, someone we most appreciated.

When we had finally exhausted ourselves and accepted that we had given everything we could still dish out, we fell into one soft heap. Nobody, not even a real doctor, could have figured out where her body began and where mine ended.

Then we slept. It was a good, long sleep, made all the more peaceful by our sweet union.

OUR JOURNEY is getting easier. The river, now left to flow naturally rather than constrained by bulkheads and seawalls, wanders gently, bordered by palm and pine and saw grass. Visible only at low tide are vast prairies of gray, openmouthed oyster beds, which, if you're unfortunate enough to run up on them, will cut your feet to ribbons. Unforgiving, primitive scalpels indeed.

Carlos and I are feeling at home. We hold hands easily. And our kisses are tinged with sweetness, as though my gall is becoming less bitter.

We're still running into areas of "progress," which I believe is a synonym for "destruction," but we are cutting through protected lands as well. At Merritt Island there were birds the likes of which I'd never seen, and some that used to frequent the keys but have been pushed north in search of new nesting grounds since their ancestral ones are now condos. I found myself wanting to ask, "Will they survive?" But I didn't let the words form, because even the fact that the question is both plausible and important is too horrible.

Carlos and I have stopped at a marina near Ponce Inlet. Folks in their one-hundred-percent-plastic vessels comment on the *Sparrow* and ask how old she is and who built her, and suddenly I am so proud. I look them straight in the eyes and say, "My granddaddy built her. He was a fine carpenter."

And everyone has agreed.

We have stopped here for two reasons. We huddled over the map and weighed our options: St. Augustine by morning or at sunset? We decided sunset because I want to see the journey in. I want to know what surrounded Mima. The river when we near St. Augustine is called Matanzas. That I want to study in the bright light of day. But I'd like my first glimpse of the town to be softened by dying light. Because I'm afraid it won't be like any of their stories. And then, my God, what will I do?

So we stopped in order to time our arrival. And also we wanted to be clean, to take startlingly hot showers and soap up our hair and maybe both dip into the Old Spice.

The moon is high and full. The sky is littered with starlight. And we are working. The *Sparrow,* we have decided, must be sparkling for her return home. I mop. And polish her wood. And wipe down the instrument panel. And Carlos replaces the hinges on her cabin door. He even found a small can of paint I didn't know I had and painted her name on new again, in a color as red as blood. People passing by say, "She's looking good."

And Carlos, unable to help himself, responds each time with, "My woman or my boat?"

And each time, instead of getting cross with him, I giggle. What's wrong with me? I'm too old to giggle.

That night, smelling of lemon oil, we make love, sharing in the gifts of the moon and stars and ancient river, with him brushing off my hard scales and me finding his tender heart and promising no harm.

In the morning we take our showers and our leave, looking as if, even as adults, we believe in our mothers' warning that if we didn't scrub good enough behind our ears, potatoes would sprout.

We hit Daytona early and get out quickly. It seems to us to be one more city full of garish hotels and not much else. There is no reason to stick around.

But north of Daytona are lands quite beautiful. Palm trees hang low and wide over the black waters that feed into a virgin river called the Tomoka. Here herons pierce the sky effortlessly, as if they cannot imagine the wilderness could ever be destroyed. But they should, for they are forewarned. Nearby are lands clear-cut, and trailers sit placidly, side by side, like endless rows of giant coffins under a relentless sun.

What would Mama and Mima say if they could be with me now? I think they would gasp at our boldness and arrogance as we take nature by the neck and spit in her face. But then again, perhaps not. Mima had seen this sort of thing before. After all, she was a little girl who watched the buffalo's descent into oblivion, who learned full well how to play the Dead Game.

But still, I try to buoy myself. I try to say there is hope, because interspersed among the new condos and housing developments—where all the houses look alike and where the retired folks probably have to leave trails in the sand to find their way back to their entertainment centers and well-stocked bars and toxic wall-to-wall carpeting made all the more pungent because in this land of luscious ocean breezes they have built look-alike homes with windows that don't open—there exist areas of quiet. Of dense hammock that suggests Africa and even of simple homes that sit back from the saw grass leading into river, rather than the developments with filled-in marsh to create pesticide-rich golf courses.

I am happy my women didn't live to see what we have done. In fact, as they journeyed south they might have wished for a bit more civilization. This makes me laugh. Once again we have missed that delicate balance.

I go below to fix us sandwiches, but Carlos hollers for me to be quick. "You'll want to see this," he yells.

I'm craving a delicacy of my youth: kosher dills with mayonnaise on white bread. So what if it sounds disgusting. Now that we know all the foods our parents loved can kill us, I've been embarrassed, even in private, to indulge. But not today. Because even though I've never before summoned the courage to go to St. Augustine, I feel as if I'm returning home. Maybe I can be a child again.

So pickle sandwiches it is. I go back on deck and give Carlos his, and I'm glad he told me to hurry, because the world here is really beautiful. The river stretches into far savannas. Water birds stand in the shallows, fishing, and on a small island on the channel's leeward side we spy a colony of roseate spoonbills. We pass by slowly and as quietly as possible, and I know that it's because my soul is far-flung, but I'm beginning to feel lucky to be traveling through a place that wears its beauty so effortlessly.

Carlos says it for me: "This is a land of grace."

We are just puttering along, enjoying the scenery, when I'm smacked in the face. Hard. Dead ahead is the fort. I say, "It can't be."

It is not at all how Mima described it. This is not a star-shaped fortress crowned by parapets and barbed with cannons. This is not a harbor looking out to the sea. A cube on the western shore, this is a small outpost steeped in solitude, surrounded by marsh and river. It's an imposing hut, not the monolithic fort of her stories. I tell Carlos, "No. This isn't right." Suddenly everything she and my mother ever told me about this place seems a sham. I begin to say, "I don't know anything. It was all lies. All of it."

But Carlos, who looks as if he knows he needs to figure something out real fast, else he's going to have a hysterical person on his hands, is frantically reaching for the map, his big-knuckled finger tracing from south to north and back. And me, I'm just gazing out at this puny fort, which under other circumstances might be interesting. I mean, it's obviously a historic structure, but it's also suggesting that whatever I was told by those two women was a crock.

Carlos interrupts my terror. "Got it," he says.

''Got what?''

He's smiling. His eyes have lost that panicked look of dread that my moods can instill in him.

''Wrong fort,'' he explains.

''Wrong fort?''

I take the map from him. He's right. This is Fort Matanzas. Mima was jailed at Fort Marion. But I'd read somewhere that they changed its name. Back to what the Spaniards who built it named it. Yes. Right up here. In thin black letters: Castillo de San Marcos.

''Thank God. I was beginning to think I'd lost my mind and that my childhood had been one long blackout. Can you imagine living someplace with all these old forts?''

Carlos reaches for a bag of plantain chips we brought with us and opens it. ''Cuba has forts,'' he says.

''Yeah—but two in one little place! It's kind of neat,'' I say.

Carlos scoops up a handful of chips. ''Those ladies didn't lie to you, Mamacita.''

''Maybe,'' I concede. ''But they might have exaggerated a lot.''

He offers me the bag. ''And maybe not.''

I turn down the chips but grab us a couple of beers out of the cooler. As I pop mine open, I look to the western shore. There is no development on this side. Not for miles. It must be protected. Nothing gets left alone on its own. ''One thing is for sure,'' I tell him.

"What's that?"

"They were definitely here. And they definitely left."

As we inch closer and closer, I tell him about my mother, what she did the night before they were to leave. "You know all those things she stole? All those glass horses and elephants and dogs and God knows what else? She said she borrowed Mr. Sammy's wheelbarrow. And she filled it up with all that rainbow-colored glass, and after the town had gone to sleep, she traveled door to door, leaving her stolen treasures on front stoops all over town."

I tuck myself up under Carlos's arm. He kisses the crown of my head. I say, "She always enjoyed that memory. I think what stayed fresh in her mind was her imagining folks going out to get their milk and finding a cheap trinket mysteriously put there just for them. She said she felt like she was leaving her scent behind, just for good measure."

"Did the people know she did it?" he asks, and he points because we've got dolphins shadowing our starboard bow.

"I don't know," I answer, and his question triggers a rush of uneasiness. What am I going to find? It's not too far now. Just a few more twists and bends in the river. But I tell myself to calm down. Mima had enough courage to come back. And enough to get on this boat with her daughter to try to make sense of their lives. "I guess they were sort of brave," I say.

"You're brave. Me too," Carlos says solemnly.

He's funny and he doesn't even know it. I lean over the rail and watch the dolphins. There are two of them, riding our wake. They breach the water in unison and I cheer, and then they are both gone, as quickly as Mama and Mima the day we buried them. My eyes tear over and I can't see a damn thing, but then, as I have so many times in my life, I hear Mima, whispering, offering her life to me through her tales that comforted me as a child and would again, if only I would let them:

LIKE A FAINT VEIL, a mist rose from the river and danced skyward the morning of our departure. Oneida and I arrived at Mr. Sammy's about six-thirty, just as the sun was dawning. I fretted all the way over, telling Oneida I was concerned about our safety, and she responded that Mr. Sammy knew what to do with his boat, and I returned that he was too old to run the whole show himself. And Oneida said bluntly, "I have dated lots of men with boats. I know the routine."

I guess we did have a lot to tell each other.

Mr. Sammy's kitchen smelled good, for he had made sweet pan bread. We sat around his kitchen table, drinking coffee and eating breakfast, and our conversation was sprinkled with laughter and excited tones, because with every tick of the clock I think we each grew more thrilled with the prospect of leaving land.

That old man and I held hands underneath the table, and I felt foolish, hiding our touching, and I thought that maybe we shouldn't be familiar in front of Oneida at all, but right as I was about to pop the last morsel of pan bread into my mouth, she said, "I know you two are holding hands." She tossed back her long hair. "And for your information, it doesn't bother me."

See, she was crusty too. Like mother, like daughter. And still, Mr. Sammy and I didn't bring our clasped hands above the table. In fact, I pulled away and folded mine neatly in front of me.

Mr. Sammy poured us another coffee and then he sat back down and cleared his throat and he said, "It's gonna be time to get going soon. You girls ready?"

Oneida and I exchanged glances. It was close to being an honest exchange, and she whispered, "Yeah, I think so."

He fiddled with his braid, which I most enjoyed watching, and he said, "Oneida, we haven't been the two most honest people with each other. I mean, I didn't have the honor of you calling me Daddy, 'cause—you know the complications. But when it came to the day-to-day, I think we always dealt squarely with each other. I was always there for you. Wasn't I?"

Oneida stared into her coffee, and I studied her. She was both solemn and thoughtful, and I let myself feel proud of her, and I was pleased that she reminded me of my mother.

My daughter said, ''You know, we never did get the labels just right, but we always took care of each other, I felt. Yeah.''

Then she looked up at him and smiled. It was good to see.

He turned to me and said, ''Woman, you and I, we've had a wild journey together. Let's not regret any of it. Let's just say it was all okay.''

I searched his lovely, wise face. The one that if I'd been able to pull myself together sooner I could have spent a lifetime adoring. I knew I could not easily do what he was asking of me, to not regret our years apart, but I knew I had to try. ''Yes,'' I said, ''it was all okay.''

And then, looking first at me and then at his daughter, he announced, ''Ladies, I think it's time. Let's get going.''

We gathered ourselves up and headed out the back door. ''Oh, look!'' I said, because there she sat, in the river, a handsome boat indeed, bearing my name. My concerns for our safety were replaced with a yearning to be afloat and to wander. I'm going to love my little stint as a sailor, I mused.

When we reached the river's edge, Mr. Sammy said, ''You know what to do, Oneida, girl, don't you? You've told me you've handled lots of boats. It's true, isn't it?''

''This boat? You're asking me if I can handle this boat? Nothing to it,'' she assured him.

But I didn't like the question. "Mr. Sammy, what are you saying here?"

He took my hands and he held them tight and it did not escape me: this look of happiness, of peace, that had settled so comfortably across his high fine cheekbones. He said, "Sweetheart, this is your journey. And your daughter's journey."

He gazed at me, it seemed, from so far away, from some far loftier perch. "Do this for me," he said. "Go and find each other."

Of course, my impulse was to argue. But in my absence he had grown powerful. In the blink of an eye he knew everything. I looked at Oneida, and she said, "Mama, I think he's right."

And I looked back at him. He was smiling at me gently, and I knew he loved me, and then he said, "Take all the time you need. I'll be here."

He kissed his daughter and hugged her so hard I had to look away.

This was not playing out the way I had thought, the way I had dreamed. A part of me wanted to insist he come with us, but a far wiser edge of my soul perceived the beauty of his plan. This trip was for Oneida and me. It was our time, my daughter's and mine.

Mr. Sammy turned from Oneida and took me in his old frail arms. We kissed and hugged and I breathed in as deep as I could because I didn't know how long it might be before I'd smell his jasmine-sweetened skin again.

We waded into the river, our skirts blossoming

out around us like two giant flowers, mine blue and Oneida's yellow. My daughter got on board and then, with Mr. Sammy shouting suggestions from shore, she managed to help me roll aboard as well. My ascent to the *Sparrow* wasn't graceful. But I got there, by God.

And while Oneida pulled anchor herself and started the motor just as if she really did know what she was doing, I stood silent and still, watching my Mr. Sammy. We drifted slowly toward the channel, and Oneida and I each raised a hand, a final wave, to the dear man staying on land.

I watched him grow smaller and smaller, the mist enveloping him in its soft white veil.

I have to tell you:

We never saw Mr. Sammy again.

We just kept going, fearful that if we stopped the boat and put our feet on firm soil, something most horrible would happen to us. And we did begin to discover each other, to share the secrets and sorrows of our lives.

I wrote to Mr. Sammy, but I don't know if he ever got the letters. You see, before we reached Hawk Channel, I was having dreams. I dreamed he'd turned into that gator he'd searched so long for.

I knew that meant he was dead. I knew this quietly, with a certainty born in the marrow.

But then, Sadie, there we were, Oneida and I. The longer we sailed, the closer we grew. It was as if mother and child were giving birth to each other.

And when one day in a Key West bar she ran into

John Looney, the father of her sons—whether it was providence or happenstance I cannot say—she and I conspired. For there was something about that bastard. Sure, she'd slept with other men in her time, but this Looney fellow had something about him. I don't know what it was, but her womb accepted his seed even as it sealed itself against all others. The man was not cut out for the responsibilities of fatherhood, but he and Oneida certainly had the right chemistry.

And Oneida and I thought that if she could have another baby it would be most perfect.

That's how you came into the world, Sadie, through a mother and a daughter who loved each other the best two women can, conspiring with an unwitting ne'er-do-well to give you life.

Little girl, listen to your Mima. Making sure you were born was an act of love and devotion, and the most honest thing either one of us ever did.

AS WE BEGIN to enter the harbor, I am no longer in my right mind. Maybe menopause has finally kicked in. Maybe my exhilaration and fear are nothing but hormonal. All I know is that the closer we get, the more determined I am to go ashore and take off my shoes, like those two barefoot dancing women, and see for myself if any hint of them, or my granddaddy, is still here. I'm going to sniff in all the dark corners and see if I can't find some light.

I look at Carlos and he is smiling. He says, "This is so good, Mamacita, us coming here."

I run my fingers along the cypress handrail. Mr. Sammy's fine old boat. He'd be pleased to see her now, returning home, looking so clean and proud.

We have read up on St. Augustine. The travel brochures support Mama's and Mima's descriptions. We know it's got cobblestone streets and old Spanish courtyards and flower-heavy balconies. It's got old houses and some of our nation's earliest tourist traps.

But does it offer any glimmer of my people? I mean, if they were able to be with Carlos and me as we walk the ancient streets for the first time, would they say, "Oh yes, here is the store where I bought my first candy bar," "Here is where I beat up that little boy," "Here is where your brothers used to play tag," "Here is where I went to school"? Or would they say, "I don't remember any of this. Nothing. I don't remember any of it at all"?

Maybe it's the river journey, or Carlos's gentle insistence that I'm not a bad person, but I'm feeling stronger, as if I might be able to handle whatever we discover.

The sun is just beginning to cast splashes of purple and orange down the backbone of this town, and I catch my breath, for it is far lovelier than I imagined. Terra-cotta spires rise above gabled rooftops. And homes with porticoes and colonnades and walled courtyards suggest that there are vestiges of the past still here.

A marina is on our left, but just ahead is an old bridge that arches gracefully across the bay. I think I know what is on the other side. It has to be. "Go on through the bridge," I say.

We are walled in with shadow and then an oval of sunlight.

And I'm right! There it is. The fort. As I look at its massive gray walls that rise so solidly against the sky, I am filled with bitterness. Tour coaches crowd the parking lot, and tourists look like ants as they scurry around its top level, taking pictures and climbing on cannons. It does have a silent beauty, and even from afar I know that the ingenuity of its construction is something to marvel at. But still, here it sits like a giant anchor tying this town to its past, and I am not so concerned with its existence as with the misery it housed. For me, it is a fortress of sad memories, a prison where my grandmama's soul was cut away.

Carlos puts his arms around me and whispers, "See, it is all true. The good and the bad."

I look eastward from the fort and—exactly as Mima and Mama described it—there is the mouth of the harbor, the Atlantic just beyond, kicking up in a flourish of white foam and blue water. That would have been the view, my grandmother's first glimpse of the sea. For some reason I think of the poor mute child we've carried with us all this way. A silent passenger entrusted with dreams and burdens far too wide for his thin shoulders. I think of my grandmama being burdened with that awful and false moniker "savage." I know what that did to her, but I don't—and I suspect I never will—understand why we don't just let people be.

"I have an idea," I say. Without explaining, I run below, and first I take the heron wings out of the freezer and then I retrieve the baby from the footlocker. Also I gather twine and scissors.

I go back on deck. Carlos looks at the bizarre assortment of items I'm carrying, and his black eyes give him away—deep pools of sadness and regret—but I know he won't give in to tears. I say, "Don't you think a burial is in order?"

"You have a very good idea," he agrees. He touches my hair and says, "Such courage it takes to believe in ourselves sometimes. Such pain to get to where we want to be."

It's like a kick in the face: I'm in love with this man and there's no getting past it. An urge to comfort him wells up in me. "Carlos, I know I can be a real hard-ass, but believe me, you have one of the sweetest souls I've ever seen."

He takes the coffin and the wings from me, and a look of resolve shoos away the threat of tears. He says, "Mamacita, let's get to work."

We maneuver to a spot in the harbor that's a direct shot to the ocean, about halfway between the fort and the Atlantic. Carlos takes the baby from the coffin, and I enclose his hard brown body in a cradle of heron wings. We tie them around the child. I make sure my knots are secure and the twine is taut. We are working swiftly and efficiently, because to do otherwise might blow the lid off our emotions. After all, we're here not to fall apart but to gather in our scattered pieces.

Carlos balances the wing-wrapped baby and then says, "No, this won't do. We cannot let him float away. Someone will find him. Maybe a person that gives him to scientists or a museum. So he still has no rest. We have to weigh him down."

I'm not sure how to do it. We can't attach anything heavy to the wings because it would tear them away. So we opt for returning the baby to the mahogany box, wings and all. Carlos is saying, "I don't know. What do we have that's heavy but not big?"

I momentarily draw a blank, but then the light bulb goes on. "The *Sparrow,*" I answer.

"What?" he says, looking at me as if I'd answered a question other than the one he asked.

I open the hatch on a storage bin that doubles as a seat, which I constructed years ago. He looks in and smiles as he says, "Ahh, the *Sparrow.*"

The bin is full of worn-out bits and gears and bolts—I've never thrown away any part of this boat. We carefully fill the coffin with these charms, these pieces of lead and steel. They do the job.

Carlos and I hold the weighted coffin out over the water. Despite the lateness of the hour, the sun is intense, so I'm squinting as I look to Carlos and say,

"Whatever you believe happened to you as a child did. And it happened because of the goodness of your spirit. That hasn't changed."

He looks back at me boldly, as though he has always known me, and says, "Your ghosts are mine. We will chase them down together. And we will love, Sadie."

Then I mutter, "We need to say something about the baby."

Carlos nods, and I can see the thoughts flickering, shadowing his eyes, and I think he's replaying his whole life in his head. Seabirds circle overhead, casting dark patches on the water, but I keep my focus on Carlos and the child. "Baby," he says, "we don't know who you are or where you came from. We just know that you once lived and your presence touched people. Maybe only your parents. Maybe your village. It doesn't matter. Just that you breathed the air of earth, which is the spark of God—that is what matters. Now it's time for your rest."

We let go of the coffin and I watch the water swallow the baby, as if it is hungry for him. I whisper, "Fly, fly, fly."

Carlos reaches for me. We hold on to each other, flesh to flesh, watching the coffin disappear into the sea.

We look up from the water, past the fort, and to the cluster of wood-shingled bayfront shops and homes. The setting sun casts a bright, even glow over this town that seems inviting and oh so familiar.

Carlos sweeps me up in his arms and begins gently to guide me, coaxing me into movement. He's singing softly in my ear, and I love the sound of those Spanish words. Before I know it we are spinning, 'round and 'round, a dance born from the ability to dream.

I touch my hand to his cheek—our dance slows—I'm about to suggest we dock and go ashore. I imagine myself stepping into a world where Mama and Mima and Mr. Sammy still live. But then I stop.

And listen.

Perhaps it is only the wind blowing, or time come home to roost, but for a second or two I hear them: those plaintive fiddles weeping, as on the day we buried my women.